PRIVILEGED
CONVERSATION

EVAN

PRIVILEGED CONVERSATION

HUNTER

WARNER BOOKS

A Time Warner Company

Warner Books, Inc., 1271 Avenue of the Americas, New York, NY 10020

 A Time Warner Company

Printed in the United States of America
First Printing: February 1996
10 9 8 7 6 5 4 3 2 1

Library of Congress Cataloging-in-Publication Data

Hunter, Evan.
Priveleged conversation / Evan Hunter.
p.   cm.
ISBN 0-446-52028-4
I. Title.
PS3515.U585P75   1996
813'.54—dc20   95-11148
                                                              CIP

Book design by Giorgetta Bell McRee

This is for
Otto Penzler

New York City is real, and so are Boston and Martha's Vineyard and Radcliffe and Mass General and *Cats* and *Les Misérables* and *Miss Saigon* and the American Psychiatric Association and Mount Sinai Hospital and the New York City Police Department and any other civic or cultural institution mentioned herein by name.

But Kathryn Duggan and David Chapman and all of the other characters in this novel are fictitious, as is each and every narrated event.

PRIVILEGED
CONVERSATION

1: *friday, june 30–sunday, july 16*

He has eight patients in all, evenly divided between those in analysis and those in therapy—the "Couches" and the "Chairs," as he often refers to them in private to Helen. All told, he puts in a thirty-hour week at the office. Well, they're only fifty-minute hours, of course, but still, he makes all his phone calls during the ten minutes between patients, so it really can be considered a full work hour. The rest of the week he teaches and supervises at Mount Sinai, just a few blocks up on Fifth Avenue.

On his lunch hour, he usually grabs a quick sandwich and coffee at the deli on Lex, and then goes for a walk in the park. The weather this June has been miserable thus far, the customary New York mix of heat and humidity broken by frequent thunderstorms; today is muggy and hot, as usual, the perfect finale to a perfectly ghastly month, not an ideal day for walking, but his little jaunts in the park are more for relaxation than for true exercise. Nor does he experience any feelings of guilt over these leisurely, peaceful strolls, his brief respites from the often tortured narratives unreeling all day long in his office.

The girl up ahead seems to appear out of a shimmering haze. Where a moment ago the path was empty, there is now a young girl on a bicycle, fifteen or sixteen years old, he guesses, sweaty and slender, wearing green nylon running shorts and an orange cotton tank top, tendrils of long reddish-gold hair drifting across her freckled face. Smiling as she pedals abreast of him, she calls, "Good morning, sir!" and is gone at once in a dazzle of sunlight—although it is already afternoon, and he will not be forty-six till the end of July, thank you.

A trifle perplexed, David wonders if his new glasses make him look older than he actually is (but Helen picked out the frames), wonders, too, if the girl who just whisked past on her bike was in fact much younger than he'd taken her for, not the fifteen or sixteen he'd originally supposed, but perhaps twelve or thirteen, in which case the "sir" is understandable, though barely.

He looks at his watch.

It is almost a quarter to one, time he started back. Arthur K is *always* on time. Never even a second late. Frowns scoldingly if David doesn't open the door to his office *precisely* on the hour. Listening to Arthur K, listening to all of his patients, David tries to visualize the enormous cast of characters they conjure for him, the boiling events, real or imagined, around which their lives are structured. Listening, he tries to understand. Understanding, he tries to—

The scream is molten.

It hangs hot and liquid and viscous on the still summer air—and then abruptly ends.

David whirls at once, his heart suddenly racing. Standing stock-still in the center of the path, he keeps listening, hears only an insect-laden silence, and then scuffling noises around the curve up ahead, the rasp of feet scraping gravel. The same voice that not moments ago brightly chirped, "Good morning, sir!" now shrilly shouts, "Let *go* of it, you . . . !" and is cut off by the unmistakable sound of a slap, a smack, flesh against flesh, and then, immediately afterward, a duller, thicker sound—a punch? This is Central Park, David thinks, you can get killed here, he thinks. Strangers can *kill* you here. From around the bend in the path now, out of sight, he hears the sounds of earnest struggle, the scuffling, grunting, shouting noises of battle, and suddenly there is another scream as jangling as the sound of shattering glass, and just as suddenly he is in motion.

They are still locked in grim and sweaty confrontation on the gravel in the center of the empty path, the black boy repeatedly punching at her as he tries to wrest the bicycle from her grip, the slender girl with the reddish-gold hair clawing at him as she tries with all her might to stop the theft. "Hey!" David shouts, but neither of them seems to hear him, so intent are they on their fierce combat. The boy hits her again with his bunched right fist, his left hand still tugging at the handlebar as if in counterpoint. This time the blow sounds thuddingly sincere. The girl lets out a short sharp gasp of pain, releases the bicycle, and staggers backward, moaning, falling to the ground on her back. The boy yells "Yaaah!" in triumph, and instantly wheels the bike away, a sneakered foot already on one of the pedals, gathering speed, and then whipping his leg over the seat and sliding down onto it.

"Hey!" David yells again.

"Fuck you!" the boy yells back, and pedals away furiously, wheels tossing gravel, around the curve just ahead, out of sight.

The summer's day goes still again.

Hot.

Hushed.

Insects rattling.

The girl lies motionless on the ground.

Kneeling beside her, David asks, "Are you all right, miss?" and then, for no reason he can properly understand—the last time he'd treated anyone for a *physical* disorder must have been twenty years ago or more, when he was still an intern at Mass General—he adds, "I'm a doctor."

She says nothing.

Looking down at her, studying her closely now, he realizes she isn't a girl at all, although these days he's likely to consider anyone under thirty a girl, but is instead a woman of . . . what, twenty-five, twenty-six? . . . the lightly freckled face, the fine wispy red hair, gold hair, the long coltish legs in the loose green running shorts, the small high breasts in the damp orange tank top, all conspiring to lend her a much younger appearance.

She is very pretty.

Sunlight filters down through the leaves, dappling her face, the high pronounced cheekbones dusted with tiny freckles—he does not at first notice that one of her cheeks is bleeding—the slender elegant nose and full mouth, its upper lip tented to reveal even white teeth, except where one is chipped. He wonders if the black boy's insistent blows to her face broke the tooth. Or anything else. That is when he notices the abrasion on her cheek, oozing a thin line of blood, bright red against her pale white face. Her eyes are still closed—is she unconscious?

"Miss," he asks again, "are you all right?"

"I think so," she says tentatively, and opens her eyes.

The eyes are as green as new leaves. Delicately flecked with yellow. A cat's eyes. He and Helen once owned a cat with eyes like that. Before the children were born. Sheba. Killed by a neighborhood Doberman. Sheba the cat. Eyes like this girl has. This woman.

"Did he get my bike?" she asks.

"Yes."

"The son of a bitch," she says, and sits up. Green shorts hiking up a bit. Long long legs, freckled thighs. White socks and white athletic shoes. Green cat's eyes.

"Your cheek is bleeding," he says.

"What?" she says, and reaches immediately for her right cheek, and touches it, and looks at her hand, the palms up, the fingers together, and frowns, puzzled. She touches the other cheek at once and feels the oozing wetness there, and mutters, "Oh shit," and looks at her fingertips and sees the blood now, and says again, "The son of a bitch."

"Here," David says, and offers her his handkerchief.

She hesitates, considering the pristine, meticulously ironed square of white cloth in his hand, her own hand covered with blood. "Are you sure?" she asks.

"Yes, go ahead."

She takes the handkerchief, gingerly presses it to her cheek.

"Where else did he hit you?"

"Everywhere."

"Anything feel broken?"

"How does something feel when it's broken?"

"It hurts like hell."

"I *do* hurt like hell, but I don't think anything's broken. That bike cost four hundred dollars."

"Where?"

"A shop on Third and . . ."

"I meant where do you hurt?"

"Oh. My face mostly. He hit me a lot in the face. I'll look just *great* tonight, won't I?"

"Anywhere else?"

"My chest."

She takes the handkerchief from her cheek, glances at the bloodstains on it, shakes her head, rolls her eyes in apology, and then asks, "Is it still bleeding?"

"Just a little."

She puts the handkerchief to her cheek again. With

her free hand she begins probing her chest, gently pressing her fingertips here and there, searching for pain.

"Hurts here," she says.

"The sternum," he says.

"Whatever."

He notices the sharp outline of her nipples against the
thin sweaty fabric of the orange top. He turns away.

"Maybe we ought to get you to a hospital," he says.

"No, I'll go see my own doctor. God, I hope this
doesn't keep me out. How's it look now?" she asks,
taking the handkerchief from her cheek again.

He turns back to her.

"I think it's stopped."

"Look what I did to your hankie."

"That's fine, don't worry about it."

"I'll wash it and send it back to you."

"No, no, don't be . . ."

"I want to," she says, and tucks the bloodstained handkerchief into the elastic waistband of the green shorts.
Still sitting on the ground, ankles crossed, she bends
over from the waist, clasps her ankle in both hands, and
carefully studies her left leg. She is wearing Nike running
shoes with white cotton Peds, a little cotton ball at the
back of each sock. "I hit the ground kind of funny,"
she says, "I hope I didn't hurt my leg."

He is still kneeling beside her. Dappled sunlight turns
her eyes to glinting emeralds. Strands of golden-red hair
drift across her face like fine threads in a silken curtain.
The side-slit in the very short green nylon running shorts
exposes a hint of white cotton panties beneath.

"It's beginning to swell," she says, probing the leg. "That's just what I need."

"We ought to report this, you know," he says.

"I will. Soon as I get home."

"You'd do better at a police station."

"I want to see my doctor first."

"You should go to the police."

"Why? They won't get it back, anyway," she says, and shrugs. Narrow shoulders in the orange tank top shirt, delicate wings of her collarbone sheened with perspiration. "Four hundred bucks. I hope he enjoys it."

"He'll probably pawn it."

"A junkie, right?"

"Maybe."

"I prefer thinking he really *wanted* the damn bike. To ride, I mean. Could you help me up? I want to make sure I don't fall right back down on my face."

He gets to his feet and extends his hand to her. She takes it. Her palm is moist. Gently, he eases her off the ground, toward him. She lets go of his hand. Balances herself tentatively, testing.

"Everything feel all right?" he asks. "Nothing broken?"

"Are you an orthopedist?" she asks.

"I'm a psychiatrist."

"Really? Do you know Dr. Hicks?"

"We've met."

"I love her. Jacqueline Hicks."

"She's supposed to be very good."

"Well, she really fixed *my* head."

"Good."

"What's *your* name? In case I see her."

"David Chapman," he says.

"Dr. Chapman, huh?"

"Yes."

"Dr. David Chapman," she says. "I'll tell her you saved my life. If I see her."

"Well, I think all he wanted was the bike, actually."

"Thank God," she says. "You have to give me your card. So I can mail you the handkerchief."

"You really don't have to . . ."

"Oh, but I *do*," she says. "Your wife would kill me, otherwise."

"She probably would," he says, and reaches into his pocket for his wallet, and wonders how she knew . . . well, the wedding band, of course. "I always run out of them," he says, "I hope I . . . yes, here we are." He slips a card from its slot in his wallet and hands it to her.

"Right here on Ninety-sixth," she says, studying the card, head bent, mottled sunlight setting her hair aglow again. "Your office."

"Yes."

"I live on Ninety-first," she says.

"We're neighbors," he says.

"Practically."

"Let me give you my home address, too," he says, and retrieves the card and finds a pen in his jacket pocket and scribbles the Seventy-fourth Street address on the back of the card. He hands the card to her again. Caps the pen. Puts it back in his pocket. Looks at his watch. "Will you be all right?" he asks. "I'm sorry, but I have a . . ."

"Oh, yes, fine."

". . . patient coming in at one."

"I'm okay, go ahead, really."

"Let me know if you need me to testify or anything."

"Oh, they'll never catch him," she says airily.

"Well, *if* they do."

"Sure. Meanwhile, I'll send you the handkerchief."

"Thank you."

"Thank *you*," she says, and extends her hand.

They shake hands awkwardly.

"I really have to go," he says.

"So go," she says, and shrugs, smiling.

As he walks off, he hears her call behind him, "Hey! My name is Kate."

The conversation in this office is privileged; that is to say, disclosure of anything said in this room cannot be forced on the witness stand. State statutes, case law, and federal rules of evidence label it "privileged communication," this private and exclusive conversation between patient and doctor. But the privilege extends beyond legalities.

David has been granted the privilege of trust.

He does not accept this privilege lightly. He understands the gravity of it, knows that what his patients confide in him goes to the very core of their beings. They may be "Chairs" and "Couches" when he is separating them anonymously for Helen, but here in this deliberately neutral office they are the incontestable stars of the wrenching memories and dreams they relate, episodes past and present, revelations, admissions, confessions, which David sorts and re-sorts in an attempt at comprehension.

He is no longer shocked by anything a patient tells him. His notes—which he makes during each session in a spiral notebook with lined yellow pages—are linked to informal storyboards he himself sketches, the way a director would before filming, except that David's illustrations are made *during* the act of creation; he is hearing the dialogue—a monologue in most instances— and visualizing the scene, while at the same time recording it on paper. His little drawings frequently resemble sketches for an Edvard Munch painting. A small boxed rectangle showing a cartoonlike figure of a screaming woman running from a racing locomotive will immediately recall for David the key episode or scene in a dream or a memory. Coupled with his scrawled interpretive note beneath it, the picture will instantly bring back the session and its essential matter. His sketches are quite good, actually. For a psychiatrist, anyway.

Today Arthur K is telling him again about the time he taught his younger sister to kiss. He has got over his pique at David's five-minute tardiness, has poutingly forgiven him, and is lying on the sofa perpendicular to David's desk. Arthur K is one of David's Couches, a neurotic who suffers from extreme bouts of anxiety bordering on panic disorder. Eyes owlish behind thick-lensed glasses whose frames are almost as big and as bold as David's own—but Helen chose them—Arthur K relates casually and with seeming indifference an episode David suspects is at the very heart of his problems. It is as if David is seeing the same movie for the fourth or fifth time.

In the movie, Arthur K is seventeen years old, a high school senior still living with his mother, his father, and his sister Veronica, who is two years younger than he is. Veronica is blond. Arthur K may have been blond at the time; his thinning hair can look somewhat blondish even now, when the light hits it a certain way, but this may simply be graying hair that is turning an unsightly yellow. Back then . . .

This was fifty years ago.

Arthur K is now sixty-seven years old, a white American neurotic male whose beloved sister Veronica died in a car crash twelve years back, exactly when all of Arthur K's problems seem to have started. It did not take a Freud or a Jung to make an almost immediate diagnosis when the man first began relating his woes in David's office this past January.

Now the movie is unreeling again.

Listening, David merely consults his previous sketches and notes. Arthur K's movie is identical each time; there is no need for fresh illustration. Even the words are the same, Arthur K's subdued monologue, the privileged conversation he shares with his analyst in this office he considers safe. David knows the man hates him, and is pleased by the knowledge; it means that transference has already taken place.

The opening shot is of Arthur K unlocking the door to an apartment and stepping directly into a kitchen. The family lives on the second floor of a two-story walk-up in the Wakefield section of the Bronx, not yet Puerto

Rican or black at the time, a neighborhood largely composed of Jewish and Italian families. Arthur K is Jewish. There is a smell in the kitchen that he will always associate with Jewish cuisine, such as it is, a heavy aroma David can well imagine, his own mother not being among the world's greatest chefs.

No need to sketch Arthur K's kitchen, David knows it intimately. No need to look at the clock on the wall; it is midnight. And there, sitting at the kitchen table, just as Arthur K has conjured her for him many times before, is a fifteen-year-old blond, blue-eyed girl wearing a pink angora sweater, a dark blue pleated skirt, a string of pearls, bobby sox and saddle shoes; this is fifty *years* ago, but Arthur K recalls everything in vivid Technicolor. The cup of dark brown chocolate pudding on the table. Topped with frothy white whipped cream and a red maraschino cherry. The glass of bone-white milk. Veronica's ivory-white skin. The blue-white pearls around her neck.

As David listens, his mind begins to wander.

Another movie intrudes.

The girl seems to appear out of a shimmering haze. Where a moment ago the path was empty, there is now a young girl on a bicycle, fifteen or sixteen years old, sweaty and slender, wearing green nylon running shorts and an orange cotton tank top, tendrils of long reddish-gold hair drifting across her freckled face . . .

He yanks his attention back to the present, Arthur K's movie that is already condensed here on the lined yellow pages in the notebook on his desk, recalled again as his patient recites it for perhaps the hundredth time.

Well, not that often; the man has only been seeing him for the past six months. But certainly a dozen times, perhaps thirteen or fourteen times, and yet Arthur K seems unaware that he keeps remembering this same scene over and over again, perhaps *fifty* times, yes, a *hundred* times, bringing it back in identical detail each and every time. *All you did was kiss your sister,* David wants to scream. *That isn't such a terrible crime, it didn't cause her death in an automobile!*

But, no, he says nothing of the sort. For now, his task is to encourage Arthur K to talk about his problems—among which is an inordinate fear of driving his own car—to listen in a nonjudgmental manner, to support and to reassure. Later, when Arthur K has fully accepted David's seeming unresponsiveness as an essential part of the therapeutic "coalition," so to speak, then *perhaps* David can begin to offer tentative interpretations of *why* Arthur K (or any of his patients for that matter) experiences such feelings or *why* he acts or reacts in such and such a manner on such and such an occasion.

For now, Arthur K's movie.

Again.

Arthur K sits at the table beside his sister. Veronica seems distracted as she pokes at the chocolate pudding with her spoon, red juice from the cherry staining the frothy whipped cream.

David's earlier notation on the lined yellow page reads *Virgin.*

Veronica the Virgin sips at her milk, white against her virginal white skin, blue-white pearls at her throat. Arthur K has taken a second chilled dark brown chocolate pudding from the refrigerator and he sits beside his sister now, both of them eating, he hungrily, she disinterestedly, almost listlessly. Their family is among the first on their block to own a "fridge" rather than an icebox, and his mother keeps it full of desserts like chocolate puddings, or rice pudding with raisins (over which they pour evaporated milk) or lemon meringue pies, or juicy apple tarts.

"She was a terrible cook," Arthur K says now, "but she gave great sweets."

David makes no comment.

This is the first time he has heard this particular reference. On his pad he sketches a woman's lips descending on what is unmistakably a penis.

Beneath the drawing he scrawls in his tight, cramped hand: *Tarts = Veronica + Mother?*

Arthur K's voice is still narrating **Veronica's Lesson**, the big hit movie of 1945. David's attention is asked to focus yet again on a two-shot of Arthur K and Veronica in close-up. Arthur K is asking his sister what's troubling her, why does she seem so gloomy tonight? "Gloomy" is Arthur K's exact word; David has surely heard it four hundred and ten times by now. Why is Veronica so *gloomy* tonight? And Veronica shakes her head and replies, "Oh, I don't know. It's just . . . I don't know."

Arthur K covers her hand with his.

"What is it, Sis?" he asks.

"Howard told me I don't know how to *kiss!*" she blurts, and suddenly she is sobbing.

Arthur K puts his arm around her, comfortingly.

She turns her head into his shoulder, sobbing.

In the other movie that intrudes again, unbidden, the girl with red hair, golden hair, in the sun more red than gold, is sitting on the ground, both hands holding her ankle, bent from the waist, studying her left leg.

"I hit the ground kind of funny," she says, *"I hope I didn't hurt my leg."*

David is all at once a costar in this bottom half of the double feature, entering the shot, kneeling beside the girl.

Dappled sunlight turns her eyes to glinting emeralds. Strands of golden-red hair drift across her face like fine threads in a silken curtain. The side-slit in the very short green nylon running shorts exposes a hint of white cotton panties beneath.

"It's beginning to swell," she says.

David looks at the penis he has drawn on the yellow lined pad, a woman's lips parted above it.

His mind snaps back to:

Veronica's Lesson
a Gothic Tale of Sibling Incest
... Almost

Veronica is telling her brother for the eight hundred and thirty-second time about the young man who took her to the synagogue dance that night, the very same dance Arthur K had attended, but which he'd left early so he could "make out"—Arthur K's language—with a brown-eyed, black-haired girl named Shirley in the backseat of his father's Pontiac sedan. Shirley, coincidentally, is also Arthur K's *mother's* name. Should David's notation be amended to read Tarts = Veronica + Mother + *Shirley?*

"My father was a car salesman," he says now. "He sold Pontiacs. I always drove new Pontiacs."

He never fails to interject these words at this point in the story, a voice-over narrator in a movie David knows by heart. Years later, Veronica will be killed driving a Chevy Camaro. Perhaps this is why Arthur K insistently mentions that he himself has always driven Pontiacs, would drive a Pontiac today, in fact, except that he is scared to death of getting behind the wheel of *any* car.

In Arthur K's movie, his sister is saying "Howard Kaplan told me . . ."

No names, please, but the damage is already done. A thousand times over, in fact.

". . . I don't know how to *kiss!*"

And bursts into tears again.

"Come on, Sis, stop it," Arthur K says. "You don't have to cry over somebody like Howard Kaplan."

There is a close shot of his face, solemn, sincere . . . pimply, too, as a matter of fact . . . his dark eyes intent behind the thick glasses he is wearing even as a youth.

"What the hell does *he* know about kissing, anyway?" Arthur K says soothingly, his arm around his sister, patting her shoulder, the blue robe slightly open to show . . .

Wait a minute, David thinks.

. . . her luminous pearls.

Wait a minute, what happened to the pink angora sweater and the pleated blue skirt? How'd she get in a blue robe all of a sudden? Did the costume designer . . . ?

"Jackass could use a few kissing lessons himself," Arthur K says.

"I wish somebody would give *me* lessons," Veronica says, her eyes brimming with tears, which the camera catches rolling down her flushed cheeks in extreme close-up.

The key words in the movie.

I wish somebody would give me *lessons.*

The essential words in Arthur K's retelling of a steamy Bronx interlude fifty years ago, almost missed this time around but for the fact that David has memorized every frame, every line, every word, every inflection in this saga of adolescent lust and desire.

I wish somebody would give me *lessons.*

In a blue robe this time around.

Slightly open, no less.

To show luminous *pearls.*

David is drawing a pair of breasts on a fresh page in his notebook when Arthur K suddenly stops his narrative.

Perhaps he, too, has recognized that he's changed his sister's long-ago attire, has put her in a *robe* instead of a pink angora sweater and a pleated blue skirt. Perhaps he is realizing that a slightly open robe lends sexual intensity to the kiss that inevitably follows in this well-remembered story, the kiss he teaches her at her request. Perhaps he is discovering that what they have here is a young girl ardently kissing her brother at midnight while wearing what now turns out to have been a *robe*, slightly open to show the *luminous* pearls around her neck. "Just part your lips, Veronica," he has repeated in previous retellings of the tale, after which he proceeds innocently to teach her—like the dutiful older brother he is—how to kiss, a calling for which she demonstrates tremendous natural aptitude, by the way. At midnight. In a merely slightly open robe.

But the film has stopped.

The projectionist has gone home.

"Isn't it time?" Arthur K asks.

"We have a few more minutes."

"Well," Arthur K says and falls silent.

He remains silent as the minutes tick away.

And finally David says, "I think our time is up now."

They both rise simultaneously, David from his black leather chair behind the desk, Arthur K from the black leather sofa at right angles to it. Before he leaves the office, Arthur K hurls a glare of pure hatred at him.

David leafs back through his lined yellow pages.

Sure enough, the first time he ever heard of Veronica eating chocolate pudding, he drew a picture of a girl with long straight hair, wearing a shaggy sweater and a pleated skirt, pearls around her neck.

Now she's in an open robe that shows those luminous pearls.

We're making progress, he thinks, and is almost sorry he will be flying up to Martha's Vineyard tonight, and will not see Arthur K again until after the long Fourth of July weekend. He glances again at the breasts he'd started to draw in his notebook. Two smallish globes, a dot in the center of each.

All at once, he remembers the sharp outline of the girl's nipples . . .

Hey! My name is Kate.

. . . Kate's nipples against the thin sweaty fabric of the orange top.

Remembers, too, the way he turned away.
And closes the spiral notebook.

Helen and the children are all wearing white T-shirts, the two girls in matching white cutoff shorts, Helen in a long wraparound skirt in a printed blue fabric. He spots them the instant he begins crossing the tarmac to the terminal building, such as it is. They all look even browner than they did last weekend, each the butternut color of the sandals they're wearing, each grinning, their teeth seeming too glisteningly white against their faces.

The kids have inherited Helen's ash-blond hair, thank God, and not his "drab" brown, he guesses you might call it, although "mousy" brown seems to be the pejorative adjective of choice for women's hair of that color. The girls' hair is cut short and somewhat ragged for the summer months. Helen wears hers falling sleek and straight to the shoulders, bangs on her forehead ending just a touch above the eyebrows. She is an extravagantly beautiful woman, and he is stunned each time he discovers this anew. David is the only one in the family who doesn't have blue eyes. His are brown to match the drab hair. Helen insists *her* eyes are gray, even though no one has gray eyes except in novels. David calls the kids the Blue-Eyed Monsters. They burst into giggles whenever he quavers the words and backs away from them in mock fright; it is easy to delight daughters of their age.

Annie, the six-year-old, begins telling him at once and excitedly all about the shark they'd seen off Chilmark, and Jenny, her elder by three years, immediately puts her down, telling David it was only a *sand* shark and a small one at that.

"Yeah, but it was a *shark*, anyway," Annie says, "wasn't it, Mommy?"

"Oh, it most certainly was," Helen says, and squeezes David's hand.

"I nicknamed him Jaws," Annie says.

"How original," her sister says.

Chattering, hopping from foot to foot in front of him, walking backward, squeezing in to hug him every now and then, they make their disorderly way toward where Helen has parked the station wagon. A sharp wind blows in suddenly off the field, puffing up under the wrap-around skirt, opening it at the slit to reveal long slender legs splendidly tanned by the sun. *So damn beautiful,* David thinks, and she catches his glance, and seemingly his inner observation as well, for she smiles over the heads of the little girls and winks in wicked promise as she flattens the skirt with the palm of her left hand, her golden wedding band bright against her tan.

The summertime rate for a direct flight from Newark to the airport near Edgartown is two-seventy-five round-trip, and the flight takes an hour and twelve minutes, to which he has to figure another hour to the airport from the city—all told a journey well worth it. He left his office at two-thirty this afternoon, and it is now only twenty past five. They have been renting here on the island for the past seven years now, from when Helen was pregnant with Annie. And even though the place is overrun with writers, movie stars, and politicians, among them—God help us—even a president of the United

States, David still finds in their Menemsha cottage a haven truly distant from the stresses of the city and the incessant turmoil of his patients. Here among the pines and the inland marshes and the soaring skies and sheltering dunes, he feels honestly at peace with his family and himself.

Lobster dinners are a tradition every Friday night. Then again, anything the Chapman family does more than once becomes an instant tradition with Annie. Sucking meat from a claw, she listens wide-eyed as David relates the tale of this afternoon's bicycle theft in Central Park.

"You should have minded your own business, Dad," Jenny says. "What you did was extremely dangerous."

"It was," Helen agrees.

Each of them looks so gravely concerned that he feels like leaning across the table and kissing them both. On the other hand, Annie wants to hear more.

"Did he kill her?" she asks.

"No, honey. Just hit her a lot."

"Urgh," Annie says, and pulls a face, and then asks, "Mommy, can you crack this for me, please?"

Helen takes the claw Annie hands across the table.

"Who was she, do you know?"

"Kate something."

"There's a girl named Kate in my class," Annie says.

"This isn't the same Kate," Jenny informs her.

"Duhhhhh, no kidding?" Annie says, and twists her forefinger into her cheek, a repeated gesture David has never understood.

"Kate what?" Helen asks.

"I don't know."

"Well, didn't you *ask?*"

"No."

"Suppose she *needs* you?"

"For what, Mom?"

"Suppose they catch the guy?"

"They won't," David says.

"They won't," the girls echo simultaneously.

"Won't you have to testify?"

"I doubt they'll pay much attention to a stolen bike."

"They better not steal *my* bike!" Annie says, and makes a threatening gesture with the lobster claw.

"Still, Dad," Jenny says, "you could have just called the cops or something. You didn't have to rush in like a hero."

"I *am* a hero," he says, and flexes his muscles like a weight lifter.

"Some hero," Helen says. "The guy got the bike, anyway."

"Ah yes, but I *yelled* at him," David says. "At the top of my lungs."

"Daddy *is* a hero," Annie says.

"He is, darling," Helen agrees. "But he should have been more careful."

"Suppose he had a gun or something?" Jenny asks, frowning now.

"Daddy would've yanked it away from him."

"Pow!" David says, and swings his fist at an imaginary assailant.

"One out of every two teenagers in New York has a gun," Jenny says.

"Where'd you hear that?" Helen asks. "Who wants more corn?"

"Me."

"Me."

"In the *Times*. It's a fact. Me, too."

"This one didn't have a gun," David says.

"How do you know?"

"Because I didn't get shot, did I?"

"Daddy didn't get *shot*, did he?" Annie says, nodding, buttering her corn.

"Or a knife," Jenny persists. "He could've had a knife."

"Daddy would have grabbed it like Crocodile Dun*dee*."

"Is she going to report it to the police?" Helen asks.

"She said she would."

"She should."

"I told her."

"I'd be afraid," Jenny says.

"No, something like that *should* be reported."

"I'd be afraid," Jenny says again.

"Not me," Annie says. "Could I have the salt, please? If *I'd've* been with Daddy, I'd've broken his *head*."

"You'd have broken my *head*?" David says in mock alarm.

"Not *yours*," Annie says, and begins giggling.

"Who's for dessert?" Helen asks, and begins clearing.

"Me!" Annie says, raising her hand at once.

"Me!" Jenny says, raising hers a beat later.

"Let me help you, hon," David says, pushing back his chair.

"I've got it," Helen says.

A look passes between them.

Private, almost secret.

"Sit," she says, and smiles and goes out into the kitchen.

There is a spectacular sunset that night.

Annie calls each night's sunset a tradition.

The house they are renting affords lavish views of both Menemsha Pond and the Bight. They stand on the deck overlooking both, the pond in the near distance, the bight and Vineyard Sound further to the northwest. The pond has already turned pink. The waters of the sound are still a fiery red. As they watch, the sky turns first a dusky purple and then a dark blue that becomes yet deeper and darker and eventually black and finally . . .

"Boop!" Annie says.

They put the children to bed and then sit on the screened porch, listening to the clatter of the summer insects and the murmur of the distant surf. Whispering in the stillness of the star-drenched night, they hold hands as they had when they were young lovers in Boston, discovering that city together, and themselves as well, discovering themselves through each other in that city. She was thinner when he'd met her, perhaps too thin, in fact, with incongruently abundant breasts— well, 34C, she told him, the first time he'd fumbled with her bra—and hips made for childbearing, she also told him. She is still slender, what he considers slender, although she constantly complains that she can stand to lose a few pounds. As they whisper in the hush and the dark, he keeps remembering the wind blowing her long skirt back over her lovely bare legs.

In bed later, the little black hook-latch fastened on the white, planked, wooden bedroom door, she spreads her legs for him, the sleek smooth legs he loves to touch, the feel of them under his searching hands, the children asleep down the hall, stroking her legs, his hands gliding up to the secret flesh high on her inner thighs, the soft hollows hidden on either side of her pubic mound. As she did the very first time they'd made love in a rented room on Cape Cod, she gasps sharply when his fingers part her nether lips, and raises her hips to accept his gently questing fingers, touching, finding her, moist and ready.

If Annie knew—and perhaps she does—what transpires each Friday night in this bedroom with its salt-dampened sheets and its windows open to the ocean winds, she would most certainly call it a tradition. For here in Helen's fiercely welcoming embrace, David finds again the young girl he once knew, and the desirable woman she's become, and is replenished by both. Overwhelmed by her beauty, stunned by her passion, moved almost to tears by her generosity, he whispers as he does each time, "I love you, Helen."

And she whispers against his lips, "Oh, and I love you, David, so very very much."

He has already forgotten the golden-haired redhead whose bike was stolen in Central Park.

★ ★ ★

But, of course, at parties all during that long weekend of the Fourth, Helen keeps urging him to tell the story of what happened in Central Park. And with each retelling of the story, even though David reports the facts essentially the same way each time, the story assumes mythic proportions in his own mind, the movie playing there differing from the actual script as much as if a director had arrogantly tampered with a writer's original creation to make it indifferently his own. At a cocktail party in Edgartown that Saturday, as David retells the basic story as it happened, he visualizes something quite other in his imagination, and is surprised to hear himself relating a tale that is, by comparison, fundamentally mundane.

In his fantasy, the bicycle thief (good title for a movie, he thinks, thank you, Mr. De Sica), in **The Bicycle Thief**, then—*David's* movie and not De Sica's—the robber is no longer a scrawny sixteen-year-old black kid struggling almost unsuccessfully to wrench a bike from a slip of a girl who couldn't have weighed more than a hundred and ten pounds, but is instead a brawny tattooed (Mom in a heart) black ex-con wearing a tiny gold earring in his left ear, sweaty T-shirt bulging with impossible muscles courtesy of Weight Lifting 101 at Ossining, New York. The girl, too, whereas not the fifteen- or sixteen-year-old he'd first thought she was yesterday in the park, becomes in the Never Never Land of his unconscious a girl of nineteen, technically a teenager but precariously poised on the cusp of womanhood, certainly a more appropriate victim for the brute assault-

ing her in this neorealistic black-and-white remake of
Beauty and the Beast, a far far better prey, unquestionably more innocent, and therefore more defenseless than
a woman of twenty-five would have been (if, in fact,
that was her age).

As David tells the story to an interested circle of listen-
ers on the deck of a house larger than the one they
are renting in Menemsha, yet another glorious sunset
provoking ooohs and ahhhs of appreciation, he does not
exaggerate in the slightest his behavior yesterday in the
park. He carefully explains that he did not run to the
rescue until he'd examined the possible risk of such
intervention . . .

"Well, of course," his host says, raising an understanding eyebrow. "You were in Central Park."

"Exactly," David replies.

. . . and even then, all he did was yell "Hey!" which
had no effect at all on the struggle, and then "Hey!"
again when the boy was already pedaling off. This being
Edgartown, he does not mention that the boy yelled
"Fuck you!" in exuberant farewell. This being Edgartown, someone immediately begins talking about the
absurdity of the Black Rage defense, and someone else
suggests that if they *catch* this little monster he should be
chained to a bicycle and forced to ride up and down
the streets of New York with a sign on his back reading
BICYCLE THIEF.

"Good title for a movie," someone says with a sly
wink, as if David hasn't already thought of it.

"Thank you, Mr. De Sica," someone else says.

That, too, David thinks.

But . . .

In retelling the tale that evening, and again at a Bring-the-Kiddies outdoor barbecue in Chilmark that Sunday, where—it being Chilmark—a heated discussion ensues regarding therapy programs for underprivileged minorities, and yet again at a West Chop picnic on Monday ("Of *course*, bring the kids!") and yet again for the last time . . .

Or at least what he *hopes* will be the last time, if only Helen would quit urging him to tell about **The Mugging in Central Park**, *her* title for the episode, which in truth is beginning to bore him even in the extravagantly distorted version inside his head. Yet retell it he does, for what actually *does* turn out to be the last time, at yet another cocktail party on the deck of a house overlooking Vineyard Haven Harbor and affording a splendid view of the fireworks display that starts as darkness falls and the world grows hushed in expectation.

But . . .

In all of these retellings, the fantastic story unfolding in his *mind* has him not only rushing to the adolescent girl's side, not only struggling with the brawny animal trying to steal her bike and rape her in the bargain— her costume torn, one breast showing where he's ripped the orange tank top from her shoulder, the adolescent nipple erect in terror—not only *struggling* with this weight-lifting specimen twice his size, but actually exchanging *blows* with him, the girl standing by breathlessly, her hand to her mouth, the green eyes wide in fear and concern, the freckled face flushed, until at last her attacker hits David a good one upside the head, in

29

his mind, anyway, and knocks him to the ground, in his mind, and kicks him while he's down, in his mind, and races off shouting the words David had not thought wise to repeat in Edgartown, nor even here in Vineyard Haven, for that matter.

Over the harbor, fireworks burst into the sky, trailing glowing shivering sparks toward the dark waters below.

Arthur K's sister is once again wearing her pink angora sweater, dark blue pleated skirt, string of pearls, bobby sox and saddle shoes. This is now the fifth of July, a hot and sultry Wednesday morning. It has been five days since Arthur K's Friday afternoon session; apparently the long Fourth of July weekend has blown all memories of the open blue robe from his mind. He revisits the scene in the kitchen again and again, tiptoeing around it like one of the ballerina hippopotami in *Fantasia*, but they are already thirty minutes into the hour and the blue robe has remained adamantly closed over Veronica's luminous pearls.

Arthur K is now telling David that he really had a *lousy* time at the synagogue dance that night long ago, and that, in fact, he *hadn't* made out with Shirley in the backseat of his father's Pontiac, or anywhere else, for that matter.

"I guess that was some sort of fantasy I made up," he says. "I guess that was what I *wished* would happen, but it didn't."

David says nothing.

"Does that make you angry?" Arthur K asks.

"No, no."

"My lying to you?"

"*Do* you feel you were lying to me?"

"No. I *told* you it was just a fantasy, didn't I? How is that lying? I was only sixteen at the time. It was just a fantasy."

In his notebook, David writes *Shirley Story a Screen*, and then waits, his pen poised over the lined yellow page.

"Nothing wrong with fantasies," Arthur K says. "I'm sure you have fantasies, don't you?"

They are perpendicular to each other, Arthur K on his back on the couch, looking up at the ceiling, David sitting in the chair behind his desk.

"By the way, how do you determine what's important and what's not?" Arthur K asks. "How do you know what to write down?"

David does not reply.

"I guess *Shirley*'s important, hm?" Arthur K says. "You always make a little note when I mention her, I can hear your little pen going, zip, zip, zip. Is that because she had the same name as my mother? *Has*, for all I know. She may still be alive. She'd be an old woman by now, of course . . . well, sixty-five, sixty-six, for a woman that's old. She was very beautiful back then, it was easy to fantasize about her, you can't blame me for fantasizing about her. I realize that what I told you . . . about the car and about her and me on the backseat . . . isn't something I fantasized back then when I was *sixteen*, of course, but something I made up *now* . . . well, not *now*, not this very *minute*, but whenever it was I first mentioned it to you. What I'm saying is I *know* I was telling you something I made up, I *know* I was lying to you, if that's what you choose to call it, telling you a lie about making out with Shirley when actually all I did was drive her home and say goodnight to her. Didn't even *kiss* her, in fact. Just said goodnight. I don't think we even shook hands. Just G'night, Shirley, G'night, Arthur, and I went home. I think I had a hard-on, I'm not sure. She was so fucking beautiful, it was impossible to go anywhere near her without getting a hard-on. I'm *sure* I must've had a hard-on."

This is the first David is hearing of Arthur K's hard-on. In previous tellings of that steamy adolescent night long ago, gawky Arthur K and sultry, dark-haired, dark-eyed Shirley were necking in the backseat of the Pontiac and suddenly Shirley's blouse was unbuttoned and her skirt was up above her waist. Until now David had naturally assumed there'd been an erection, else how could Arthur K have "made out"? He'd also assumed that Arthur K had gone home sated and *sans* erection, there to discover his sister Veronica sitting at the kitchen table weeping and spooning chocolate pudding into her mouth.

But now, all at once, a hard-on.

Ta-ra.

"I think she had that same effect on everyone," Arthur K says. "Shirley. Well, she was so fucking beautiful, you know. Blond hair and blue eyes, Jesus, she looked like a shiksa, I swear to God, you'd never know . . ."

You'd never *know*, David thinks with shocking clarity, that in every version he's heard of Arthur K's story so far, Shirley has had long black hair and brown eyes, and—in at least one telling—crisp black pubic hair. But now she is a *blonde*, and David forges an immediate connection which he scribbles into his notebook as *Blonde= Shirley = Veronica* . Arthur K doesn't hear him writing this time around because he is too busy staring up at the ceiling in David's office, where apparently he is visualizing his blond, blue-eyed Shirley-Veronica shiksa . . .

". . . half sitting, half lying back against the pillows, crying her eyes out. Her room was on the way to mine," he says, "this was a railroad flat, you had to walk through one room to get to the next one, there was like a corridor running straight through the apartment from one end of it to the other, with the rooms strung out along the way. Her light was on, she used to have this little lamp with a shade on it, on the table beside her bed. The door was open. I could see her lying back against the pillows, sitting there sobbing, her legs stretched out, she was barefoot. Wearing this little skimpy blue robe she always wore, a pink nightgown under it, I could see her pink nightgown, there was lace on the bottom of it, the hem. I said, 'Sis?' Whispered it, actually, because my parents were sleeping right down the hall, there was Veronica's room first, and then mine, and then the big bedroom where my parents slept. 'What's wrong?' I asked her. 'Sis? What's wrong?' And I went inside and sat beside her on the bed."

Arthur K falls silent.

David waits, scarcely daring to breathe.

"A lot of guys felt the same way I did about her," Arthur K says at last. "Shirley. She was the class cock-tease, in fact."

And the moment is gone.

And soon the hour is over.

On Wednesday morning, just as his second session that day is ending, the telephone rings. His patient, an obsessive-compulsive named Susan M, asks as she does after each session, changing only the day each time, "So I'll see you on Friday, right?" and when he says, "Yes, of course," she says, "Same time, right?" and he says, "Yes, same time," and the telephone rings. He is picking up the receiver as Susan M, waggling her fingers in farewell, closes the door behind her.

"Dr. Chapman," he says.

"Hi, it's Kate."

"Kate?" he says.

"Duggan. Rhymes with huggin'."

"Duggan?"

"Or, come to think of it, *muggin'* might be more appropriate."

"I'm sorry, I . . ."

"Kate. From the park. The victim, remember?"

"Oh. Oh, yes. How are you, Miss Duggan?"

"Kate. I'm fine. They caught him," she says. "At least, they *think* it's him. Guess where they got him?"

"Where?"

"In the park. Trying to steal somebody *else's* bike."

"Did they find yours?"

"No, he'd already sold it. He's a junkie, we were right."

We, he thinks.

"What happens now?"

"I have to go to the precinct later, identify him. That's why I'm calling. Do you think you could come with me?" she asks at once, and somewhat breathlessly, as if knowing in advance he will say no. "I told the police there was a witness, and they said it would help if they could get a positive ID from someone other than the victim. That's me. The victim."

"Well . . ."

"I know you must be busy . . ."

"Well, as a matter of fact I've been away, and . . ."

". . . but this won't be till six tonight. The lineup. *I* work, too, they know that. The cops. I told them that's the earliest I could get there. They've already got him on the attempted robbery, the one in the park yesterday, but they *really* want to nail him if it turns out he's the one who stole *my* bike, too. So if you could come to the precinct, it really would help. If you want to, that is. As a public service, that is."

"Well, actually, I won't be free till *almost* six. So . . ."

"That's okay, you could meet me at the precinct, it's not far from your office. And I don't think it'll matter if you're a few minutes late."

"Well, you see, Miss Duggan . . ."

"Kate," she says.

"Kate," he says. "I'm not sure I . . ."

"Please?"

He does not know why the image of her sitting on the ground, ankles crossed, flashes suddenly into his mind, the side-slit in the very short green nylon running shorts, the hint of white cotton panties beneath.

"Say yes," she says.

The stage is behind a thick plate-glass window which the detective running the lineup assures them is a one-way mirror, or a two-way mirror as it is sometimes called in some precincts, he says, go figure. What it is, *they* can see into the next room where there's the stage with height markers on the wall behind it, and a microphone hanging over it because the detective plans to ask all the people they parade to repeat the words the suspect said in the park last Friday—"First to you, Miss Duggan, and then to you, Dr. Chapman"—but nobody in the next room could see them where they were sitting here in the dark. None of the people in the other room would be able to hear any of the conversation in here, either, the conversation in here would be private and confidential.

The detective goes on to explain that all of the people they'll be looking at will be black men of about the same age as the suspect. This was so no smart-ass lawyer could come in later and say the identification process had been rigged, like say they put six Vietnamese fishermen and the one black kid on the stage there, some choice *that* would be, huh? The detective wants them to take their time, look everybody over carefully, nobody can see them or hear them out here in the dark, there's no danger of anybody coming after them and trying to do them harm later on. Just take your time, he tells them, see if you recognize anybody on the stage there, see if anybody's voice sounds familiar, okay?

Sitting in the dark here in the small room equipped with several folding chairs facing the glass, David has the feeling he's already read this scene, or viewed this scene, and by extension has been an integral *part* of this scene a hundred times over—except for the fact that Kate Duggan is sitting beside him here in the dark.

She is wearing for this earnestly official occasion a flimsy pale green garment he is sure he's seen at the dentist's office in the pages of *Vogue* or *Harper's Bazaar*, a costume he usually associates with very young women, gossamer enough to show long slender legs through the long skirt, a darker green shirt rescuing modesty beneath the dress's sheer bodice but failing to disguise the fact that Kate isn't wearing a bra, something all of the precinct detectives seemed to notice the moment she walked in—ten minutes late, by the way.

Her feet are in sandals strapped part of the way up the leg. Her legs are crossed. She is jiggling one foot. Her toenails are polished a green to match the dress; he wonders if she paints them a new color each time she puts on a different outfit. Her perfume conjures visions of tall pale skinny girls rushing across fields of heather and crushing themselves against the chests of extraordinarily tanned and muscular young men. He is sure he has smelled Kate's perfume on television. He thinks suddenly of Arthur K's blond, blue-eyed fifteen-year-old sister lying back against the pillows on her bed, skimpy blue robe parted over her short pink nightgown, bare legs showing, and all at once he feels intensely and uncomfortably aware of Kate sitting beside him in the dark as if they are here alone together to watch a pornographic movie.

Fortunately, they are spared the ordeal of having to sit too long through this police cliché, he and Kate both identifying her assailant virtually at once, by sight and also by the sound of his voice when he repeats first the words he'd spoken to her by way of introduction, "Give me the fuckin bike, bitch!" and then the words he'd hurled at David in farewell, "Fuck you!," his vocabulary and his repertoire being somewhat limited. They are out on the street again by a quarter to seven.

"I really appreciate your doing this," she says.

"I was happy to help."

"Well, most people wouldn't have bothered. Thank you. Really."

"Don't be silly."

He feels oddly removed from her all at once.

Last Friday, they shared a traumatic event that forged some sort of tentative bond between them. Today, they shared yet *another* experience, but now that justice has triumphed, the matter is over and done with, and they are once again strangers in a city of strangers, walking side by side in silence as the hot and humid evening closes in upon them.

"I haven't got around to your handkerchief yet," she says.

"Oh, don't worry about . . ."

"But I will," she says, and shrugs. There is something very girlish, almost childlike about the shrug and the small moue that accompanies it, her narrow shoulders rising, her tented mouth pulling into a grimace. There is no lipstick on that mouth. Her green eyes are shadowed with a blue that makes them appear even more green. Her breasts are tiny in the sheer dress. A girl's breasts. A girl's tentative nipples puckering the fabric. "I'll mail it to you as soon as . . ."

"That isn't necessary. Really."

"You saved my life," she says simply.

"What do you think'll happen to him?" he asks, and realizes he is merely making conversation; the episode is over, the tentative bond was broken the moment after they made positive identification.

"They're pretty sure he'll plead to a lesser offense."

"Like what?"

"Gee, I don't know," she says, and shrugs again. "Stealing roller skates?"

David smiles.

"Well, Miss Duggan . . ." he says.

"Kate," she says.

They both seem to realize at exactly the same moment that, really, there is nothing more to say.

"Well, Dr. Chapman . . ." she says.

"David," he says.

"David," she says.

There is a very long silence.

"See you around the pool hall," she says, and walks off.

He doesn't expect he will ever see her again.

But on Saturday morning, Stanley Beckerman calls.

★ ★ ★

"I understand we're both bachelors this weekend," he says.

"I've been meaning to call you . . ."

David has *not*, in fact, been meaning to call him, even though Helen has mentioned that Stanley will be alone in the city all this week and next and has suggested it might be "nice" if they had dinner together one night. David doesn't particularly enjoy Stanley's company, and Helen knows this. But Stanley's wife is in Helen's aerobics class, and the two of them are constantly hatching misbegotten dinner dates far too often, even though Helen *knows* how David feels about his colleague, such as he is.

Like David, Stanley is a psychiatrist. In fact, he is one of many in the profession who cause David to feel that *most* psychiatrists are attracted to the practice only because they themselves are crazy. All oblivious to his own nuttiness—"Well, he *is* a bit eccentric," Helen concedes—Stanley casually refers to his patients as the "Crazies" or, alternately, the "Loonies," descriptions David finds appalling. Stanley is about David's age, perhaps a year or so older, forty-seven or -eight, David guesses, but this is all they have in common, the practice of psychiatry notwithstanding. And whereas David would be content to have the relationship end with their few chance encounters at this or that seminar, Helen and her pal Gerry, bouncing around at Rhoda's Bodyworks on East Eighty-sixth and Lex, simply will not be deterred. So here is Dr. Stanley Beckerman now, on a hot Saturday morning in July, calling to say that one of his Loonies has given him two tickets to *Cats* for tonight's performance . . .

"I only saved him from committing suicide," Stanley says, "the cheap bastard . . ."

. . . and would David like to go with him to dinner and the show afterward?

"Dinner will be Dutch, of course," Stanley says. "The tickets are on me."

Or on your Loony, actually, David thinks.

He does not know why he accepts the offer.

Perhaps because it is easier to do so than to have to listen to Helen later wondering aloud how he could have been so *rude* as to turn it down.

Stanley is growing a beard while his wife and kids are in North Carolina for the summer. It is coming in scruffy and patchy, an uneven mix of mostly white, red, and gray hairs, with only a scattering of dark brown hairs that match the thinning, straight hair on his head. He is a short man, overweight to some extent, who wears rimless eyeglasses and a perpetual sneer, as if he knows secrets of the universe he would not reveal upon pain of torture or death. Tonight he is wearing khaki slacks, an altogether rumpled plaid sports jacket, brown loafers without socks, and a white button-down shirt open at the throat, no tie.

By contrast, David, wearing a neatly pressed tropical-weight suit with a pale blue shirt and a striped summer tie, feels absurdly overdressed. But he believes that dressing for the theater still warrants something more elegant than a bowling shirt and blue jeans. Then again, he supposes Stanley thinks he *does* look elegant. Or, more likely, Stanley doesn't give a shit *how* he looks.

What he looks like, in fact, is a beachcomber who's been washed ashore in far Bombay. Sneering instead like a British regimental commander entering a leper colony, he leads the way into the French restaurant he has chosen without consulting David, even though he has already informed him that they will be splitting the check, perhaps hoping David will insist on paying for *both* dinners, since, after all, the tickets are on Stanley, hmm?

Stanley has a habit of saying "Hmm?"

The mild query threads his conversation like a bee buzzing in clover, hmm?

Like Jackie Mason, Stanley has imperiously refused the first table offered to them—"Is this a table for a man like me?"—which seemed perfectly okay to David. As they accept another table, David again wonders why in hell he's here tonight, about to have dinner with a totally obnoxious human being, about to see a musical everybody else in New York has already seen, a show he didn't even *want* to see when it first opened because he has no particular affection for human beings pretending to be cats. He has read the Eliot book of poems, of course; he tries to keep up with *everything*, a hopeless task, in the expectation that a patient's dream might one day obliquely refer to something, anything, in the common realm. Movies, novels, essays, plays—even a musical like *Cats*, he supposes—are all grist for his analytic mill, the interpretation of dreams often hinging on obscure references like . . .

Well, for example, the one that had come up during a session with Alice L, who'd related a terrifying dream of water rushing through a sluice, totally mystifying until David recalled that such a gate was called a penstock, and lo and behold, one association led to another until the penstock became Guess What, and the rush of water became her husband's premature Guess What, live and learn, my oh my.

If David's three o'clock patient—a man named Harold G, who's been complaining about his itchy balls for the past three sessions, and who, David guesses, is afraid he may have caught some dread disease from the black prostitutes David suspects he's been frequenting—were to come in next Monday afternoon to disclose a dream about Jellicle Cats and Jellicle Balls, would this not in some way relate to his thus far unrevealed fears? David doesn't expect this will *really* happen—Harold G may be the only other person in New York who hasn't yet seen *Cats*—but *if* it did, wouldn't he be justified in surmising a reference to Eliot's descriptions of Jellicle Cats as white and black, black and white, and didn't Jellicle cross-rhyme with testicle, after all, and isn't a *jig* mentioned in the poem . . . well, a gavotte, too . . . but jig is certainly slang for . . .

". . . skirt up to here," Stanley is saying. "Sits across from me with half her ass showing, how am I supposed to take *that*, hmm? If I were a less principled man, Dave . . ."

No one ever calls David "Dave."

". . . I would most certainly take advantage of the situation. I'm only human, after all . . ."

A matter for debate, David thinks.

". . . mere flesh and blood, hmm? What would you do in a similar circumstance?"

"I would remind myself that I'm supposed to be a doctor," David says, sounding prim even to himself.

"You haven't seen this girl," Stanley says.

"Her appearance has . . ."

"*Or* her pussy," Stanley says.

Which comment, David hopes, will serve as a segue to the subject matter of the musical they're about to see together.

"Sits there like Sharon Stone," Stanley says relentlessly, "legs wide open, no panties. What looks good to you?" he asks, and picks up the menu.

David is happy for the respite.

But Stanley seems determined to pursue the matter further. Standing on Broadway outside the Winter Garden Theater with its banners proclaiming in black and white CATS NOW AND FOREVER, as if anything but cockroaches can be forever, and its three-sheets with the big yellow cat eyes in which the pupils are formed by dancing figures, David finds his mind wandering again as Stanley begins describing in detail the patient he is certain is trying to seduce him.

This is a particularly unattractive location for a theater, lacking all of the showbiz hubbub of the marquee-lined side streets west of Broadway. Instead, the theater is adjacent to a Japanese restaurant whose austere front looks singularly uninviting. Furthermore, it stands directly opposite a tall black featureless office building across the avenue, and faces diagonally to the northwest a similarly unattractive red brick Novatel Hotel with a Beefsteak Charlie's restaurant on its street level. The sidewalk outside the theater is packed with an inelegant crowd all dressed up for Saturday night, probably bussed in from New Jersey. Most of them are smoking. David always takes this as a sign of lower-class ignorance, although Stanley himself is smoking and he is a man with many years of education and training who was raised in a home with a geneticist mother and a college-professor father.

Smoking his brains out, he tells David—while assorted New Jersey theater-partygoers crane ears in their direction—that Cindy, for this now turns out to be her name, has been dressing more and more provocatively for each of their sessions, coming in just yesterday . . .

"I swear to God this is the truth, Dave, I wouldn't be telling you this if you weren't my closest friend . . ."

. . . wearing the short mini Stanley has earlier described, no panties under it, and a flimsy little top that shows everything God gave her . . .

"And believe me, Dave, God gave her plenty. She is overabundantly endowed, I would give my soul to rest my weary head between those voluptuous jugs . . ."

And here a man smoking a vile cigar turns toward Stanley in open interest.

". . . if only I weren't such a dedicated healer," he says, and smiles like a shark surfacing to devour a hapless swimmer. "What do you think I should do, Dave?"

"See a shrink," David says.

"Just between us . . ." Stanley says.

Privileged conversation, David supposes.

". . . I think I'll fuck her."

And the man from New Jersey almost drops his cigar.

The show starts with pairs of white lights blinking in the onstage dark and spilling over to enwrap the audience beyond the proscenium arch. It takes David a moment or two to realize that all those blinking white lights are supposed to be the eyes of cats shining in the dark. The lights, or the cat eyes, all suddenly wink out, to be replaced by strings of red lights that only faintly illuminate the garbage-dump stage. These resemble the lights strung on a Christmas tree. David wonders why Christmas-tree lights are strung all over a garbage dump and why they are all red. While he is trying to figure this out, someone in the audience lets out a gasp and then begins laughing. David realizes it is because human beings dressed as cats are now crawling on all fours down the aisles and through a two- or three-row gap deliberately left between the row ahead and the row in which he and Stanley are seated.

These are very good seats, even though Stanley has labeled as a "cheap bastard" the suicidal patient who gave them to him. They are, in fact, *house* seats, Stanley's patient being not only a cheap bastard, but also a friend of one of the show's wardrobe supervisors, a job that has to be monumental judging from the elaborate costumes on the twenty or thirty feline humans now gathering in midnight conclave on the stage. The seats are *so* good, in fact, that one of the marauding cats prowls to within a foot of where David is sitting in seat K102, directly at the intersection of the center aisle and the gap between the rows, and peers directly and somewhat unnervingly into his face before crawling away again to scamper onto the stage.

On the stage now, something cylindrical in shape and lighted all over its underside begins rising from the floor like the spaceship in *Close Encounters of the Third Kind*, to what purpose David, clever analyst that he is, cannot immediately discern. The assembled *cats*—for David realizes at once that he must begin thinking of these crawling, creeping, back-arching, furry, fake-tailed humans as cats if the show is to have any credibility at all—begin singing an introductory number titled "The Naming of Cats," which seems taken entirely from the Eliot poem of the same title, but which is an ill-conceived notion since the names spilling from the stage in full choral unison are cutesy-poo names like Mungojerrie and Skimbleshanks and Jennyanydots and Bombalurina, names no cat-lover in the universe would ever foist upon any self-respecting feline. The cat he and Helen had owned was named simply Sheba, an honorable name harking back to King Solomon's time, ultimately killed by a Doberman appropriately named Max, the Nazi bastard.

All of these preposterous cat names seemed okay, if undeniably cute, on the printed page. But here, being belted by twenty-four, twenty-five people in cat makeup and cat costumes, they are virtually incomprehensible, followed as they are by a number titled "The Invitation to the Jellicle Ball," which repeats the word jellicle over and over again, to the utter mystification of anyone unfamiliar with *Old Possum's Book of Practical Cats*, a rather cutesy-poo title in itself, Eliot should have stuck to Prufrock.

It does not take long for David to realize that this is a show essentially without a book. This is a show, in fact, that merely sets these fundamentally second-rate Eliot poems to music, with no attempt to tie them together into any dramatic semblance of beginning, middle and end. At its basic worst, this is a show about people trying to look like cats and behave like cats. Accept that silly premise or go home. David cannot accept that anyone on this stage—well, maybe the female cat in the white costume—moves like any cat he has ever known. He cannot go home, however, because Stanley seems inordinately and childishly engrossed, tapping him lightly on the arm each time a chorus girl in sleek leotard and tights slinks across the stage.

The girl in the white costume seems to be performing in a world of her own. She seems to believe she really *is* a cat. There are many choreographed cat moves in the show, actions that the cast performs simultaneously in response to music cues, but David feels certain the little personal bits of cat motions were improvised by the individual members of the cast during rehearsal and have now become mannerisms indigenous to performances set in concrete. The girl in white, however . . .

He squints through the program during a well-lighted song-and-dance number that spills some illumination to where he is sitting, trying to identify her in the jumble of cats with names that are non-names, all of them leaping about the stage, often hissing, sometimes baring fake claws. He cannot for the life of him determine which character the girl in white is portraying.

But she continues to hold his interest.

She seems truly in a world apart, obviously having owned a cat at one time, or perhaps having devoted hours to the study of cat behavior, now translated to subtle dance poses, or perhaps indeed having *been* a cat in some previous life long ago, perhaps even Sheba the cat, although Sheba was a great big fat tabby, all gray and black with a fluffy white tummy, and not this slender pristine white cat who really seems to *be* one.

She is dressed entirely in white, white leotard and tights with snippets of fake white fur fastened in tatters to the shoulders and bosom of the costume. A white fur hat covers her hair, hiding it completely, fastening under her chin, topping the costume and capping her head, little peaked ears poking up out of it. The makeup on her face is a chalky white, highlighted with black liner that emphasizes cat eyebrows and a cat nose and cat whiskers.

She is wearing low, flat-heeled shoes undoubtedly rubberized to grip what appears to be a polymered stage floor across which she and the other cats frequently body-slide as if on ice. Over the tights and partially flopping onto the dancing shoes are leg warmers a shade darker than the stark white of the costume, more a pearly gray by contrast. She wears on her arms, from her wrists virtually to her elbows, coverings of the same type, what appear to be long knitted wristlets or the upper parts of graying white dinner gloves. Real gloves, cut off at the fingers and thumbs, grayer than the wristlets, lend her hands, or rather her paws, a grubby alley-cat look, in contrast to her otherwise sleek appearance. A narrow belt around her waist holds a long tail of the same grayish color as the leg warmers.

She is every inch a cat.

Moreover, she seems to be a cat who is only intermittently caught up in the inanity of this plodding musical, going about her own catlike business, licking her paws, or snapping her tail, or cocking her head to watch this or that bit of action, or swatting at an invisible insect, or rolling over on her back, only to sit upright an instant later when some further piece of business or song erupts nearby, sometimes startled by what she sees, sometimes merely bemused by the fact that she is here at *all*.

Since she is the only white cat on a stage full of varicolored cats often indistinguishable one from the other, it is easy to follow her every movement. She seems to have captured Stanley's attention as well; he lightly taps David's arm in the "Jellicle Ball" scene near the end of the first act, alerting David to her form as she is lifted over the head of a male dancer, her long legs gracefully dangling. When the grizzled cat—of course named Grizabella—sings "Memory," the show's one and only memorable song, the white cat is lying on her side stage left, utterly still, as rapt as the audience, completely absorbed in lyrics that truly evoke the emotions of Eliot's *real* poetry. For the first time since the show began, David takes his eyes off the white cat, and finds himself moved beyond comprehension when the aging glamour cat sings of her lost, irretrievable youth.

PRIVILEGED CONVERSATION

★　★　★

While Stanley goes outside to enjoy an intermission smoke, David leafs through the program, trying to zero in on the name of the dancer playing the white cat. There is no White Cat, as such, listed anywhere. He tries to imagine whether Eliot would have named this cat Jellylorum or Rumpleteazer or Demeter or . . . wait a minute. Here are four cats, two male, two female, listed simply as "The Cats Chorus," but he has no idea whether the white cat is one of them. He looks up their bios in the *Who's Who In The Cast* section of his Playbill, but finds no clues there, either. He seems to remember, but perhaps he's wrong, that one of the cats singing right up front and center in the Ball-Invitation number at the top of the show was the *white* cat . . . wasn't she? He checks back to the listing of scenes, and finds three cats credited by name for that particular song, two of them male cats respectively called Munkustrap and Mistoffelees—boy oh boy—and the third a female cat named Victoria. *Victoria?* How'd such a sensible name sneak in here? He looks across the page to see who is playing this oddly named creature. The line reads:

Victoria . . . . **Kathryn Duggan**

He looks at the name again.

Kathryn Duggan.

Hey! My name is Kate!

Kate.

Duggan. Rhymes with huggin'.

But no. It can't be.

But yes, right *there*, Kathryn Duggan.

51

Well, wait a minute. He flips forward again to the biographical listings of the cast. A loudspeakered voice announces that the curtain will be going up in three minutes. The cast is listed alphabetically. He hastily reads:

KATHRYN DUGGAN (Victoria) returns to *Cats* after the national tour of *Miss Saigon*. Prior to that, she was seen in *Les Miz* London, and was assistant dance captain and performed in *Cats* Hamburg. She wishes to thank her sister Bess and especially Ron for their support and encouragement.

"Anything interesting happen while I was gone?" Stanley asks, and slips into the seat beside him just as the lights come up again.

And now David cannot possibly take his eyes from her. Whenever she disappears from the stage, as frequently she does, he wonders where she has gone, and renews his scrutiny when suddenly she reappears. He keeps hoping she will come down into the audience as some of the other dancers do every now and then, crawling up and down the aisles on all fours, but either she is hidden behind a Siamese cat mask in the "Growltiger's Last Stand" number—at least he *thinks* it's Kathryn and therefore perhaps Kate because he spots the grayish-white leg warmers under the Oriental garb—or else she's paying homage to the cat named Deuteronomy, sitting on his lap and stroking his aged face, or else she's pretending to be part of a locomotive's piston assembly in yet another number, stroking the huge piston back and forth as if it is the head of a penis, nice association, Dr. Chapman. But none of this brings her close enough for him to get a good look at the face disguised by that dead-white makeup, until—as if some cat-God high up in cat-Heaven is granting a secret wish—she comes down off the stage in the "Macavity" number, comes off from the side ramp on the right of the theater, surprising him when she crawls through the wide space in front of row K, and then in her catlike way, sits up, seemingly detecting a human presence, seemingly startled, jerking her head around and looking directly into his face, her green eyes wide.

She shows not the slightest sign of recognition.

She is a cat, thoroughly immersed in her own cat existence, and she is off again in an instant, scampering away, gray-white tail twitching.

Toward the end of the show, when Grizabella sings the searing words "Touch me," David's eyes fill with tears.

At eleven o'clock on Sunday morning, shortly after he's called Helen on the Vineyard, the intercom buzzer sounds, and Luis the doorman tells David there's a delivery for him.

"Some young lady leaves a package," he says.

"A package?"

"*Sí.* But a leetle one."

"Can someone bring it up?" David asks.

"This is Sunday. I'm here only myself."

David is still in his pajamas. The Sunday *Times* is spread all over the dining alcove table. He tells Luis he'll be down for the package later and then realizes this has to be his handkerchief, and that the young lady who delivered it was surely Kate Duggan, who last night had prowled all over the stage of the Winter Garden Theater in rather good imitation of a predatory feline. He has already decided he'll go out for brunch in an hour or so, and he figures he can pick up the handkerchief then. Surely there's no urgency. But nonetheless he throws on undershorts, jeans, a T-shirt and a pair of loafers, and, unshaven and unshowered, takes the elevator down to the lobby.

The package is a small clasp envelope with his name hand-printed on it in thick red Magic Marker letters. **DR. DAVID CHAPMAN**. Luis gives him a big macho Hispanic grin and all but winks at him as he hands over the envelope. The grin suggests that not everyone in the building has "leetle" packages delivered by beautiful redheaded girls at eleven o'clock in the morning. David ignores complicity with what the rows of glistening white teeth imply. He thanks Luis for the package, answers politely when Luis asks how Mrs. Chapman is enjoying the seashore (slight raising of a Puerto Rican eyebrow, faint suggestion again of the male-bonding grin under the black mustache) and then walks across the lobby to the elevator bank. He feels certain Luis's dark eyes are on his back, and feels suddenly guilty of whatever crime Luis is imagining. In the elevator, he resists the temptation to open the envelope. It seems to take forever for the elevator to crawl up the shaft to the tenth floor. It seems to take forever for him to unlock the door. The keys feel suddenly thick in his hands.

He carries the envelope to the table in the dining alcove off the kitchen, and sets it down on the front page of the Arts & Leisure section. The red letters spelling out his name are ablaze in bright morning sunshine. He sits at the table. Picks up the envelope again. Turns it over. Lifts the wings of the clasp. Opens the envelope.

The handkerchief has been laundered and ironed, folded once upon itself, and then once again to form a perfect white square. He is disappointed when he realizes there is no note attached to the handkerchief. He peers into the envelope, spots a small white business card in it, and shakes it free onto the table. The card is imprinted with her name, her address on East Ninety-first, and two telephone numbers, one below the other. He turns the card over. Handwritten in blue ink scrawled across its back are the words:

Don't you dare ever blow your nose in it! Thanks again.

Kate

He smiles.

He does not go immediately to the telephone, but he knows he will call her sometime later this morning, before he goes down for brunch—what time is it now, anyway, eleven-fifteen, eleven-thirty? He looks at his watch. It is twenty past eleven. He'll call her later, as a courtesy, thank her for her kindness, her thoughtfulness, mention how much he enjoyed her performance last night.

He goes back to reading the *Times*.

His eyes keep flicking to the card lying on the table beside the freshly laundered handkerchief.

Don't you dare ever blow your nose in it! Thanks again.

Kate

He looks at his watch again.

Eleven twenty-five.

He rises abruptly, decisively, walks into the bathroom, undresses, glances at himself briefly in the mirror, and then steps into the shower. He studies his face carefully as he shaves. His eyes meet his own eyes often. He realizes he is rehearsing what he will say to her when he calls. Naked, he pads into the bedroom and puts on a black silk robe with blue piping at the cuffs, a gift from Helen last Christmas. Wearing only the robe belted at his waist, the silk slippery against his skin, he sits propped against the pillows on the unmade bed, and dials the first of the numbers on her card. A recorded voice tells him he has reached the Phillip Knowles Agency, and that business hours are Monday to Friday from nine A.M. to six P.M. He puts the phone back on its cradle.

Oddly, he thinks of Arthur K's sister in her blue robe, propped against the pillows in her midnight bed.

Arthur K's arm around her.

He takes a deep breath and dials the second number.

"Hello?"

Her voice.

PRIVILEGED CONVERSATION

"Kate?"

"Yes?"

Somewhat breathless.

"This is Dr. Chapman. David."

"Oh, hi. I just came in the door. Did you get the . . . ?"

"Yes, that's why I'm . . ."

"I washed and ironed it myself, you know. I didn't take it to a laundry or anything."

"Well, thank you. That was very thoughtful. Truly."

"Considering what a lousy ironer I am . . ."

"On the contrary . . ."

". . . I think I did a pretty good job."

"Very professional, in fact."

There is a silence on the line.

"I saw you last night," he says.

"Saw me?"

"Your performance. In *Cats*."

"You did?"

"Yes. You were very good."

"Well, thank you. But . . ."

A slight pause.

"How'd you even know I was in it? Did I mention . . . ?"

"Actually, I . . ."

"Because I don't remember tell—"

"It was just an accident. My being there."

"Gee."

"I enjoyed . . . seeing you. Your performance. I thoroughly enjoyed it."

"Gee," she says again.

He visualizes her shaking her head in wonder. The golden-red hair. The hair so effectively hidden by the white fur cap last night.

"Everybody *else* saw me in it ages ago," she says. "Everybody I know, anyway." She pauses again. "How was I?" she asks. "I don't even know anymore."

"Terrific."

"Did I look like a cat?"

"More so than anyone else on stage."

"Really?"

"Really."

"Tell me more," she says, and he can imagine a wide girlish grin on her freckled face. "Tell me I should be the star of the show . . ."

"You were really very . . ."

"Tell me how beautifully I dance . . ."

"You do."

"And sing . . ."

"Yes."

"Take me to lunch and flatter me."

He hesitates only an instant.

"I'd be happy to," he says.

He is surprised to learn that she's actually twenty-seven.

"Which is old for a dancer, right?" she says.

"Well, no, I don't . . ."

"Oh, sure," she says. "Especially a dancer who's been in *Cats* forever," she says and rolls her eyes. Green flecked with yellow. Sitting in slanting sunlight at a table just inside the window of the restaurant she's chosen on the West Side. Eyes glowing with sunlight. "Now and forever, right?" she says. "That's the show's slogan, the headline, whatever you call it. Cats, Now and Forever. That's me. I'll probably be in that damn show when I'm sixty-five. Every time I go for an audition, they ask me what I've done, I say *Cats*. That's what I've done. Well, that's not *all* I've done. I was in *Les Miz* in London, the Brits call it *The Glums*, did you know that? And last year I toured *Miss Saigon*. But *Cats* is the big one, *Cats* is Broadway. I've been in that damn show practically since it opened, seventeen years old, little Dorothy in her pretty red shoes, I don't think we're in Kansas anymore, Toto. That's right, we're in a goddamn show called *Cats!*"

He realizes he is nervously checking out the restaurant as she talks, trying to remember how many people he and Helen know here on the West Side, preparing a cover story in advance to explain why he is here with a young and beautiful girl while his wife is up there in the wilds of Massachusetts. He remembers all at once what Kate said that first day in the park, referring to the handkerchief she'd bloodied and offered to launder— *Your wife would kill me*—and wonders if she'd been fishing that day, trying to learn if he was available. Well, he's flattering himself, for Christ's sake. Why would anyone as beautiful as she is, as young as she is—well, twenty-seven, he's just learned—why would anyone like Kate wonder whether a forty-six-year-old man, a man *about* to be forty-six, was married or single or divorced or whatever the hell? Besides, he'd been wearing the wedding band, just as he's wearing it now, plain to see on the ring finger of his left hand—see, folks, I'm married, nothing fishy going on here, nobody trying to hide anything, I'm married, okay? So of course, she'd already known. She'd seen the ring, and she'd known he was married. Still, he wonders why that *particular* remark if it wasn't a fishing expedition. Or maybe a warning. I know you're married, mister, so no funny moves, okay?

"Where in Kansas?" he asks.

"What?"

"You said . . ."

"Oh, that was just an expression. Don't you know the line from *Wizard of* . . . ?"

"Yes, of course. But I thought . . ."

"No, I'm not. From Kansas."

"Then where are you from? You said . . ."

"Westport, Connecticut. But I've been living in New York since I was seventeen. Ten years last month, in fact. That's when I got the job in *Cats*. Before then, I was studying dance in Connecticut. No *wonder* I'm still in that damn show. Where are you from?"

"Boston."

"I thought you sounded a little like a Kennedy."

"Do I?"

"A little."

"Is that good or bad?"

"It's good, actually. It's a nice sound, that Massachusetts accent. Or dialect. Whatever you call it. Regional dialect, I guess. Anyway, I like it."

"Thank you."

"You promised to flatter me. Tell me about last night."

He tells her how he'd been invited to see the show

with a man he despised, someone whose wife is in *his* wife's aerobics class, venturing to mention his wife, watching her eyes to see if anything shows there, but nothing does, and anyway, why should it? This is simply a Sunday brunch in broad daylight, a married man wearing his wedding band for all to see, two people who'd happened to share an unusual experience together, now sitting and chatting in the innocent light of the sun, nothing going on here, folks, see the ring, wanting to waggle the fingers of his left hand so the ring would catch the light of the sun and flash like a beacon to anyone entertaining suspicious thoughts.

He tells her all about how she'd captured his attention because she was so very good . . .

"Tell me, tell me," she says, and grins again.

. . . perfectly capturing a cat's, well, *essence*, he supposes one might call it, in a show that was otherwise, well, he hates to say this . . .

"Say it," she says. "It sucks."

"Well, there were things about it . . ."

"Name one," she says. "Besides 'Memory.'"

" 'Memory' was very moving."

"I played Sillabub in Hamburg. I got to do the *other* version of the song. The younger, more innocent version than the one Grizabella sings. In a sort of high, piping voice, you know? For contrast."

"Yes."

"But aside from 'Memory,' what else is there? It isn't even a *dancer's* show, you know, like *Chorus Line* or any of the Fosse shows when he was alive, which is odd because you'd think the very notion of cats *dancing* would inspire all sorts of inventive choreography. None of the dances seem to me like anything a *cat* would dance, do they to you? Do you have a cat?"

"Not now."

"I have a cat, well, you'll meet her, and believe me, if they allowed her to get up on that stage and dance, it wouldn't be like anything *we're* doing up there. It's a shame when you think of it, the opportunities squandered . . ."

He is thinking about what she said not ten seconds ago, *I have a cat, well, you'll meet her,* and misses much of her dissertation, or what sounds like one, sounds like something she's said many times before to many other people, about the way cats naturally *seem* to be dancing whenever they move, the glides, the leaps, the turns, "Even in repose," she says, "a cat looks like a dancer resting," but he is thinking *I have a cat, well, you'll meet her,* her green eyes unwavering as she leans across the table toward him, fervently intent on making her point, the reddish-gold hair falling loose about her face, he wonders why they didn't make her a tawny cat, didn't use her own hair and a rust-colored costume instead of dressing her in white like a virgin, and why the name Victoria, he doesn't recall any Victoria in the Eliot . . .

"Was there a cat named Victoria in the poems?" he asks suddenly. "Excuse me, I didn't mean . . ."

"That's okay, I was just rattling on, anyway. When he talks about the names families give their cats, he gives *Victor* as an example, but not Victoria. And also, he mentions that Mungojerrie and Rumpleteazer live in

Victoria Grove, which is an actual section in London, have you ever been to London?"

"Yes, many times."

With my wife, he thinks, but does not say.

"But what's interesting is that Victoria is the only *straight* name in the show," she says. "All the other cats are given what Eliot calls their par*tic*ular names. Which he rhymes with *per*pendicular, by the way. Have you read the poems?"

"Yes."

"Mediocre, right? Like the show. God knows why it's a hit. Dress people up like cats, and you've got a hit, go figure, no matter how boring it is. Would you like to go to the crafts fair? When we're finished here. Or do you have other plans?"

"No," he says. "I have no other plans. Who's Ron?"

"Ron? I don't know. Who's Ron?"

"In the program, you thanked . . ."

"Oh. *That* Ron."

"You thanked your sister . . ."

"Bess, yes. Well, Elizabeth, actually."

". . . and especially Ron . . ."

"My God, did you *memorize* that dumb thing?"

". . . for their support and encouragement."

"Ron was someone I used to know." Her eyes meet his. "Why?" she asks.

"I just wondered. I've never understood why performers *thank* people in the program notes . . ."

"It's stupid, I know."

". . . sometimes even *dedicate* their performances to this or that person . . ."

"Absolutely idiotic. How can you dedicate a performance? Mom, Dad, I dedicate this next *pas de deux* to you. Unless my partner objects. In which case, I dedicate the *entrechat*."

"And yet . . ."

"I know, I know, you surrender to the stupidity. Everyone else is thanking everyone in sight, you figure the people *you* know and love will be hurt or offended if you don't thank *them*. They put that in the program when I rejoined the show in January. After the *Miss Saigon* tour ended in Detroit. If you liked me in a white fur hat, you should've seen me in a black wig and slanty eyes."

"Was Ron in *Miss Saigon?*"

"Well, yes, actually. He played the Engineer." Her eyes meet his again. The Green Lantern's eyes. Flashing across the table at him like a laser beam. "Why?" she asks again.

"Just wondered."

"Mm," she says. Eyes refusing to let go of his. "I had a dream about you," she says. "Last night, when I washed and ironed your handkerchief, isn't that odd? The very night you saw the show. That's very peculiar, don't you think?"

"Yes."

"I washed and ironed it when I got home. It must've been two in the morning by then, some of us had gone out for Chinese after the show, we're always *starving* after the show. Anyway, I washed and ironed it last night because I planned to drop it off either today or on Tuesday. There's a three o'clock matinee today, but I pulled something in my leg last night, so I'm off, aren't we lucky? We're dark on Tuesdays and Thursdays, we have a very abnormal Broadway schedule. Anyway, it was on my mind, you see. That I hadn't yet returned it to you. Which is probably why I dreamt about you last night."

"What'd you dream?"

"I dreamt you and I were making love in front of my mother's house in Westport."

David says nothing.

"On the lawn," she says.

He still says nothing.

"Naked," she says. "Well, in the dream, I'm wearing a white blouse, but that's all. You're entirely nude. And we're making passionate love. Which is odd, since I hardly know you."

David nods. He feels suddenly as if he is taking unfair advantage of her. He is a skilled analyst, a person *trained* to interpret dreams. He should not be listening to . . .

"My mother comes out with a huge pail of cold water and throws it on us. The way they do with dogs who get stuck, you know? But we keep right on going. I guess we were enjoying it."

He nods again, says nothing.

"So how do you interpret that?"

"How do *you* interpret it?"

"Oh-ho, here comes the shrink."

"Force of habit," he says, and smiles unconvincingly.

He is feeling suddenly very threatened.

And guilty.

He is feeling that he'd better get the hell out of here

fast because his wife and two adorable daughters are too far away on Martha's Vineyard and he has no right sitting here with this beautiful *dancer*, never mind the wedding band on his left hand, never mind the purity of eggs over easy on an English muffin, side of bangers, please, sitting here openly and innocently in the noonday sun for all the world to see, but with a faint tumescence in his pants nonetheless, hidden under the table, a dangerous and guilt-ridden hard-on covertly ripening in his pants because this girl, this woman, this delicate and desirable creature sitting opposite him has dreamt of them making *love* together, making *passionate* love, as she'd put it, in fact *enjoying* it so much that not even a huge pail of cold water could break them apart.

Oh yes he *knows*, of *course* he knows that the forty-six-year-old man in her dream could easily stand for her father, and he knows yes of course that the intercourse on her mother's lawn, naked on her mother's lawn, could stand for a flaunting of whatever unresolved Electral feelings she may still nurture. And he knows, yes yes *quit* it already, that her mother throwing water on them, trying to stop them, most likely stands for society's taboos against incest, he *knows* all of this, he realizes all this, but the developing hard-on in his pants keeps reminding him that the person she chose to be Daddy's stand-in and stuntman is none other than David himself.

Moreover, she has confessed it to him, she has revealed her unconscious choice . . . well, not *confessed* it, surely. She has only *mentioned* it to him, actually, rather matter-of-factly, as if she'd dreamt of the two of them merely having tea at the Plaza—but mentioned it nonetheless.

Which means, the way he interprets it to his now insistent hard-on, that she'd *wanted* him to know, wanted him to *understand* that the person she'd chosen for her fantasy, albeit unconsciously, the person with whom she elected to fuck her brains out on her mother's lawn was none other than David Chapman, M.D., P.C.

"You come all over the blouse," she says. "In the dream. Your semen stains my blouse. I guess that refers to the handkerchief, don't you think? My getting blood on your handkerchief?"

"I . . . would imagine," he says.

"In the dream, I have to wash my blouse to get the stain out. Your semen. In the dream, I'm standing topless, washing my blouse and then ironing it."

They are staring at each other across the table.

"Do you really want to go to the crafts fair?" she asks.

Her cat is named simply and sensibly Hannah.

She is a great fat tubby thing that Eliot might have called a Gumbie Cat, her coat "of the tabby kind, with tiger stripes and leopard spots." She sidles up to Kate the moment she enters the apartment, rubbing against her, and then looking up at David as if knowing in her infinite cat wisdom that he will soon be making love to her mistress. David knows this, and Kate knows it, and the cat knows it, too.

Her apartment on East Ninety-first is a one-bedroom, for which Kate—she tells him as she opens a can of food for the cat—paid a hundred and ten thousand dollars four years ago, and which she is now trying to sell for seventy-nine thousand, if she can get it, so she can move to the West Side and be closer to the theater section. The cat keeps rubbing against her as Kate uses the can opener. Kate keeps saying, "Yes, darling, yes, baby," tossing the lid of the can into the garbage pail under the sink, and then spooning its contents into a red plastic bowl, "Yes, baby," all the while telling David that the closest offer she's had so far is forty-five thousand, which means she'd be losing thirty-four thousand non-tax-deductible dollars, "Yes, baby, here you are," she says and sets the bowl down on the floor near the refrigerator and comes immediately to David and drapes her arms over his shoulders and leans into him and kisses him.

Sitting beside her on her bed, his arm around her, Arthur K hears his sister's plaintive cry for help, *I wish someone would give* me *lessons*, and the words break his heart. She is so very beautiful and innocent and vulnerable that he is enraged by just the *notion* of someone like Howard Kaplan kissing her and telling her later that she doesn't even know how. Sitting beside her on her bed, his arm around her, her head on his shoulder, the bedside lamp bathing them in a soft indulgent glow, he keeps patting her shoulder and saying, "No, no, Sis, don't cry, there's nothing to cry about," all at once afraid her crying will awaken their parents down the hall, though surely there is nothing wrong going on here in her room, a brother comforting his sister is all, there is nothing wrong with that. So why is he worried about them waking up?

"I can teach you in a minute," he hears himself say.

And she answers, "Then do it."

★ ★ ★

"Yes, do it," Kate says, her mouth under his, her lips murmuring against his lips, "Do it, do it." They have kissed their way to the sofa against one wall of the living room, awkwardly moving in embrace toward the sofa heaped with pillows against the wall. The wall itself is hung with three sheets of the shows in which she's performed, the *Cats* poster in the center with its big yellow eyes pupiled with dancers in black, and the *Miss Saigon* poster with its rising helicopter that looks like Asian calligraphy, falling blindly onto the pillows, their lips entangled, "Yes, do it," she keeps saying, though he scarcely knows *what* he is doing anymore, his hands all over her, his lips on hers, do it, do it, and the *Les Misérables* poster with its French waif and her dark soulful eyes.

Her blue eyes are wide in expectation. Her long blond hair frames her face, delicate strands electrifying the back of his hand when he brushes her hair away to reveal the pale oval of her face. From the corner of his eye, below, he can see the flimsy pink nightgown with its intricately laced hem where the blue robe has parted over it, her long white legs. He catches a fleeting glimpse of her left breast as she turns to him, the robe gapping slightly, and is suddenly enraged by what Howard Kaplan did to her, or tried to do to her, hurting her that way, the anger coursing through his veins, causing his temples to throb, causing his cock to swell suddenly inside his pants.

"Part your lips, Veronica," he says like the good older

69

brother he is, and she lifts her face to his and does exactly as he says.

Her kiss is surprisingly adept. He wonders, but merely for an instant, if she was lying to him about Howard telling her she didn't know how to kiss. Then again, what the hell does Howard know, the jackass? His sister—he remembers that she is his sister and that he is merely performing a brotherly service that will enable her to cope more effectively in any future boy-girl relationship—his sister immediately and expertly draws in her breath in the same instant that he does, their simultaneous inhalations creating a tight seal that fiercely joins their lips and causes him to remember, yet again, that she *is*, after all, his sister, although the insistently clamoring erection in his pants seems determined to prove otherwise.

Nonetheless, he is here to teach her, sister or no, and so he gently inserts his tongue into her mouth, meaning to pull away an instant later—but the seal is so tight— to explain that tongues play as important a role as lips in this serious business of kissing, fully intending to explain the procedure step by step, but suddenly her own tongue is alive in his mouth, actively seeking his tongue, coiling around his tongue like a serpent, even though she said she didn't know how to kiss. Or, more accurately, all she said was that *Howard* told her she didn't know how to kiss, she didn't say that she *herself* believed she didn't know how to kiss.

In fact, she now seems ferociously determined to demonstrate that Howard was wrong, that for all her tender years—but she's fifteen, after all, and so was Shirley in

the backseat of his father's Pontiac who dug her fingernails into the back of his hand the moment he cupped
her chin preparatory to kissing her and ordered him to
take her home right that very minute. His sister Veronica,
his little sister Veronica, his blue-eyed blond and beautiful baby sister Veronica is the same age as big-titted
Shirley Fein who'd sent him home all desolate and for-
lorn, a condition his sister with her questing mouth and
writhing tongue is rapidly reversing. The hard-on he'd
had in the Pontiac, subsequently shriveled by Shirley's
rejection, surprisingly revived when his sister leaned in
to accept his kiss and the robe momentarily opened to
show that single small white breast with its little pink
nipple—she *is* his sister, he keeps reminding himself, she
is his goddamn *sister*.

Which is perhaps why his indecorous and inappropriate hard-on causes a sudden wave of terror to sweep
over him, almost nauseating—suppose his parents wake
up? Because now, you see, this isn't just a dutiful brother
comforting a distraught sister, patting her shoulder and
trying to still her fears of inadequate osculatory technique. This is a seventeen-year-old boy and a fifteen-
year-old girl kissing passionately, their arms wrapped
around each other—yes, but don't forget we're just *sitting*
here, we're not *lying* on the bed, we're not pressed against
each other or anything, no matter how it may look, the
robe somehow having ridden up over the lace-hemmed
nightgown, the nightgown itself having somehow ridden up over Veronica's long white naked legs. Suppose
his *mother*, God forbid, comes down the hall and finds
them, well, *kissing* this way, suppose his mother *sees* the

hard-on straining in his pants, a hard-on provoked by the sight of his own sister's girlish breast and nipple, a hard-on bulging not inches from where Veronica's hand rests upon his leg, her robe somehow slipping off her left shoulder now to fully expose this time the breast and nipple he merely glimpsed earlier.

In that instant he becomes utterly confused.

"It was like a dream," he will later tell David. "I don't know where I am in the dream, I don't know who it is I'm with, there is just . . ."

. . . this beautiful girl whose mouth is insistently, whose tongue is demandingly, forgets in that instant, but only for an instant, that she truly is his sister, her hard pink nipple erect under his grasping fingers, fearful she will reach up at once to remove his hand as forcefully as Shirley had when he, but she doesn't. Instead, her own hand drops to where his cock is seething inside his pants, and suddenly he doesn't care if she's his sister or his aunt or his mother or his grandmother, suddenly his hands are inside the robe and under the gown and she reaches past him and over him, turning slightly, lifting herself slightly, her right hand still tight on his cock inside his pants, and turns out the light with her free hand, and then lies beside him in the dark and opens her robe to him and opens herself to him.

There is a frenzy to their joining.

It is as if they have been waiting all their lives, each and separately, for this moment to arrive, and now that it is here, they must cling to it desperately and drain it of every last passionate drop. They writhe on her pillows in shafts of light slanting through open blinds across the room, glide in silvery sunlight as if through something wet and viscous, yellow cat eyes watching from the wall behind them, helicopter rising against a yellow moon on the wall behind them, little French-girl eyes peering curiously from the wall behind them. And Hannah. Hannah the cat. Watching indifferently.

Only once does his wife cross his mind, briefly, her name, his wife's name, Helen, and then her face, her blue eyes, Helen's face and eyes, but he banishes her at once, excluding her from all he has already done to this woman in this room, all that he is doing now to this woman in this room, all that he will continue doing to this woman, in this room, in frenzy, forever—or at least until the afternoon shadows start to lengthen and all at once it is dark and time to go home.

"Stay the night," she says.

"I can't."

They are standing just inside her door. He is fully dressed. She has put on a man's white tailored shirt, which she wears unbuttoned and hanging loose, the sleeves rolled up. He wonders whose shirt it was, or perhaps whose shirt it still *is*. Does the shirt belong to Ron? Is it Ron's shirt she wears after sex on a Sunday afternoon? Old "Especially Ron," who together with sister Bess offered such support and encouragement?

"When will I see you again?" she asks.

"When do you want to see me?"

"Tomorrow morning. The minute the sun comes up."

Standing barefoot inside the doorway, looking up at him, green eyes and blue fingernails, wearing only Ron's or whoever's white shirt open over her breasts, the nipples still erect and looking angry and raw, the tangled patch of red pubic hair showing at the joining of her long naked legs.

In the dream, I'm wearing a white blouse, but that's all. You come all over the blouse. In the dream. Your semen stains my blouse.

He pulls her fiercely to him.

He does not leave her apartment until eleven that night.

By the time he gets home, it is too late to call Helen.

On the phone early Monday morning, he tells Helen that shortly after he'd spoken to her yesterday he'd gone over to the crafts fair on Amsterdam Avenue, where he'd eaten his way serendipitously from food stand to food stand.

"I didn't see anything I wanted to buy," he says, "not even for the kids. I went over to the office afterward, to study some notes I'd made, and then I went back to the apartment and took a nap before dinner."

"Did you eat in?"

"No, I went to a place over on the West Side," he says, and names the restaurant where he and Kate had brunch.

"The West Side *again?*" Helen asks, surprised. "How come?"

"There was a movie I wanted to see over there."

"Oh? What movie?"

The Arts & Leisure section of yesterday's *Times* is open before him on the desk in what they both laughingly call "the study," a room that had been a butler's pantry at one time, but which they converted into a windowless office when they bought the apartment. He has circled with a felt-tipped pen a foreign movie playing at the Angelika 57, and has underlined the time of the screening that would have got him home sometime between eleven and eleven-thirty, which was when he *had* got home, eleven-twenty to be exact, he'd looked at the kitchen clock when he walked in. He reels off the name of the movie casually now, tells her it wasn't all that good, and is starting to ask how the kids are, when Helen says, "I was wondering why you didn't call."

"I thought you'd be asleep," he says. "I didn't get home till eleven-twenty."

Which was the God's honest truth.

"Actually, I was still awake," she says.

"I didn't want to risk . . ."

"I was worried. I hadn't heard from you all day."

"Honey, I spoke to you . . ."

"I meant after that."

"I'm sorry, I was just on the go all . . ."

"I know."

"I'm sorry, really."

"Did you call Stanley to thank him for the evening?" she asks, abruptly changing the subject.

"Do you think I should? He let me pay for dinner, you know. Even though he said we'd be going Dutch."

"Yes, but the tickets came to more than that, didn't they?"

"Honey, the tickets were *free*. A *patient* gave him the tickets."

"Even so."

"Well, I'll see. I really don't like to get into conversations with him, Helen. I really don't like the man."

"Well . . ." she says, and lets the rest of the sentence trail.

"How're the kids?" he asks.

"Fine. Well, I'm not sure. Annie may be coming down with something."

"What do you mean?"

"She has the sniffles. I kept her out of the water yesterday, and she got very cranky. Well, you know Annie."

"Tell her I love her."

"Tell her yourself," Helen says, and shouts, "Annie! Jenny! It's Dad!"

Annie is the first one to come on the line.

"Mom wouldn't let me go in the water yesterday," she says.

"That's cause your nose is running."

"No, it isn't. Not *now*, it isn't."

"That's because Mom wouldn't let you go in the water."

"What does that mean?"

"It means you got all better."

"Sure, Dad. When are you coming up here?"

"Friday."

"Jenny has a boyfriend."

"I do not!" Jenny screams in the background, and

snatches the phone away from her. "Dad? I do *not* have a boyfriend. Don't listen to her."

"How are you, sweetie?"

"I'm fine, but I don't have a boyfriend. I'm going to *kill* you, I swear to God!" she shouts.

"You can plead temporary insanity," David says. "I'll testify on your behalf."

Jenny begins giggling.

Annie grabs the phone from her.

"Why is she laughing?"

"She's temporarily insane," David says.

"Permanently," Annie says, and bursts out laughing at her own sophisticated joke.

"Let me talk to Mom."

"Bye, Dad, I love you, see you Friday!" Annie shouts.

Jenny grabs the phone from her.

"Bye, Dad, I love you," she echoes. "See you Friday!"

"Love you, too, honey. Put Mom back on."

"What was all that about?" Helen asks.

"Temporary insanity," he says. "What are you doing tonight?"

"Why, you want to take me out?"

"I wish."

"I'm going to dinner at the McNeills'."

"Who's baby-sitting?"

"Hilda."

"She's not the one with the wooden leg, is she?"

"Oh, come *on*, David, we haven't used her in *years!*" she says, laughing.

"Remember the time she lifted her skirt to show the kids that leg?" he asks, laughing with her.

"Oh dear," she says.

Their laughter trails.

"What time will you be home tonight?" he asks.

"I don't know. Ten, ten-thirty."

"I'll call you tomorrow morning then," he says.

"Not too early, please."

"After my nine o'clock, okay?"

"Yes, good."

"Give my love."

"I will. I miss you, David."

"I miss you, too."

"I love you, darling."

"I love you, too."

The week drags by in sullen torpor.

Kate does not call him that Monday or on Tuesday or Wednesday, and he does not try to reach her. He endures the sweltering city like a penitent monk wearing a hair shirt, relieved when the entire week passes without a word from her. On Friday, he goes up to the Vineyard again, and somehow manages to look Helen in the eye, turning aside the dual knowledge of having betrayed her and lied to her afterward. By the time he flies back to the city on Sunday night, whatever happened between him and Kate seems to have happened in a past as distant as the one Arthur K continuously relates, its details already fuzzy, its parameters defined by a vague memory of impetuous madness.

2: *tuesday, july 18–friday, july 28*

". . . like a dream," Arthur K is telling him. "I don't know where I am in the dream, I don't know who it is I'm with, there's just this beautiful girl whose tongue is in my mouth, I don't know who she is, her kisses are driving me crazy."

It is almost one-thirty on this hot Tuesday afternoon. After his disclosures early last week, Arthur K has been unwilling to touch with a ten-foot pole—so to speak—his memory of what happened on his sister's bed that night long ago. His reluctance has persisted until today. Today, he is entrusting David with the true memory of what happened, never mind the drawn curtains, never mind the screens. Arthur K is at last facing the truth.

"I know she's my sister, of course," Arthur K says, "I mean I'm not a fool, I *know* she's my sister—or at least I know it *now*. What I'm saying is I didn't know it *then*, when I was feeling her up. I mean, this was just a *girl* there on the bed with me, not my sister, does that make any sense to you? I'm not trying to make excuses here, I'm just trying to explain that I was seventeen years old and this was a very beautiful girl here whose breast I was touching, and she was suddenly reaching for my cock, and right then I didn't care if she was my sister or my aunt or my mother or my grandmother or who*ever* the hell. I was intoxicated, delirious, crazed, depraved, call it whatever you like. I don't care *what* you call it. I almost came in my pants when she reached over to turn off the light, my hands were all over her by then, inside her robe, under her nightgown, oh God I was crazy with wanting her. And all at once it was dark, and in the dark she could have been anyone, in the dark she was opening her robe and spreading her legs, warm and wet and pulling me into her. If you ask me did I know she was my sister, I would have to say yes. At some point in time, I realized I was fucking my own sister."

She calls at exactly ten minutes to two. Arthur K is barely out of the office when the phone rings. David's heart begins beating faster the instant he hears her voice.

"Hi," she says.

"Hi."

"Did you miss me?"

"Well . . ."

"I know you did. How are you?"

"Good."

"Me, too. What are you doing?"

"My one o'clock patient just left."

"That's what I figured. The show's dark tonight. Can you meet me? For dinner or whatever? My treat, I owe you one."

"Well, we'll see about that," he says.

"But do you *want* to?"

"Yes. Yes, of course," he says at once.

"I'll pick a nice quiet place," she says. "I realize you're married."

The restaurant she's chosen is a small Thai newcomer on Eighty-fifth Street, between First and Second Avenues, virtually equidistant from his office on Ninety-sixth and the apartment on Seventy-fourth. There are perhaps eight tables in the place, a bit too crowded for the comfort of a soon-to-be-forty-six-year-old married man sitting with a beautiful young redhead virtually half his age, who paints her fingernails and toenails in colors to complement her clothes, and who's told him on the phone that the service here is very fast and they should be out in less than an hour, "which'll give us plenty of time afterward." But the place is dimly lighted and hung with beaded curtains that somewhat shield the tables one from another, and moreover he doubts that any of his friends or acquaintances would choose this pleasantly unimpressive spot for a seven o'clock Tuesday night dinner on the Upper East Side.

The restaurant does not serve liquor. They have both ordered white wine and they sit now, sipping it, waiting for their food to arrive. The pale gold of the chardonnay echoes the outfit she is wearing this evening, a wheat-colored mesh linen vest with a sort of sarong skirt in crinkled silk with a sheer leaf print that matches the color of her nail polish.

"What color are they in the show?" he asks.

"What do you mean?"

"Your nails."

"Oh. A sort of pearly white. But they're fake, I put them on before each performance. Because they have to look very long and curvy, like claws, you know. We unsheathe our claws and bare our teeth a lot in that show. And hiss like cats, you may have noticed. Such bullshit," she says, and sips at the wine.

He is beginning to feel his first real sense of remorse for what he's done and is about to do, and yet he knows he will go ahead with it, anyway, knows without question that he and Kate will make love again tonight. This restaurant, the food which now comes steaming on heaped platters, the idle chatter they make, all of this is really just vamping till ready, a social exercise that denies the true purpose of why they are meeting again.

He tries to assuage the guilt by telling himself it was she who initiated this evening—just as she'd initiated their Sunday afternoon encounter, by the way—that it was *she* who called today, nine days later, to invite him to dinner or *whatever*, "My treat, I owe you one," which certainly seems to indicate that she's feeling some of the same things he himself is feeling right this moment, though he can't imagine why she should be interested in *him*, this young and beautiful girl, this far too beautiful woman.

But she does indeed seem interested in mild-mannered, bespectacled Clark Kent sitting here all suntanned, wearing a casual blue blazer and gray slacks, white shirt open at the throat, blue socks and loafers. Perhaps she knows he has a Superman erection in his pants, caused by the knowledge of what they are going to do the moment they get out of this opium den—"The service there is very fast. We should be out in less than an hour, which'll give us plenty of time afterward," his heart leaping when she'd said those words.

Temporary insanity, he thinks.

Oh, yes, he can understand Arthur K quite well, he has been trained to understand people like Arthur K. But presumably, he's been trained to understand his *own* feelings as well—*how* many goddamn years of analysis?— and he cannot now fathom why he is jeopardizing so much, lying to Helen, putting himself at risk by perhaps one day having to defend the lie, thereby escalating the deception and, yes, putting the marriage at risk, yes, jeopardizing the marriage. And for what? What he felt two Sundays ago, what he feels now, has nothing to do with love, he is not so foolish or naive as to believe he is in love with this girl. This woman. Two Sundays ago, that was not lovemaking, that was plain and simple *fucking*, and not so simple at that, pretty *fancy* at times, in fact. And that is what it will be tonight. And that is what he wants. He is here because that is what he wants. That is *all* he wants. As the incestuous Arthur K put it this afternoon before leaving the office, "A stiff prick has no conscience, Doc." Unless later on your sister gets killed in a car crash and you can't enter an automobile anymore.

"So do you do this a lot?" she asks out of the blue.

"Eat Thai food? Every now and then."

"Sure," she says, and picks up the long-stemmed glass and sips at the wine again, a faint amber glow reflecting from the glass to touch her chin. She looks more catlike tonight than she did on the stage of the Winter Garden, the reddish-blond hair swept back from her face and caught with a ribbon that matches her eyes, the green looking deeper than it had before, the eyes burning with an intense inner glow, the yellow flecks complementing the bright umber gloss of her fingernails and the earth colors of her gossamer costume. She is wearing sandals. Her toenails are painted in the same subtle brownish-yellow color. She puts down her glass and says, "Which means you fool around, right?"

"No," he said.

"Then why the Thai evasion?"

"Good title," he says. "The Thai Evasion."

"There it is again," she says.

"No, I do not fool around."

"I don't care except that I'm not eager to catch some dread disease. You don't have any dread disease, do you?"

"No."

"Like AIDS, for example?"

"I do not have AIDS."

"Ron had herpes. I didn't catch it because I was very careful. But we didn't use any protection last week . . ."

"You and Ron?"

"Sure, me and Ron. Why do you do that?"

"I don't know. Why do I?"

"You're the shrink, you tell me."

"I guess I'm a little embarrassed by this conversation."

"You shouldn't be. I know too many people in the business who died of AIDS."

"Does Ron have AIDS?"

"No, just herpes. We both tested HIV negative in Detroit."

"You were that serious about each other, huh?"

"That was eight months ago."

"But you were serious enough to . . ."

"I guess we were serious. But that was eight months ago, I just told you."

"Yes."

"And this is now."

"Yes."

"So if either you or your wife fool around . . ."

"We don't fool around."

"Then why the Thai Evasion? Which *is* a very good title, you're right, but it's still ducking the question. If you haven't done this a lot, have you done it a *little?*"

He looks across the table at her.

"Thank you, I have my answer," she says.

"No, you haven't. But I don't feel like discussing it in a room this size, where everyone . . ."

"My apartment isn't much bigger," she says. "But let's go, you're right. If I don't kiss you soon, I'll die."

Her air conditioner is going full blast, but the sheets beneath them are wet from their earlier passionate thrashing on what has turned into another sodden summer night. The apartment is on the third floor of a doorman

building, and he can hear the traffic moving below on
First Avenue, horns honking in this city where noise
pollution is illegal, but who cares, ambulances shrieking
in this city where murder is as inevitable as sunset, but
who cares? Who cares, he wonders, that we ourselves
are murderers of a sort in this bedroom with its drawn
blinds and its noisy air conditioner, who cares that we are
together nullifying and rendering void a sacred covenant,
while Helen—sworn second party to the same pact—
sleeps peacefully in Menemsha?

Let it come down, he thinks.

First Murderer. Macbeth.

He has done something like this . . . well, not *really*
like this . . . only once before in all the time he's been
married, just that once in Boston . . . well, not *anything*
like this, in fact nothing at *all* like this. In fact, he cannot
recall *ever* having been this excited by any woman he's
ever known, not Helen, not any of the girls he'd known
before he met Helen . . .

"Do I really excite you?"

"You know you do."

"I *want* to excite you. Is that her name? Helen?"

"My wife, yes. Helen."

Saying her name in this room. Saying it aloud where
he has just made love to a passionate woman not his
wife, whose arms are still around him.

"My mother almost named me Helen," she says.

"You're joking."

"No, no. Helen was my grandmother's name. She
almost named me after her. Does your wife excite you
the way I do? Does Helen excite you this way? Say."

"No."

Murderers, he thinks. We are both murderers here.

"Did this woman you met in Boston . . . ?"

"No, certainly not her. No one. Ever."

"That's because I love you," she says. "More than any woman you've ever known."

"No, you don't love me," he says.

She can't love me, he thinks.

"Wanna bet?" she asks, and kisses him again.

There's just this beautiful girl whose tongue is in my mouth, I don't know who she is, her kisses are driving me crazy.

She breaks away breathlessly. They are lying on her bed, naked, and whereas they'd made love not ten minutes ago, he feels again the faint stirrings of renewed desire as she gently lifts her mouth from his, their lips clinging for an instant, stickily, the taste of his own semen on her lips, parting. She looks deep into his eyes, her face inches from his, and says, "Tell me all about your woman in Boston. What were you doing in Boston?"

"There was a convention up there. Of psychiatrists. The American Psychiatric Association."

"Was *she* a psychiatrist?"

"Yes."

"Oh God, another shrink!"

"Yeah."

"Was she beautiful?"

"Not very."

"How old were you?"

"I don't know, this was seven years ago."

"Well, you must know how *old* you were."

"I guess I turned thirty-nine that July."

"Midlife Crisis," she says at once.

"Maybe."

"Fear of Forty," she says.

"Maybe."

"Incidentally, I have a great title for Erica Jong's *next* book."

"Tell me."

"*Sex at Sixty*. How old was she?"

"Who, Erica?"

"Sure, Erica. Your bimbo in Boston."

"She wasn't a bimbo. She was just this lonely woman . . ."

"This *shrink*, you mean. God, she wasn't Jacqueline *Hicks*, was she?"

"No, no."

"You almost gave me a heart attack. If she'd turned out to be Jacqueline . . . well, it couldn't have been her because you said she wasn't beautiful. I think Jacqueline is *very* beautiful, don't you?"

"I never noticed."

"Is that the truth?"

"That's the truth."

"I love Jacqueline. I was really crazy when I started going to her, you know. She really helped me a lot. I'm glad it wasn't her you fucked in Boston."

"No, it was just a woman who . . . found me attractive, I guess."

"You are attractive."

"Thank you, but I wasn't fishing."

"I *love* your looks."

"Thank you."

"Do you love *my* looks? And I *am* fishing."

"I adore the way you look."

"Do you like my being a redhead?"

"Yes."

"Do you like my being red down here, too?"

"Yes."

"I used to hate it. I was shocked to death the first time I saw a girl with red pubic hair."

"When was that?"

"In the locker room at school. I was eleven, I had nothing down there at all. This was an upperclassman. Woman. Person. An eighteen-year-old *girl*. She had red hair, too, on her head, I mean, much redder than mine. Seeing her naked scared hell out of me. I thought, Jesus, is *that* what I'm going to look like when I grow up? Those great big tits and that flaming red hair down there, Jesus! I never did get the tits, as you can see, but I sure as hell got the rest. This is my summer trim. You should see it when it runs rampant. It's like a forest fire. Tell me about your Boston shrink."

"There's not much to tell. We met at one of the seminars, and discovered we were both from New York . . ."

"Both married . . ."

"Yes, both married."

"How did I know that?"

"Maybe because I told you she was lonely," he says, and wonders why such an association would have come to mind. "Anyway . . ."

"Are *you* lonely?" she asks at once.

"I may have been back then."

"How about now?"

"No."

"Then why did you start up with me?"

"I don't know. Anyway, we had dinner together, I forget who asked who to dinner . . ."

"*Whom.* And I asked *you* to dinner, don't forget," she says. "And *lunch*, too. Don't ever forget that. I was the one who wanted *you*," she says, and kisses him again.

Her kisses make him dizzy.

Her hand drops to his naked thigh, rests there, the fingers widespread.

She pulls her mouth from his.

Looks into his face again.

"Tell me," she says.

"We ended up in her room," he says, and shrugs. "She wanted to be in her own room, in case her husband called."

"Did he call?"

"No."

"Did your wife call? Helen? Did she call *your* room?"

"No."

"Did you stay the whole night with her?"

"No."

"Was it good?"

"Yes."

"Better than me?"

"No one's better than you."

"Mmm, sweet," she says, and her hand moves onto him. "Did you ever see her again?"

"No."

"Why not?"

"I felt too guilty."

"Do you feel guilty now?"

"No."

"Good," she says, and gives him a friendly little squeeze.

"I almost told Helen about her," he says. "When I got back home."

"Don't ever tell her about *me*," she says, and squeezes him again, hard this time, in warning.

"I was glad in the long run. If I'd told her, it would have meant the end of our marriage. We had just the one child then, Jenny. Annie wasn't even on the horizon. If I'd told her . . ."

"You have two children, is that it?"

"Yes."

"Two little girls."

"Yes."

"How old?"

"Six and nine."

"Annie, you said?"

"And Jenny."

"Jennyanydots," she says at once. "Put the names together . . ."

"Yes, I guess they do, come to think of it."

"Oh, no question. Jennyanydots. That's one of the cats in the show."

"I know."

"So you're how old? If you were thirty-nine . . ."

"I'll be forty-six this month."

"Oh? When?"

"The twenty-seventh."

"We'll have a party. Do you believe in fate?"

"No."

"I think we were fated."

"Then I believe in it."

"I'm not Glenn Close, by the way."

"I didn't think you were."

"I mean, I'm not going to boil Annie's pet rabbit or anything."

"She doesn't have a pet rabbit."

"Or Jenny's. Or anybody's, anydots. This isn't Hollywood, there isn't just one plot in the entire world, you know. Oh, it's *Fatal Attraction*, I get it! But with a psychiatrist and a dancer, right? Wroooong! This isn't that at all. If you think that's what this is . . ."

"I don't."

"Good. Because you don't have to worry about me, I know you're married. In fact, I'm *glad* you didn't tell her about that shrink in Boston. Because then she'd be suspicious, and I don't want her ever finding out about us."

"I'm glad, too. She'd have left in a minute. And for what? A meaningless one-night . . ."

"Am *I* a meaningless one-night stand?"

"This is our *second* night," he says.

"I'd better *not* be meaningless," she says, and kisses him fiercely, biting his lip, and then pulls her face back, and stares into his eyes again as unblinkingly as a cat, and bares her teeth an instant before biting him again. She is straddling him an instant after that, sliding onto him warm and wet and demanding, and an instant later he comes inside her.

PRIVILEGED CONVERSATION

I was intoxicated, delirious, crazed, depraved, call it whatever you like.

I don't care what you call it.

His nine o'clock patient has just left the office.

David dials the number at the Menemsha cottage and listens to it ringing, four, five, six times, and is about to hang up, relieved, when Annie picks up the phone.

"Chapman residence," she says in her piping little voice, "good morning."

"Yes, may I please speak to Miss Anne Chapman?" he says, disguising his voice so that he sounds like a rather pompous British barrister.

"This is Miss Chapman," Annie says solemnly.

"Miss Chapman, you have just inherited a million pounds from your aunt in Devonshire."

"A million pounds of what?" Annie asks.

David bursts out laughing.

"Is that *you*, Dad?" she asks.

"That's me," he says, still laughing.

"A million pounds of *what?*" she insists.

"Feathers," he says.

"I'm busy eating," she says. "Did you want Mom? She's still in bed."

"Wake her up, it's five to ten."

"When are you coming up here?"

"I told you. Friday night."

"We'll have lobster," Annie says, and abruptly puts down the phone.

When Helen picks up the extension upstairs, she sounds fuzzy with sleep.

"Hullo?" she says.

"What are you doing in bed?" he asks.

"I know what I *wish* I was doing in bed."

"Late night?"

"Oh sure, a drunken brawl. I was in bed by ten, but I just couldn't fall asleep. When are you coming up here?"

"Must be an echo in this place."

"Everybody misses you."

"Who's everybody?"

"Me," she says.

"I *have* to lay out my clothes in advance, or I'd *never* get dressed," Susan M is saying. "You know that, I've told you that a hundred times already."

She is one of David's so-called Couches, a twenty-four-year-old "obsessive-compulsive," or "obsessional neurotic"—you pays your money and you takes your choice unless you happen to suffer from a disorder where choice seems obstinately denied.

Susan M has been suffering from her disorder for the past three years now. Her disorder was what forced her to drop out of college. Her disorder is what brings her here twice a week, to discuss over and over again the ritual that keeps at bay her personal hounds of hell.

What Susan M does, compulsively, is lay out in advance the clothing she will be wearing for the next two weeks. Every flat surface in her apartment—tables, chairs, countertops, floors—is covered with the neatly folded garments she will wear on Monday, Tuesday, Wednesday, and so on, this week and next week, each careful little stack labeled with a note naming the day and date. Two weeks ago today, Susan M knew what she would be wearing to this ten o'clock session on Wednesday morning, the nineteenth day of July. She knows, too, what she will be wearing on Wednesday of *next* week. She has told David she will be wearing the blue shirtdress with a red leather belt and red French-heeled shoes. Her bra and panties will be white. That is the uniform of the day for the twenty-sixth of July, a day before David's forty-sixth birthday.

Susan M doesn't know this. She knows scarcely anything about David, except that he listens patiently behind her while she details her lists, frequently planning her wardrobe aloud, well in advance of actually laying it out in her apartment. Counting the hours she spends talking it over with David—"I don't *really* need blue underwear with the blue dress, do I? I mean, it's still summertime"—she will often have her wardrobe planned three weeks in advance of when she actually will be wearing it.

"You lay out *your* clothes, don't you? Everybody I *know* decides in advance what he or she is going to wear to work tomorrow, or to school tomorrow, or to a party that night, or even to *bed* that night. My mother always made sure I wore clean panties to school because a person never could tell when she'd get run over by a car and have to be taken to the hospital. A clean bra, too, when I got old enough to wear one. I was very big for my age . . . well, that's obvious, I guess . . . I started developing at the age of twelve, very early on, I had to watch what I wore, the boys could be so cruel, you know. What bothers me is why I should be so *concerned* about performing a simple act everyone else in the world performs. Why should I worry so much that if I don't get it *right*, something terrible will happen?"

Silence.

She has said this before.

She knows she has said it before.

"Look," she says, "I know this is all in my *head*, why the hell else am I here? I *know* my mother's not *really* going to die if my shoes don't match my bag next Friday or whenever the hell. She's in Omaha, how's she going to *die* if I don't have everything laid out? What is this, voodoo or something? Which thank God I *do* know— what I'm going to wear next Friday, I mean—because I wouldn't want *that* on my conscience, believe me. The white sandals with the white leather sling bag I bought at Barneys and the white mini and white tube, a regular virgin bride, right? That's next Friday, I'm pretty sure it is, anyway. I have the list here if you don't mind my checking it, I'd like to check it if you don't mind."

She sits up immediately, not turning to look at him, embarrassed by this behavior she knows to be irrational but is unable to control, digging into her handbag, green to match the green slippers she's wearing, and locating her Month-At-A-Glance calendar into which she relentlessly lists all her wardrobe schedules. Still not looking at him, she says, "Yes, here it is, Friday the twenty-first, white bag, white sandals, yep, all of it's right here, I guess you won't get hit by a bus, Mom," and laughs in embarrassment at her own absurdity and then lies back down again and sighs in such helpless despair that she almost breaks David's heart.

She falls silent for the remainder of the hour.

When at last he mentions quietly that their time is up, she rises, nods, and says, "I know I've got to get over this."

"Yes," he says.

"Yes," she says, and nods, and sighs heavily again. "So we're back to the regular schedule now, right? Until August first, anyway."

"Right," he says.

"So I'll see you on Friday, right?"

"Yes, of course."

"Same time, right?"

"Yes, same time."

She seems more anxious when she leaves his office than she did when she came in this morning.

He is not at all sure that she *will* get over this.

He tries Kate's number several times that day.

The voice on her answering machine chirps, "Hi. At the beep, please."

The third time he hears it, he wants to strangle the machine.

He knows she had a performance this afternoon, and further knows she has to be at the theater again by six-thirty tonight, she has explained all this to him. Kate's makeup isn't as intricate as what some of the other cats wear, but it nonetheless takes her a full half hour to do her face and another twenty minutes to get into costume. She spends the rest of the time before curtain stretching and warming up; a dancer can really hurt herself, she's told him, if she goes on cold. Half-hour is at seven-

thirty. Fifteen is at a quarter to eight. Five is five minutes
before curtain, and then it's show time, folks. He tries
her apartment again at ten to six, immediately after his
last patient leaves the office, and again at six sharp, on
the walk home from his office, from a pay phone on
Lex. He gets the same damn brief chirpy message each
time. To get to the theater by six-thirty, Kate will have
to leave her apartment by six-ten at the very latest. He
calls from another pay phone at five past, and gets the
same infuriating message again. Frustrated, he realizes he
will not be able to talk to her until she gets home later
tonight.

If she gets home.

"We shouldn't be having this conversation," Stanley
is telling him, even though he is the one who called
David to say he simply *had* to talk to him. The two men
have eaten dinner in a Turkish restaurant on Second
Avenue, and now they are strolling along like two old
men in the park, a bit flat-footed, their hands behind
their backs, though they are not in any park, and David
certainly doesn't think of himself as old, either. Not
now, anyway. Not anymore.

Kate has promised him a party on his forty-sixth
birthday.

It occurs to him that she doesn't yet know he'll be
leaving for Martha's Vineyard the day after that.

Or that he'll be gone the entire month of August.

The night is sticky and hot.

The heat has driven everyone outdoors, and the avenue is thronged with pedestrians. Somehow, the city seems softer and safer tonight. At sidewalk tables outside colorfully lighted restaurants, diners seem engaged in spirited conversation, and there is laughter and a sense of gaiety and old world sophistication here on the privileged Upper East Side where for a little while the entire world is strung with Japanese lanterns and everyone is sipping French champagne and dipping Russian caviar and Vienna waltzes float dizzily on the still summer night.

He supposes he's in love with her.

"I think I'm in love with her, hmm?" Stanley says. "This is ridiculous, I know. For Christ's sake, Dave, she's only nineteen years old, if she were a little younger I'd go to jail. I'm a *doctor!* I'm her *psychiatrist!*"

Although I don't even know her, David thinks.

How can I love someone I don't even know?

"I couldn't believe we were doing it right on the office couch," Stanley says. "I'm so ashamed of myself."

He does not, in all truth, appear terribly ashamed of himself. He is, in fact, beaming from ear to ear as he makes this admission, wearing tonight the same beachcomber outfit he wore to *Cats*, but perhaps it's the only good beachcomber outfit he owns. The same khaki slacks, and rumpled plaid sports jacket, the same brown loafers without socks again, the same white button-down shirt open at the throat, no tie. David is positive it's the same shirt because there are still stains on it from the duckling *à l'orange* Stanley ordered that night. His beard has grown several thousandths of an inch since then, but it is still an unsightly tangle of hairs of another color.

His grin appears in these incipient whiskers like a flasher opening a raincoat; Stanley is *proud* of the fact that he seduced a nineteen-year-old patient on his office couch.

"I leave for Hatteras on the twenty-ninth," he says now, the smile vanishing to be replaced by what he supposes is a look of abject sorrow but which comes across as a clown's painted-on mask of tragedy, the mouth downturned, the eyes grief-stricken. "I haven't told her yet. I don't think she knows that psychiatrists take the month of August off, I don't think she's read the Judith Rossner novel."

Has *Kate* read the Rossner novel? David wonders.

"I don't know how to tell her," Stanley says.

But haven't you already told *all* your patients? David wonders. Haven't you been preparing them all along for the traumatic month-long separation to come, *more* than a month, actually, since sessions won't begin again till the day after Labor Day, the fifth of September?

I have to tell Kate, he thinks.

"I don't want to go," Stanley says. "If I can find some excuse to stay in the city, I'd do it in a minute, hmm? Can you imagine being on my own here for an entire month, no patients to worry about, Gerry way the hell down there in North Carolina, just me and Cindy Harris . . ."

Might as well break *all* the rules of the profession while you're at it, Stan.

". . . rollicking in the hay up here? Oh God, I'd give my *life* for that. A whole month with her? *More* than a month? I'd give my left *testicle*."

The men fall silent for several moments. The swirl of pedestrian traffic engulfs them. A buzz of conversation hovers on the thick summer air, snatches of words and phrases floating past as they move silently through the crowd. David is wondering whether it would, in fact, be possible to find some reason to stay in the city during the month of August . . . well, certainly not the entire month, but perhaps *part* of the month . . . no patients to worry about, just him and . . .

And realizes that Stanley is undoubtedly wondering the same thing.

And wonders how there's any difference, really, between the two of them.

"Would you be willing to alibi me?" Stanley asks.

"Alibi you? What do you mean?"

"If I said, for example, that I had to come down for a conference or something. A seminar, for example. Whatever."

"I don't think I could . . ."

"Because I *know* I can't stay here the whole damn month, Dave. I'm just looking for an excuse to come up for a week or so, hmm? Even two, three days."

"Stanley, there *are* no conferences in August."

"We could invent one. Or a seminar. Something."

"I don't think . . ."

"A series of lectures. Anything."

"Stanley . . ."

"Somebody visiting from England or wherever the hell. Australia. Some big psychiatrist taking advantage of his summer vacation."

"It's winter in Australia."

"Wherever. He's here by invitation, France, wher-ever. They take August off in France, don't they?"

"Well, yes, but . . ."

"Italy maybe. He's from Italy. They take August off there, too, am I right?"

"Yes."

"There are psychiatrists in Italy, maybe this one is a big shot who's been invited here to speak to a select group of people, hmm? You, me, a handful of other shrinks Gerry doesn't know. Helen, either, I guess. If it's going to work. I mean, if you're willing to alibi me, that is. It would have to be people neither of them know. The lecturer could be giving . . ."

"Stanley, really, I couldn't possibly . . ."

". . . a series of lectures, who the hell knows where?" Stanley says, stroking his scraggly beard and narrowing his eyes like Fagin about to send his little gangsters out to pick pockets. "Let's say they start in the middle of the week, hmm, the lectures, a Wednesday night, let's say, and they continue through Friday night, three lec-tures in all, I've seen plenty of programs like that, I don't think something like that would sound too far-fetched. That would make it reasonable to come up on the Tues-day before and stay till Saturday morning. Four full days and nights with her, Jesus, I'd take a suite at the Plaza, I swear to God, fuck her every hour on the hour, go back down to Hatteras on Saturday morning. I think that would *work*, you know? I honestly think it would *work*, Dave. But only if . . ."

"I couldn't lie to Helen that way," David says.

"You're my best friend, Dave."

Sure, David thinks.

"At least think about it, will you?" Stanley says.

"Well, I'll think about it."

"Will you promise to think about it?"

"I promise, yes."

"You don't know how much it would mean to me, Dave."

"I'll think about it."

"Please."

"I will."

But he already knows it would work.

Curtain is at eight o'clock. The show lets out at ten-thirty. He tries her again at eleven and then again at eleven-thirty. When she does not call by midnight, he begins to believe he will never see her again.

He falls asleep wondering if Especially Ron, the Herpes King, has resurfaced.

The telephone rings at one o'clock in the morning.

He fumbles for the ringing phone in the dark, thinking at once that something has happened to Helen or the kids, a terrible accident, someone has drowned, knocking the receiver off the cradle, finding it again in the dark, picking it up, "Hello?"

"Hi."

He does not know whether to feel irate or relieved. He does not turn on the light. He does not want to know what time it is, but he asks immediately, "What

time is it?" and she says, "One, a little after one, am I
waking you?"

"Yes," he says.

"Oooo," she says, "angry."

He wonders if she's been drinking.

"I've been calling you," he says.

"All those hangups," she says, "and no messages."

"I didn't know who might be listening with you."

"Who do you *think* might be listening with me?"

There is a silence on the line.

He waits, hoping she will be the first one to speak
again. The silence becomes unbearable. He wonders if
she will hang up.

"Where were you?" he asks.

"When?"

"Well, for starters, how about all day long?"

"Oooo, angry, angry," she says.

There is another silence, longer this time, broken at
last by an exaggeratedly tragic sigh and then the sound
of her voice again. "First, I went to see my agent," she
says. "That was at ten o'clock, but I slept late and had
to rush out, which is why I couldn't call you before I
left the apartment. Anyway, I left at twenty to, and my
window of opportunity wouldn't have been till *ten* to,
correct, Doctor? After my agent . . . he thinks he may
have a movie for me, by the way, not that I guess it
matters to you in your present frame of mind. Anyway,
after my meeting with him, I went to my Wednesday
morning dance class, I have dance three times a week.
Then I went to the theater for the matinee performance,
and had a sandwich and did a little shopping with a

girlfriend afterwards, and went back to the apartment to drop off the things I'd bought, and then I took a nap, and let me see, I went out for a carrot shake, alone, at that health food deli on Fifty-seventh, and walked to the theater to get ready for the evening performance. Then I did the show, naturally, and went out for a bite with some of the kids afterwards, and then I came home. And here I am."

"No phones any of those places, huh?"

"None at precisely ten minutes to the hour."

"How about before you went to the theater?"

"I tried your office but you were already gone."

"Did you leave a message?"

"I didn't know who might be listening with you," she says.

Touché, he thinks, and almost smiles.

"Did you try the apartment?"

"Yes. There was no answer. You were probably on the way there."

"What time was that?"

"Around six. And I called again from the theater at seven-thirty, after I was in costume and doing my warm-ups."

Which was when he'd gone down to dinner.

"I'm sorry we kept missing each other," she says.

"Was Ron with you?"

"Ron?"

"When you went out for a bite with the kids?"

"Ron's in Australia. *Ron?*"

"So who were these kids?"

Her calling them "kids" makes him feel like Methuselah. On the twenty-seventh of the month, he will be forty-six years old. His grandfather was forty-six when he died of lung cancer. Now *he* is forty-six. Well, *almost* forty-six. And Kate is twenty-seven and she goes out for a bite with "kids" from the show.

"The girl who plays Demeter," she says, "and the girl who plays Bombalurina and the guy who plays Munkus-trap. He's gay, if you're wondering. You have nothing to worry about," she says. "I love you to death. I thought of you all day long."

"I thought of you, too."

"There are two pay phones backstage," she says. "I can let you have both numbers. So something like today won't happen again. Our missing each other."

"I guess I should have them," he says.

But he wonders how he can possibly use either number. Call backstage and have someone other than Kate answer the phone? Risk *that?* Who shall I say is calling, please? Whom? Who. Who*ever*, it definitely ain't *me*, mister. A married man named David Chapman calling a showgirl in a cat costume, are you kidding?

"I'm sorry I woke you," she says. "But I just got home."

He's wondering why she didn't call *before* she left the theater. From one of the pay phones backstage. But he imagines they're all ravenously hungry after a performance, all those cats leaping around for two and a half hours, well, not quite that long when you count inter-mission, but even so. They must all be eager to change into their street clothes and get the hell out of there, put some food in their bellies. He wonders what she wears when she goes to and from the theater. Blue jeans? He wonders if anyone recognizes her when she's walking in the street—Hey, look, Maude, there goes that girl from *Cats*. He supposes not. He himself didn't recognize her in makeup, and he'd already known her before he saw the show.

". . . shooting it in New York," she is telling him, "or I wouldn't even *think* of considering it. Leave you to go on location? No way. It's a costume drama, where I'd be playing the confidante of the female lead who's having an affair with a Russian diplomat. She's British. So am I, if I get the part. What it is, they've taken *Ninotchka* and changed the Russian girl to a Brit and the American guy to a Russian diplomat, and they've set it all back in the eighteenth century. At least, that's the way the producer described it to me. In Hollywood, they can only think of movies in terms of *other* movies. Tunnel vision, it's called. Which, by the way, *was* a movie, wasn't it? *Tunnel Vision?* Or a book? Or something? I'd have to learn a British accent again, I had a pretty good one when we did *Lady Windermere's Fan* in high school. British accents are easier to learn than almost . . ."

He tries to imagine what she's wearing now. What color are her fingernails today? Has she already undressed for bed? But no, she just got home after a bite with the kids. He visualizes her bed. Visualizes her *in* her bed. Does she wear a nightgown when he's not there making love to her? Is she wearing a nightgown now?

". . . why you never ask me about myself," she is saying now. "Don't you want to know how I became a dancer, how I happened to land in *Cats* when I was only seventeen? Don't you want to know if my parents are still living together, or if they're divorced, or if I have any sisters or brothers . . . well, you know I have a sister, you read that in the program notes. But don't you want to know anything at *all* about me, David? You're supposed to love me so much . . ."

But he's never told her that.

". . . and yet you never ask me anything about myself. Why is that?" she asks.

Why *is* that? he wonders. He also wonders if she expects him to ask her about herself at one, one-thirty in the morning, whatever time it is now. *Are* your parents divorced? If so, are they remarried? Where does your sister live, or did you tell me? What is Ron doing in Australia, and does he send you an occasional postcard? Maybe I don't *want* to know about you, he thinks. Maybe the *less* I know about you . . .

". . . never even said you love me, when I know you do," she says.

There is a silence.

"Don't you?" she asks. "Love me?"

He hesitates.

"Yes," he says, "I love you."

"Of course you do," she says.

His first patient is scheduled to arrive at nine this morning. He likes to get to the office at eight-thirty or so, check his notes from the patient's previous session, generally prepare himself for the long day ahead. The mail is delivered at nine, nine-thirty. He usually goes out to the lobby mailboxes after his first session, leafs through it during the ten minutes before his next appointment. His office routine is rigid and proscribed. In that sense, he is a well-organized man, dedicated— he likes to believe—to the arduous task of helping these people in dire need.

He has set his alarm, as usual, for seven forty-five.

When the telephone rings, he is in deep sleep and he thinks at first it is the alarm going off. He reaches for the clock, fumbles with the lever on the back, but it is still ringing, and he realizes belatedly that it is the telephone. The luminous face of the clock reads six forty-five A.M. He grabs for the phone receiver.

"Hello?" he says.

"Hi."

Her voice signals a violent pounding of his heart each time he hears it.

"Are you awake?" she asks.

"I am now."

"Come make love to me," she says.

The uniformed doorman outside her building is with another man in a short-sleeved striped shirt and dark blue polyester slacks. This is now seven-thirty in the morning, and they are standing in bright sunlight, idly chatting, watching the passersby hurrying along on this busy street. They interrupt their conversation and turn to him as he approaches.

"Miss Duggan," he tells the doorman.

"Your name, sir?"

"Mr. Adler," he says.

This is the name he and Kate agreed to on the telephone, though she truly couldn't see any reason for him to use a false name. Adler. After the famous *Alfred* Adler, one of Freud's friends and colleagues who left the psychiatric movement rather early on.

The doorman buzzes her apartment. "Mr. Adler to see you," he says. David cannot hear her answer. The doorman replaces the phone on the switchboard hook and says, "Go right up, sir, it's apartment 3B."

A woman and a dog are already in the waiting elevator. David steps inside, hits the button for the third floor, and then smiles briefly in greeting. The woman does not smile back. Neither does the dog. The woman is wearing a quilted pink robe over a long flowered nightgown and pink bedroom slippers. The dog is a long-haired dachshund who sniffs curiously, or perhaps affectionately, at David's black loafers. This morning, David is wearing a dark blue tropical-weight suit—the forecasters have said it will be another scorcher today—with a white button-down shirt and a striped red and blue silk rep tie. He looks quite professional. He does not look like someone going up to the third floor of this building to make love to a girl who is waiting in apartment 3B for him. He cannot stop thinking of Kate as a girl. He guesses this is something he should examine. Why he keeps thinking of this passionate twenty-seven-year-old woman as a girl.

The woman in the elevator—and she is most definitely a woman, some fifty-three years old with a puffed scowling face and suspicious blue eyes—yanks on the dog's leash and says, "*Stop* that, Schatzi!" The dog, properly chastised, quits his, or her, exploratory sniffing. The woman stares straight ahead, feigning indifference to David as the elevator begins a slow, labored climb, but he knows she thinks he's a rapist or an ax murderer who is only *dressed* like a respectable physician making a house call at the crack of dawn, *sans* stethoscope or satchel. He hopes she will not be getting off at the third floor. He hopes she does not live in apartment 3A or 3C. He hopes Schatzi will not begin barking when he or she catches the scent of Hannah the cat in apartment 3B. Or the scent of Kate waiting in apartment 3B. The elevator doors slide open. David steps out without looking back at either the woman or her hound. The doors slide shut behind him.

He checks out the hallway like a sneak thief about to commit a burglary. His wristwatch reads seven-forty A.M. Sunlight slants through a window at the far end of the hall, dust motes swarming. There is the smell of bacon wafting from one of the apartments, coffee from yet another. From behind the door to 3C, he can hear the drone of broadcast voices. He visualizes television anchors announcing the early morning news. He visualizes people sitting down to quick breakfasts before rushing off to work. This is not a time for making love, but his heart is beating frantically as he presses the bell button set in her doorjamb. There is the sound of chimes within, and then the sound of heels clicking on a hardwood floor. The peephole flap snaps back. The chain instantly rattles off its hook. There is the small oiled click of tumblers falling as first one bolt and then another is unlocked. The door opens just a crack. He virtually slides into the apartment.

She is wearing high-heeled red leather pumps and nothing else. She moves into his arms at once, slamming the door shut behind him, pressing him against the door, her left hand reaching for the bolt as she grinds herself into him, the lock clicking behind him, her mouth demanding, her teeth nipping at him hungrily, his lips, his chin, his cheeks, biting, kissing, her murmured words entangled on their tongues. She smells of powder and soap. He knows her dusted body will turn his dark suit to white, but he ignores this danger and pulls her closer instead, his hands covering her breasts slippery smooth with talcum, a young girl's breasts, *this* girl's breasts, this girl, this *girl*. He lowers his head, finds her nipples, "Don't *bite!*" she warns sharply, though he isn't biting her, kisses her, licks her nipples, "Yes," dropping to his knees in his proper blue suit and smart silk tie, parting with his fingers the crisp red hair in its summer trim, parting her nether lips, kissing her there, "Yes," licking her there, *"Yes,"* savoring her there as if her swollen cleft is a smooth wet nourishing stone.

Before he leaves the apartment, she tells him if he *must* use a fake name whenever he comes here, she's thought of a more appropriate psychiatrist than Adler.

"Who?" he asks.

"Horney," she says.

He figures Stanley must know, as does any psychiatrist, that during the course of therapy a patient will recover feelings for significant people in his past and unconsciously apply them to his shrink. Stanley has read Freud. Every psychiatrist in the *world* has read Freud:

"We overcome the transference by pointing out to the patient that his feelings do not arise from the present situation and do not apply to the person of the doctor, but that they are repeating something that happened to him earlier. In this way we oblige him to transform his repetition into a memory."

Which, unquestionably, was the technique Stanley—who, like David, is a Freudian—followed with the patient he's identified as Cindy *Harris*, the better to lead her to mental health, m'dear.

But Stanley? Are you in there, Stanley? Do you remember?

"It is not a patient's crudely sensual desires which constitute the temptation. It is, rather, perhaps, a woman's subtler and aim-inhibited wishes which bring with them the danger of making a man forget his technique and his medical task for the sake of a fine experience."

Stanley seems to have forgotten, if not his technique, then certainly his medical task. By "doing it" with Cindy "right on the office couch," he has rather, perhaps, also broken the mental health profession's absolute and explicitly stated prohibition on sexual contact or sexual intimacy between patient and therapist.

Why then, David wonders, am I seriously considering whether or not I will *alibi* the son of a bitch sometime this August?

For however abhorrent he finds Stanley's behavior, he cannot ignore the fact that if he *does* become his accomplice, so to speak, he will also be serving his own interests. All day Thursday, this continues to trouble him, to the extent that he begins feeling in imminent danger himself of forgetting his technique and his medical task. His technique is to coax a patient's memories into the present, so that they can be dealt with more effectively than they had in the past. His technique is to keep his own personal anxieties, hopes, aspirations, fears, cravings or lusts out of this office and out of the therapy. In this office, he is a neutral and objective listener, an indefatigable, nonjudgmental interpreter. Here in this office, his medical task is to guide back to mental wellness eight severely troubled people.

But.

His patients' disturbing memories are most often sexual in content. As a result, much of his working day is spent listening to Arthur K or Susan M or Brian L or Josie D or any of the others as they reveal—or try to *avoid* revealing—that the symptoms of their illnesses can be traced back "with really surprising regularity to impressions from their erotic life," thank you again, Dr. Freud. David accepts this basic premise as an absolute truth. It is, in fact, the very foundation of the medicine he practices here five days a week, save for the month of August.

But.

On this Thursday morning after Stanley has made an August offer he may not be able to refuse . . .

On this Thursday morning after he has raced to Kate's apartment at seven-thirty to be with her for even just a little while before going to work . . .

PRIVILEGED CONVERSATION

On this relentlessly hot and sluggish Thursday morning toward the end of July, David listens apathetically to his patients' tales of sexual abuse or neglect or indulgence or addiction or identity or dysfunction, relating them only to his own passionate sexual entanglement and finding them by comparison merely dull and inane.

She calls him at ten minutes to eleven to say that the insurance company has sent her a check, and she'll be going out today to buy a new bicycle, would he like to go with her? The bicycle shop she's chosen is on Seventy-ninth, between First and York. He tells her he will meet her there at twelve noon.

To commemorate the occasion of the Buying of the Bike, as he will later refer to it, she is wearing what she wore in the park on the day they met. The green nylon shorts, the orange tank top shirt, the Nike running shoes and white cotton socks with the little cotton balls at the back of each. The salesman in the shop, a young man who introduces himself as Rickie, is similarly dressed; perhaps there is a bicycle race somewhere in the city today.

In any event, he is wearing red nylon shorts that do little to conceal muscular young legs, and a blue nylon tank top of a lighter shade and with the numeral 69 in white on the front of it. Hmm. The top exposes pectorals, biceps and triceps that have all had higher educations, either at the local gym or in a state penitentiary. This association comes to mind because he is sporting, on the bulging biceps of his left arm, the tattooed head of an Indian chief in full feathered headdress, and this further prompts the notion that perhaps he himself is an Indian, forgive me, David thinks, a Native *American*, of course. His skin fortifies the assumption, a rather dusky color that could be a suntan. But his hair is a shiny black, pulled to the back of his head in a ponytail and held there with a little beaded band that further confirms the idea that he may be a Sioux or a Cherokee or, more appropriate considering the fact that he's twenty-two or -three years old, a mere Ute. He and Kate seem splendidly matched in age and costume. Here in the bicycle shop, David begins feeling like a decrepit fifth wheel.

Rickie the Callow Ute starts selling her a bike, making sure to flex his marvelous muscles each time he lifts down another one from the rack. He asks where she will be doing most of her riding, and she tells him in Central Park, and then immediately informs him that all she's got to spend is four hundred dollars, so please don't start showing her bikes that cost two, three thousand dollars, which she knows some of them do.

"I think I have some good models to show you in that price range," Rickie says.

"Not in that *range*," Kate tells him. "I'm talking four hundred dollars, not a penny more, not a penny less."

"Including tax?" he asks, and flashes a mouthful of glistening white teeth which David would like to punch off his face.

"Well, I guess I can spring for the tax," Kate says and smiles back.

"Phew," Rickie says, and flicks imaginary sweat from his noble brow.

PRIVILEGED CONVERSATION

It occurs to David that they might be flirting.

Rickie displays a beautiful little number painted in a color he describes as "Wild Orchid with Blue Pearl Hyper-Highlight" and identifies as "a Cannondale aluminum bike in the 3.8 Mixte series with your hybrid frame and your TIG-welded all-chrome-moly fork," Kate listening wide-eyed, David standing by with his thumb up his ass, "and your GripShift SRT 300 shifters with Shimano Altus C-90 Hyperglide 7-speed rear derailleur and cogset," speaking a language known only to the Plains Indians and young Kate Duggan, who seems to know exactly whereof he speaks. But the bike costs four hundred and seventy-nine dollars, and Kate has already told him . . .

"Sorry, I thought I'd sneak it past you," Rickie says, and grins his boyish all-American grin again.

"You almost did," she says, and bats her lashes at him.

She climbs onto the next bike he lifts from the rack. As she settles onto a black leather seat Rickie describes as "a Vetta comfort saddle, made in Italy," the side-slit in the very short green nylon shorts exposes the now-traditional hint of white cotton panties beneath. "You keep in good shape," Rickie says, interrupting his shpiel—or at least his *bike* shpiel.

"Thanks," she says. "How much is this one?"

"About the same as the other one. Where do you work out?"

"I don't. I'm a dancer."

"Really? What kind of dancing."

"I'm in *Cats*," she says.

"No *shit!*" he says.

David wonders if Rickie thinks this older person here might perchance be Kate's brother, standing and watching this blatant little flirtation and making no comment. Or mayhap her father? What*ever* his relation to this lithe slender dancer slipping so easily from saddle to saddle, David seems to have achieved an invisibility only Claude Rains or Vincent Price or Nicholson Baker could have aspired to.

"This Tassajara in the Gary Fisher line is a bit cheaper," Rickie says, "but it's got every feature you'd . . ."

"How much cheaper?"

"Four forty-nine. But it's got your TIG-welded double-butted cro-moly frame and your Weinmann rims and Tioga Psycho tires . . ."

"I really can't spend that much."

"In that case, I've got *just* the bike for you," Rickie says and pulls down a sporty number in the Raleigh line, which he describes as "Your sweet little M60 with a chrome-moly frame and STX Rapid Fire Plus shifters and Shimano Parallax alloy hubs. Comes in the metallic anthracite you see here."

"How much is it?"

"Three ninety-nine, how's that for on the nose?"

"What else have you got?" she asks.

He spends another twenty minutes showing her bikes, at the end of which time Kate settles on a purple fade, multitrack cro-moly sport with your basic high-tensile steel stays and steel fork and your Araya alloy 36-hole rims and your white decals for a mere three hundred and forty-nine dollars.

David leaves her in the shop with her credit card

and Chief Running Mouth while he rushes back up to Ninety-sixth Street where he buys a hot dog with your basic mustard and sauerkraut on Lexington Avenue and gets to his office in time to greet his next patient, Alex J, who tells him that just when he thought he was making real progress, he's started rubbing up against girls in the subway again.

When Kate phones the apartment at twenty to seven that night, she seems to have completely forgotten the Buying of the Bike. Or perhaps *he's* the one who's exaggerated it out of all proportion. He asks her to wait a minute because he's just put his dinner in the microwave and if they're going to talk, he wants to run into the kitchen to turn it off. He takes his good sweet time doing so, letting her cool her heels even though he knows she's calling from the backstage phone, punishing her for her behavior earlier today. When at last he returns to the study and picks up the receiver, he says, "Okay, I'm back," and hopes his inflection properly conveys a sense of distance. She seems not to notice.

"We're dark tonight, you know," she says, "but I made dinner plans a long time ago. With one of the girls."

"Too bad," he says.

"Can you come over later?"

"No, I have to get up early tomorrow."

"What time does your plane leave?" she asks.

"Four o'clock."

"Will you be going from your apartment or the office?"

"The office. I quit early on Fridays."

"So you can go up there."

"Yes. Right after my last patient leaves."

"What time will that be?"

"Ten to two."

"Can I see you before you go to the airport?"

"No, I don't think so."

"Are you coming to my place tomorrow morning?"

"No, I can't. I have a patient coming in at eight. On Fridays . . ."

"Sure, a short day."

"Yes."

"How long is the flight?"

"An hour and twelve minutes."

"So you'll be up there at twelve past five."

"Well, five-seventeen. It leaves at four-oh-five, actually."

"Will Helen be waiting at the airport?"

"Yes. *And* the kids."

There is a long silence. In the background, he can hear voices moving in and out of focus. He visualizes dancers in cat costumes rushing past the phone, dancers stretching. He can hear someone running a voice exercise, phmmmm-ahhhh, phmmmm-eeeee, phmmmm-ohhhh, over and over again.

"Is something wrong?" she asks.

"Nope."

"Is it Rickie?"

"Who's Rickie?"

"The guy from the bike shop. You know who Rickie is."

"Was that his name?"

"He asked me out," she says.

David says nothing.

"I told him I'd think about it."

"Fine."

"We're not married, you know."

"I know that."

"You have a life that doesn't include me, you know."

"That's right."

"So you can't get angry if somebody . . ."

"I'm not angry."

"Anyway, I didn't say yes. I just said I'd think about it."

"Did you give him your number?"

"No."

"I appreciate that."

"You're angry, right?"

"No, I told you I'm not."

"Good. Then why don't I come to your office tomorrow?"

"I have patients all . . ."

"On your lunch hour, I mean. So I can see you before you go up to the Vineyard."

"Well . . ."

"Do you *have* to go up to the Vineyard?"

"Yes."

"Why don't you stay in the city instead?"

"I can't."

"Why don't you marry me?"

"I'm already married."

"Divorce her and marry me. Then we can make love

all day and all night. And you won't have to worry about Rickie. Or anybody else. Not that you have to, anyway. What time do you have lunch? Twelve?"

"Yes."

"That's when we met in the park."

"I know."

"Twenty minutes after twelve. On the last day of June. I'll never forget it. Do you have a couch?"

"Of course I do."

"Of course, a shrink. Is it leather?"

"Yes."

"Good, we'll do it on your couch."

I couldn't believe we were doing it right on the office couch.

"What color is it?"

"Black."

"I'll wear black panties to match."

"Fine."

"And a black garter belt."

"Fine."

"With black seamed stockings and a black leather skirt."

"Okay."

I was so ashamed of myself.

"Don't be angry, David. Please."

"I'm not."

"The doorman'll think I'm one of your nymphomaniac patients."

"Probably."

"Do you have any nymphomaniac patients?"

"I can't tell you that."

"That means yes."

"No, it means I can't tell you."

"Well, you'll have one tomorrow. Does that excite you?"

"Yes."

"Shall I call you when I get home tonight?"

"No, I want to get some sleep."

"Right, you have to leave for the Vineyard."

"Yes."

"Then I'll see you at twelve tomorrow. Who shall I say I am? If the doorman asks me."

"You don't have to give him a name. Just say you're there for Dr. Chapman."

"Oh, yes, I will most certainly be there for Dr. Chapman."

"I'll see you tomorrow then."

"You're supposed to say you love me," she says.

"I love you," he says.

"Of course you do," she says, and hangs up.

She arrives at the stroke of noon Friday.

He comes out of his private office when he hears the outside bell ringing, and finds her standing in the waiting room, studying the deliberately neutral prints on the wall. She is wearing a short-sleeved white cotton blouse and a pleated watch-plaid miniskirt with black thigh-high stockings and laced black shoes. Her hair is pulled back in a ponytail, fastened with a ribbon that picks up the blue in the blue-green skirt. He wonders if she's wearing the black panties she promised. She does not look at all like the nymphomaniac she advertised on the telephone last night. Instead, she looks like a preppie in a school uniform.

"Hi," she says.

"Come in," he says.

She prowls his office like a cat, studying his framed diplomas, running her palm over the smooth polished top of his desk, looking up at the curlicued tin ceiling painted a neutral off-white, circling the desk again, running her forefinger over the slats of the Venetian blinds behind it, studying the finger for dust, pursing her lips in disapproval as she swipes it clean on the short pleated skirt, and then at last going to the black leather couch, and sitting erect on it, her black-stockinged knees pressed together, her hands on her thighs, the palms flat.

"Would you like to know why I'm here, Doctor?" she asks in a quavering little voice, and it is obvious at once that she is about to play the role of a troubled adolescent girl here to consult an understanding shrink. He wonders again if she is wearing black panties under the skirt.

"I've already told all this to Jacqueline," she says, "Dr. Hicks, but I feel it's something *you* should know, too, don't you think, Doctor?"

Shyly lowering her eyes. Staring at her hands flat on her white thighs above the black stockings. Sitting quite erect. Like a frightened little schoolgirl.

"Oh yes, I certainly do," he says, and smiles, and joins the game. Sitting in the chair behind his desk, he tents his hands and pretends he's this troubled little schoolgirl's psychiatrist, a not altogether difficult role to play in that he really *is* a psychiatrist, although she's no schoolgirl, Senator, black panties or not—*is* she wearing black panties? Is she, in fact, wearing *any* panties at all, her knees pressed so tightly together that way, *Sits there like Sharon Stone, legs wide open, no panties. What looks good to you?*

What looks good to David is Kathryn Duggan, sitting on his office couch, here to make love to him. He has already forgotten the way she batted her eyes at the Callow Ute in the tank top yesterday afternoon. This is today, and she is here, and she is pretending to be a schoolgirl and he is pretending to be a psychiatrist. He doesn't have to pretend too strenuously, of course, since listening is what he does all day long. But pretending nonetheless, he listens as she raises her eyes to look straight at him where he sits, those startling green eyes peering unblinkingly at him, her hands never moving from her thighs, her knees tight together, a little virgin girl sitting erect on his couch, beginning her make-believe little tale of woe.

It is Westport, Connecticut, and little Katie Duggan—"That's what my parents used to call me, Katie"—is thirteen years old and working for the summer as an apprentice at the Westport Country Playhouse, a job she got through her father's best friend, who that summer was the theater's accountant or something, "I forget what his exact title was," she says, "but he was there in some sort of financial capacity, he wasn't the artistic director or anything," sounding very genuine in her little schoolgirl role, relating that she was just beginning to develop at the advanced age of thirteen the teeniest budding little breasts, "Well, look at me now, nothing's changed much," she says and lowers her eyes in mock shyness again. He does, in fact, look at her now, looks at the front of the pristine cotton blouse, and discovers that as usual she's not wearing a bra, and discovers, too, that her nipples as usual are erect against the cotton fabric, puckering the fabric, and wonders again if she's wearing panties, "although I already had pubic hair," she says, "it started coming in red when I was twelve."

"How interesting," he says. "Are you wearing panties now, miss?"

"Yes, I am, Doctor," she says, and smiles briefly, and then resumes the pose of serious little girl relating something she's already told Jacqueline Hicks, but which she feels is something *he* should know, too, don't you think, Doctor? As she begins talking again, she seems to immerse herself more deeply in the role so that he now finds himself *truly* listening intently, just as any *real* psychiatrist might, just as Dr. Hicks might have if such a story had actually been related to her, just as—he realizes with a start—Dr. Hicks *must* have when Kate first told her about that summer when she was thirteen. This is real, he is too skilled a listener to believe any longer that it is playacting. Not three minutes into the story he knows that this is what *really* happened and that she has chosen this method of revealing to him what she has already told Dr. Hicks, whom she was seeing when she was "really crazy."

Looking directly into his eyes, Kate tells him that what she decided to do that summer was lose her virginity to her father's best friend, a married man with three children, whose exact title she forgets but who came in every day to tally the box office receipts and balance the books and pay the salaries and all that in a little office he had down under the theater. "Do you know where the rest rooms are, have you ever been to Westport, to the theater there? Downstairs where the rest rooms are was where Charlie had his office, his name was Charlie. He had this little office with a desk and a chair in it, and some filing cabinets. I used to go down to the office when I'd finished doing whatever they told me to do, they give the apprentices all kinds of shit to do, and I'd sit on his desk and spread my legs for him. That was later."

In the beginning, she used to find excuses to go down there to his office to complain about how badly they were treating her. He listened patiently, he was after all her father's best friend, seemed happy in fact for any respite from the tedium of poring over figures and balancing books. She'd stop down there in cutoff blue jeans and T-shirt, nothing *under* the shirt, of course, she didn't have anything much to put in a bra except those tiny breasts that were almost entirely nipples. She was beginning to develop pretty good nipples that summer, at least recognizable as such and discernible enough for him to comment one day in a very fatherly manner, "Katie, you ought to start wearing a bra," which meant he'd noticed, which meant she was making some progress here. And, of course, her legs looked terrific in the cutoffs.

"I've always had great legs," she tells David now,

"even when I was just a little girl. But I'd been taking dance for quite a while by the time I was thirteen, and my legs were really quite long and shapely . . ."

"They still are," he says, forgetting for the moment that he is neither her real psychiatrist *nor* her fake one, remembering all at once that they are here to make love, presumably, and the time she is a-flying, and he hasn't had lunch, and his next patient will be here in forty minutes, and besides he's not even sure he *wants* to hear this story of teenage . . .

"Thank you, Doctor," she says. "Anyway, I guess *he* thought my legs were pretty spectacular . . ."

"They are," he says, a psychiatrist's ploy, a cheap trick, an unabashed *prompt*, hoping she will respond *Yes*, come put your hands on my creamy white thighs, *Yes*, come slide your hands under my schoolgirl skirt and onto my . . .

"Thank you, Doctor," she says again, "because one day he said in a very fatherly manner, 'Katie, some of the boys have been noticing your legs,' which meant *he'd* been noticing them, which was further progress. By the way, seducing him wasn't the *main* reason I was at the Playhouse, if that's what you're thinking. Actually, that was just something I decided to do because I got so *bored*. And maybe *angry*, too, because I didn't get to dance in *On the Town*, which I knew they'd be doing that summer, and which was the main reason I was there to begin with—but that's another story."

Charlie was a man in his early fifties, she guesses now . . . well, her father was forty-three that summer and Charlie was older than he was, so yes, he was either in his very late forties or his early fifties. He had a bald head and he was sort of short and stout, and he wasn't very attractive although he did have nice sensitive blue eyes, but she can't imagine now why she was so intent on having him *notice* her to begin with, which he certainly did with more and more frequency, and then *touch* her, which he finally did one rainy day in August while on stage the actors, including two of them from Broadway, were rehearsing *Who's Afraid of Virginia Woolf?* and in the workshop the other apprentices were busy painting scenery.

She rises from the couch now, as if the memory of that steamy day in August is too much for her to bear sitting still and erect on a black leather couch, rises and begins pacing his office, the pleated skirt swirling about her long legs as she walks back and forth before his desk, turning at opposite ends of the short course her long strides define, the skirt swirling, swirling. She is a dancer, she was a dancer even back then, surely she realizes that her abrupt turns are causing the short skirt to billow about her legs, to expose above the taut black stockings a wider expanse of white thigh each time—and *yes! There!* A glimpse of the now world-famous bicycle-shop white panties, not the black ones she promised on the phone, but plain white panties instead, girlish cotton panties more appropriate to the schoolgirl uniform, similar to the panties she was wearing on that dripping wet day in August when she was thirteen and she slipped down the stairs to his office wearing, yes, white panties, yes, under her habitual cutoff jeans and a thin white cotton T-shirt that had the words WEST-

PORT COUNTRY PLAYHOUSE printed across its nipple-puckered front.

He is sitting at his desk, bald head bent over the ledger spread open before him. A narrow window is on the short wall opposite the door, and rain beats steadily in a widening street-level puddle just outside of it, droplets of water splashing up onto the glass. A lamp with a green shade illuminates the yellow ledger and his bald head bent over it. Suddenly a flash of lightning turns the horizontal window glaringly blue, and there is immediate thunder in the parking lot outside. He glances up toward the window, shaking his head in awe, and then turns back to his books again. He does not yet know she is in the office. They have never been alone together in this room with the door shut. She eases the door shut behind her. He looks up when he hears the click of the lock as she turns the bolt.

"Katie?" he says.

She goes to his desk, stands in front of him where he sits in his swivel chair with his books spread before him, and takes the hem of her T-shirt in both hands and lifts it above her tiny adolescent breasts and outrageously stiff nipples.

"Kiss them," she whispers.

He says, "Katie, what . . . ?"

"Kiss them."

"Your father . . ."

"Yes, do it."

He kisses her repeatedly all that rainy afternoon— well, at least for an hour on that rainy afternoon, his hands tight on her tight buttocks in the tight cutoffs, which she refuses to remove despite his constant pleadings—and he repeatedly kisses her nipples and blossoming breasts all through the next week, while proclaiming terrible feelings of guilt for betraying his wife, and the week after that while telling her he shouldn't be doing this to his best friend's teenage daughter, he feels so guilty doing this, and the week after that while telling her he himself has a daughter her age, how can he be *doing* this, is he *crazy?* He goes even crazier when one day at the beginning of September with russet leaves drifting onto the parking lot she unzips the cutoffs for him, and removes them, and lowers her white cotton panties, and sits on his desk before him and spreads her russet self wide to him, and allows him to bury his bald head between her legs and to lick her there until she experiences a thunderous orgasm for the very first time in her life.

Abruptly, she stops pacing.

Her eyes meet David's again.

She nods knowingly, and walks to him where he sits in his chair behind his desk, and she unbuttons the white cotton blouse button by button until it is hanging open over her breasts. Standing between his spread legs, she moves into him, and pulls his head into her breasts, and says, "Kiss them." And while he kisses her feverishly, she reaches under the short pleated skirt and pulls the white cotton panties down over her waist and her thighs, slides them down over her long legs in the tight black stockings, and then sits on the desk before him and spreads her legs to him as she did to Charlie long ago, and whispers, "Yes, do it."

★   ★   ★

On Saturday morning, Helen drives Jenny into Vineyard Haven to shop for new sneakers, which Jenny says she desperately needs if she is not to become "a social outcast," her exact words. It is a cloudy, windy day but David and Annie are walking the beach together nonetheless. He is wearing a green windbreaker; Annie is in a yellow rain slicker and sou'wester tied under her chin. Her cheeks are shiny red from the cold, and the wind is causing her eyes to water. She and David are both barefoot, although it is really too chilly for that, the sand clammy and cold to the touch. Still, they plod along hand in hand. The water looks gray today, streaked with angry white crests.

"Here's what I don't get," Annie says.

"What is it you don't get?"

"How do astronauts pee?"

"Astro—?"

"I mean, *where* do they pee, actually? When they're walking on the moon in those suits, I mean."

"I guess they have a tube or something."

"The girls, too?"

"I really don't know, honey."

"That really bothers me," Annie says, and looks up at him. "Cause everybody's always asking me do I want to be an astronaut when I grow up."

"Who's everybody?"

"Anybody who comes to the house. Grown-ups. First they say How are you today, Annie? and I say I'm fine, thanks, and then they say Are you looking forward to going back to school in September? and I say Well, it's still only *July*, you know, and they say Do you *like* school? and I say Oh yeah, tons, and that's when they ask me what I want to be when I grow up."

"I guess they're just interested in you, Annie."

"Why should they care *what* I want to be when I grow up? Suppose I don't want to be *anything* when I grow up? I sure don't want to be president of the United States, which is something *else* they always ask. Are your feet cold?"

"Yes."

"Why don't we go back to the house and make a fire and roast marshmallows?" she says. "Before Jenny and Mom get back, okay?"

"Why don't I just *carry* you back to the house," he says, and scoops her up into his arms. "So your feet won't get any colder, okay?"

"Okay," she says, grinning. Her head against his shoulder, she asks, "Do I have to be an astronaut, Dad?"

"You don't have to be anything you don't want to be," he says.

"Cause I sure wouldn't like peeing in a tube," she says.

He hugs her closer, shielding her from the wind.

A woman at the dinner party that night is telling them it is the end of the criminal justice system as they've known it. "Never again will a black man in this country be convicted of a felony," she says. "All the defense has to do is make sure there's at least one person of color on the jury. That's it. A hung jury each and every time. Check it out."

She is a quite pretty brunette who looks too young to be an attorney, but apparently she is a litigator with a Wall Street firm. Harry Daitch, who is hosting the party with his wife, Danielle, is a lawyer himself and he debates the brunette furiously, but with a smile on his face, contending that justice has nothing to do with racial sympathies, and maintaining that recent verdicts were anomalies rather than true indicators. This is while they are all having cocktails on the deck, under a sky still surly and gray. A black maid is serving hors d'oeuvres. She pretends to be deaf, dumb and blind as the sun sinks below the horizon without a trace.

At dinner, Fred Coswell, who with his wife, Margaret is renting the house next door to Helen and David, mentions that David was in a situation not too long ago—"Do you remember telling us, David?"—where some black kid stole a bicycle from a girl in Central Park.

"Do you mean to say *he'll* get off?" Fred asks the woman attorney, whose name is Grace Something, and who is now seated on Harry Daitch's right, just across the table from David. All told, there are eight people at the party, including an investment broker from Manhattan who's been invited as Grace's dinner partner, and who is sitting alongside her on the same side of the table.

"I'm sure Grace meant major felonies," Harry says, and pats her left hand where it rests alongside his.

"Don't put words in my mouth," Grace says, laughing. "I'm not sure it won't apply to lesser crimes as well. Black kid steals a bike, that's petit larceny, a class-A mis, the most he can get in jail is a year. Even if he gets the max, which he won't, he'll be out again stealing *another* bike four months later. But if he hires himself a smart lawyer . . ."

"Like you," Harry says, and pats her hand again.

"Like me, thank you—*white* like me, anyway, so it won't look like a slave uprising—the defense'll play the 'Underprivileged Black' card, and then the 'Black Rage' card, and any person of color sitting on that jury'll go, 'Mmmm, *mmmm*, tell it, brother, amen,' " she says, doing a fair imitation of a call-and-response routine in a black Baptist church. David wonders all at once if Grace is a closet bigot, but the black maid who is now serving them at table seems to find the takeoff amusing. At least, she's smiling. "And he'll walk," Grace says in conclusion and dismissal, and picks up her knife and fork.

"Did that case ever come to trial, by the way?" Fred asks.

"I have no idea," David says.

"Ever hear anything more about it?"

"Well, I had to go identify him."

"You mean they *got* him?" Margaret says.

"Well, yes."

"I didn't know that," Helen says, surprised.

"I guess I forgot to tell you," he says.

"When was this?"

"I don't remember. Shortly after the Fourth of July weekend. When I got back to the city."

"Well, what *happened?*" Danielle asks.

As hostess, she is sitting at the opposite end of the table, facing her husband at this end. Helen, on her left in this not-quite-boy-girl-boy-girl seating arrangement, is leaning forward now, her head turned to the left, looking across the table, waiting for David's response. In fact, *all* attention seems to have turned from the defense to the prosecution, so to speak, everyone suddenly curious about what happened when David went to identify the young bicycle thief, an event he somehow neglected to mention to Helen in the press of further developments, small wonder. She is still staring at him, waiting.

"The police called and asked if I'd come over after work," he says. "So I did," he says, and shrugs.

"How'd they know who you were?" Fred asks.

"I guess the girl told them."

"*Was* it the guy?" Danielle asks.

"Oh, yes."

"So they got him," Margaret says, almost to herself, nodding. "Good."

"You didn't tell me this," Helen says, still looking surprised.

"I meant to," he says.

"Annie keeps asking me every *day* did they catch him."

"I'm sorry, I guess it just slipped my . . ."

"But it hasn't come to trial yet," Fred says.

"That's the last I heard of it."

Helen is still looking at him.

"Will you have to testify?" Margaret asks.

"I really . . ."

"If it comes to trial?"

"I don't . . ."

"How old is he?" Grace asks.

"Sixteen, seventeen."

"First offense?"

"I don't know."

"The case may even be dismissed," she says. "You know what a class-A mis is?"

"No, what?" her dinner companion asks. This is the first time he's opened his mouth all night long. He has flaxen hair and dark brown eyes and he is wearing a heavy gold chain over a purple Tommy Hilfiger sweater. David wonders if he's gay.

"Writing *graffiti* is a class-A mis. Unauthorized use of a *computer* is a class-A mis. *Hazing* is a class-A mis. Are you beginning to catch the drift?"

"She means it's a bullshit crime," Harry says.

"Well, he also hit her," David says, and thinks Shut up. End it. Let it die. "Kicked her. Knocked her down."

"That's assault," Grace says.

"That's a horse of another color," Harry says.

"Which is why he'll walk," Grace says knowingly.

Coming out of the bathroom, Helen says, "I can't believe Danielle can be so *blind*." She is slipping a night-gown over her head as she walks, the blue nylon cascading over her tanned body, blond hair surfacing as her head clears the laced bodice. She shakes her disheveled hair loose, a habit he loves, and then goes to the dresser. Sitting before the mirror, she begins brushing her hair. He does not know how she can brush and count and talk at the same time, but it is a feat she performs effortlessly every night. Fifty strokes before bedtime every night. Meanwhile talking a mile a minute.

"He invites her to *every* party, seats her on his *right* at every party, feels her *up* at every . . ."

"He was patting her hand," David says.

"Why do men feel compelled to defend other men who they *know* are fucking around?" Helen asks incredulously. "He was patting her hand *on* the table. *Under* the table he was feeling her up."

"How do you know what he was doing under the table?"

"I know when a man has his hand on a woman's thigh. Or closer to home. Something comes over her face."

"I didn't see anything coming over her face."

"Her eyes glazed over."

"I didn't notice that. I was sitting directly across from her, and I didn't . . ."

"Right, defend him."

"I just don't think anything's going on between Harry and Grace whatever her name is."

"Humphrey. Which I feel is appropriate."

David thinks about that for a moment.

"Oh," he says.

"Oh," Helen says, and winks at him in the mirror.

He is stretched out on the bed, his elbow bent, his head propped on his open hand, watching her. He loves to watch her perform simple female tasks. Putting on lipstick. Polishing her nails. Clasping a bra behind her back. Slipping on a high-heeled shoe. Brushing her hair.

"How does he know her, anyway?" he asks.

"Biblically," Helen says.

"I mean . . ."

"They work in the same office."

"And she's up here for the summer?"

"No, she's a houseguest. Every weekend," Helen says, and raises her eyebrows. "Hmm?"

"Well . . ."

"Mmm," Helen says.

"Do you think Danielle invites her?"

"I have no idea. Maybe Danielle has a boyfriend of her own. Maybe Danielle doesn't care *what* Harry does under the table or behind the barn. Danielle is French, my dear."

"Oh, come *on*, Hel. She's been in America for twenty years. In fact, they've been *married* that long."

"So have we," Helen says. "I can't believe you forgot to tell me."

"Tell you what?"

"About going to identify that boy."

"Well, it was a busy week. Everybody just back from the long weekend . . ."

"I'll bet they were rattling their cages."

"Anxiety levels were high, let's put it that way."

"Was this a lineup?"

"Yes."

"Where?"

"The precinct. They have a room."

"Was the girl there, too? The one he hit?"

"Yes."

"What was her name again?"

"I forget."

"She identified him, too, huh?"

"Oh, yes."

"So they've really got him then."

"Oh yes."

"Kate," she says. "It was Kate."

"Right. Kate."

"Done," she says, and puts down the brush.

"How do you do that?"

"I'm a fucking phenomenon," she says. "Speaking of which," she adds, and swivels toward him on the bench.

"I thought you'd never ask," he says.

Making love to her tonight, he remembers the way she looked that autumn day when first he laid eyes on her, sitting on a riverbank bench, head bent, totally absorbed in the book she was reading. On the Charles, a sculling team from Harvard was tirelessly rowing, he can still hear the megaphoned voice of the coxswain calling the stroke, still recall everything that happened that day as if it is playing back now in wide screen and stereophonic sound.

Leaves are falling like golden coins everywhere around her. Her straight blond hair cascades down her back, well past her shoulders, she wears it longer back then, she is still a college undergraduate, though he only sus-pects that as he stands rooted to the river path, staring. Woolen skirt and moss-green sweater, string of tiny pearls. A shower of leaves twists in the gentle breeze, silently floating, drifting, seeming to fall out of sunlight as golden as her hair. He has never seen anyone quite so beautiful in his life. And to think he's here only to pick up a book at the Coop.

Making love to her tonight on ocean-damp sheets,

he recalls all this. Sees it clearly in his mind's eye. Remembers.

"Hello?" he says. "May I join you?"

She turns to look up at him.

Eyes as blue as a searing flash of lightning.

He is twenty-six years old, a recent graduate of Harvard's medical school, and he is sporting a mustache because he thinks it makes him look older and therefore, he hopes, more authoritative in the Emergency Room at Mass General, where he is interning. He has already decided he will become a psychiatrist, but he won't begin specializing till next year, Mom, and meanwhile he's treating people who are bleeding, biting, babbling, bawling or merely broken in a hundred pieces, all flowing through the E.R. doors in a constant stream designed to instruct him in the basic truths of medicine, fundamental among which is the knowledge that any mistake he makes can prove fatal. He guesses this gorgeous blond goddess sitting here with her legs crossed and an open book in her lap doesn't know much about life and death, the way he does. He guesses she is four or five years younger than he is—actually, it turns out to be six—and he hopes as he sits beside her that the mustache doesn't make him look *too* much older or wiser, although the way her blue laser glare seems to focus in on the mustache leads him to believe she doesn't much care for "an *hairy* man," Esau notwithstanding.

"I'm David Chapman," he says.

He resists adding "*Dr.* David Chapman" because the title still seems strange to him, even though he is now officially a doctor, more or less, otherwise why is he allowed to treat all those maimed and wounded people who swarm into the E.R. day and night?

The way she keeps looking at him also leads him to believe she's unaccustomed to strange mustachioed men sitting beside her uninvited on a public bench. Out on the river, the scullers keep rowing past tirelessly. Here on the bank of the Charles, the leaves fall softly, gently, even romantically, an appropriate backdrop, he feels, for this first momentous encounter, though she doesn't seem to be sharing the same keen sense of History in the Making.

"I don't want to intrude on your privacy," he says.

Then why *are* you? her look asks.

"But . . . I'd like to know you," he says.

"Why?" she asks.

"Because . . . you're so beautiful," he says.

Lamely.

"That I know," she says.

The scullers are out of sight now. Pedestrians are idling across the Longfellow Bridge to Alston. On the other side of the river, he can see automobiles rumbling along Storrow Drive, and beyond that the big Coca-Cola sign near the entrance to the Mass Pike. The leaves continue falling silently. She has returned to her book again.

"So what do you think?" he asks.

"About what?" she says without looking up.

"About let's walk over to the Square and have a cup of coffee."

"I have a class in twenty minutes," she says, without even glancing at her watch.

"Then I guess we'll have to sit *here* and talk," he says.

She looks at him again. His daughter Annie will one day inherit her mother's intent gaze and direct manner, but he doesn't know that as yet, of course, he isn't thinking that far ahead, he isn't even thinking past her scented proximity on the bench (Tea Rose, she will later tell him) or the bee-stung temptation of her lips, pursed now in seeming displeasure, he can't imagine why. He wonders if she's noticed the stethoscope sticking out of the right-hand pocket of his jacket. If so, does she think it has perhaps been stolen from an attending physician on a psychiatric ward someplace? The reason he wonders this is because her look somehow implies he may be an escaped lunatic.

"I have a test in twenty minutes," she says in dismissal. "I don't wish to appear rude, Mr. Chapman . . ."

His opportunity.

"*Dr.* Chapman," he says.

"*Dr.* Chapman, do forgive me. But I have to . . ."

"A test in what?"

"Irrelevant," she says. "I have to study. Please."

"Can I call you sometime?"

"Why?" she asks again.

"So I can get to know your *mind?*" he suggests, and grins so broadly that she bursts out laughing.

The first time they go out together, Helen advises him to "lose the mustache" because together with the eyeglasses they make him look as if he's wearing one of those trick disguises you put on with the big nose and the shaggy brows and the glasses and mustache, though he doesn't have a big nose at all and his brows aren't shaggy. It's just that she can't imagine ever *kissing* anyone with a mustache, which, if not exactly an open invitation, does seem an opportunity he shouldn't ignore, so he kisses her for the first time and stars fall on Alabama—for him, at least. *She* says this sort of thing has got to stop. He shaves his mustache that very night.

The reason *this* sort of thing has got to stop is that Helen Barrister—her name, and an appropriate one in that both her parents are lawyers and both are of English ancestry—is engaged to someone named Wallace Ames who happens to be going to school in California, which technically makes him a GUG, shorthand for a Geographically Undesirable Girl or Guy (a Guy, in this instance), but Helen doesn't yet realize this. At the moment, she is a straight 4.0 student at Radcliffe, concentrating in journalism and hoping one day to become editor in chief of *The New Yorker*, her favorite magazine, although he suspects she reads *Vogue* as well, witness the dandy outfits she wears during this blazing Massachusetts autumn while he diligently pursues her, stealing a kiss here or there, hither or yon, when not busy stanching wounds or delivering babies, *three* of them by Christmas alone.

David feels certain his mother would be a solid Wallace Ames supporter if she knew of his existence, or even of Helen's existence, for that matter, since he hasn't yet told her about the radiant blue-eyed beauty he stumbled upon one bright October day. *Knows* without question that his mother would agree Wallace is *really* the man this nice young girl should marry, why don't you concentrate on your *work*, David, on becoming a good *doctor*,

David, instead of sniffing around a blond, blue-eyed beauty already engaged to a surfer?

To the surfer's credit—and anyway he *isn't* a surfer, but is instead seriously studying film at UCLA—it is he who decides to end this long-distance engagement to a girl he "hardly knows," as he puts it in a *Dear Helen* letter which she receives on New Year's Eve, great timing, Wally. Two weeks later, this still being the lewd, lascivious, obscene and pornographic seventies, David and Helen consummate their budding romance on a single bed in a rented room on the Cape. To his mother's credit, she accepts Helen without a backward sigh.

There is a history here.

It is a record as complex as the computer banks of their separate minds, storing and recalling memories solitary or shared, before or since. It is as pervasive as the waves gently lapping the shore beyond the sliding screen doors in this room where they make quiet love lest they wake the children, reckless love in that they cannot quite muffle their ardor.

He has shared with this woman a thousand hopes and aspirations, small triumphs, bitter disappointments. He has laughed with her and cried with her, fought with her, hated her, loved her again, abjured her, adored her again. When Jenny was born . . . oh dear God . . . and the obstetrician told him Helen had gone into shock . . . no, dear God . . . and he might . . . he might . . . he might lose her, he prayed long into the night to a deity he had not acknowledged since he was eighteen. He knows every facet of this woman's mind, every nuance of her body. He has savored each forever, and has never tired of either. He still believes she is the most beautiful woman he has ever known.

Then *why*, he wonders.

Why?

It is raining on Sunday morning.

Annie wants to go to a movie.

"That's what you do when it rains," she says and shrugs in perfect logic.

Together, she and Helen go into the kitchen to call the movie houses in Vineyard Haven. David is playing chess with Jenny in the living room. She is a whiz at the game he taught her when she was Annie's age, and she plays with intense concentration, forcing him into moves that enforce and encourage her master plan, all the while keeping up a running conversation, much as her mother does when administering her fifty magic strokes each night.

"Check," she says. "If I tell you a secret, will you promise not to tell Mom or Annie?"

"I promise."

"*Especially* Annie."

"Yes, darling, I promise."

Jenny lowers her voice. On her sweet solemn face, there is a look of such trust that he wants to hug her close and tell her he would never betray a secret of hers as long as he can draw breath. Blue eyes wide, she leans over the chessboard and whispers, "Brucie loves me."

"Who's Brucie?" he whispers back.

"Di Angelo. Next door."

She gestures with her head.

"How do you know?"

"He gave me a ring," she whispers, and pulls from under her T-shirt a tiny gold band on a golden chain. "You know what else?" she whispers, quickly sliding the ring out of sight again.

"What else?" he whispers.

"I love him, too."

"That's nice," he says.

"Yes," she says, and nods happily. "Your move, Dad."

The sun is shining when they come out of the theater at a quarter past three. His plane will be leaving at six-fifteen this evening, and will get into La Guardia at seven twenty-nine.

"Why don't you go back tomorrow morning instead?" Jenny asks.

"Cause that would be a hardship," Annie says. "Besides, Dad'll be here *forever* next weekend."

They are taking a last long walk up the beach before it's time to head to the airport. He and Helen are holding hands. The girls are running up the beach ahead of them, circling back occasionally to hug them both around the legs, skipping off again, skirting like sandpipers the waves that gently rush the shore.

"Right, Dad?" Annie says, turning to look back at him.

"Right, honey," he says, and squeezes Helen's hand.

"Forever, right?"

"Forever," he says.

Annie leaps over someone's abandoned sand castle, lands flat-footed and crouched on the other side of it.

"Boop!" she says.

And in that moment, he decides to end whatever this thing with Kate might be.

He is in the study reading when the doorman buzzes upstairs at five minutes to nine that night. Puzzled, he pads barefoot through the apartment to the receiver hanging just inside the front door.

"Hello?" he says.

"Dr. Chapman?"

"Yes?"

"Pizza delivery."

"I didn't order any pizza," he says.

"Young lady says thees pizza for you."

"Oh. Yes, I . . . yes, send it right up."

She is wearing black shorts, a red T-shirt, a red beret, red socks and black high-topped thick-soled shoes that look like combat boots. She does indeed look like someone who could be delivering a pizza, which she is in fact doing. From the looks of the carton, it is a good-sized one.

"I got half cheese and half pepperoni," she says, "I hope that's okay. Are you hungry?"

"No, I ate a little while ago."

"I'm *starved*," she says. "Why didn't you call me?"

"The plane was late."

"I'm glad you're here. Aren't you going to kiss me?"

"Kate . . ." he starts.

PRIVILEGED CONVERSATION

"Before I die?" she says and moves into his arms.

He kisses her, and then breaks away gently but almost at once, fearful that somehow Helen, all the way up there in Massachusetts, will *know* there's another woman in their apartment, will *know* he has just kissed a woman who's brought him a pizza at nine o'clock at night, will *know* this is the woman, the *girl*, he's been sleeping with, talk about euphemisms, and that she is here in their apartment right this very minute, now, dressed like a delivery person in a red beret and combat boots. As he takes the pizza carton from her and carries it into the kitchen he fully expects the phone will ring and Helen will yell, "Who's that with you, you bastard?"

But, of course, the phone doesn't ring.

"Nice," she says, looking around.

"Thank you," he says.

He is still very nervous. More than nervous. Apprehensive. Frightened that Luis . . . was it Luis at the door when he got back from dinner tonight? *If* it was Luis who passed her in, will he remember that this is the same girl who left a washed and ironed handkerchief downstairs two weeks ago, have they been sleeping together for only two *weeks?* But, of course, the handkerchief was in an envelope, so he wouldn't have known it was a handkerchief, as if *that* makes any difference, sly Luis with his big macho Hispanic grin and virtual wink, clever Luis who accepted the "leetle" package from a beautiful redheaded girl at eleven o'clock on a Sunday morning two weeks ago, but this is now nine o'clock *this* Sunday *night*, and Mrs. Chapman is enjoying the seashore up there in Massachusetts, *verdad, señor?* Will

Luis remember? If it *is* Luis downstairs? Will Luis remember—and destroy him even *after* he has ended it? But, of course, he hasn't ended it yet. Not quite yet. He has only *decided* to end it.

"We should put it in the oven," Kate says.

She seems blithely, and somehow infuriatingly, unaware of his discomfort. Doesn't she know that Helen has a nose like a beagle and that the perfume she's wearing, while admittedly seductive though inappropriate to the delivery boy guise, is the sort that will permeate upholstery and drapes and be sniffed in an instant when Helen and the children walk through the front door on the fifteenth of September, which is when the lease on the Vineyard house runs out? Bending from the waist like the dancer she is, she slips the pizza carton into the oven, turns to smile at him, and blows a kiss on the air.

"Kate," he says, "we have to talk."

"Sure," she says, and familiarly adjusts the dial on the oven, as if she has warmed pizzas in this oven in this kitchen forever, as if this is *her* kitchen, in fact. "But aren't you going to offer me a drink?"

"Of course," he says, but he is thinking he wants to get this over with, talk to her, tell her it's over, eat the goddamn pizza, get rid of the carton, end it. As he leads her into the living room, she looks around appraisingly, studying the paintings on the wall, and the silk flower arrangement on the hall table, and the furniture, and the small piece of sculpture he and Helen brought back from their trip to India three years ago, her green eyes roaming, "Nice," she says again, and sits on the couch facing the bar unit, crossing her long legs in the short black shorts and the incongruous combat boots. She knows her legs are gorgeous . . .

I've always had great legs, even when I was just a little girl. But I'd been taking dance for quite a while by the time I was thirteen, and my legs were really quite long and shapely . . .

. . . knows she can take outrageous liberties with them, probably figures as well that the shorts and the boots are an exaggerated echo of the green nylon running shorts and Nike running shoes she was wearing on the day they met.

"Could you make a martini for me?" she asks.

"Sure," he says.

"Thank you," she says. "Vodka? With a twist?"

"Sure."

He was hoping she'd prefer something simpler, Scotch on the rocks, bourbon and soda, anything but a drink that will require time-consuming preparation, because truly he wants to get this over with before . . .

Before what?

Well, before the telephone *really* rings and it'll be Helen calling from Menemsha.

He doesn't know what he can possibly say if Helen calls.

Pouring the Absolut, adding a dollop of vermouth, skimming a bit of lemon peel from the big yellow lemon he takes from the refrigerator, the phone hanging on the wall behind the counter, fearful the phone will ring, *Oh, hi, Helen, I was just making myself a martini*, but the phone doesn't ring. He carries the drink back into the living room, where Kate has taken off the combat boots and now sits on the couch with her legs tucked under her and one arm draped across the back of the couch. She has also taken off the beret. Her red hair shines under the glow of the ceiling spot that illuminates the abstract painting behind her. He carries the drink to her . . .

"Aren't you having something?"

. . . pours himself a little Scotch over ice, goes to the couch to clink glasses . . .

"To us," she says, and smiles up at him.

"Kate," he says, "we . . ."

"Mmm," she says, sipping at the drink.

He sits beside her. The couch is blue. He hopes she hasn't powdered herself after showering, hopes she won't leave traces of her powder, her perfume, her *scent* in this apartment for Helen to discover after Luis casually mentions this little nocturnal visit from a redhead.

"So what is it?" she asks, and turns her head and her eyes to him. He takes a long swallow of Scotch.

"Kate," he says, "I think you should know I'll be leaving for the Vineyard as usual this Friday night . . ."

"Yes?"

". . . but this time I'll be gone the entire month of August."

"Yes, I know."

He looks at her.

"You're a shrink, you'll be gone all of August, I realize that. We still have the rest of the week. Anyway, why don't you just marry me? Then you won't have to go to the Vineyard at all."

"Kate . . ."

"Or at the very least, why don't you go up there on

Saturday instead? Or even Sunday. Why do you have to rush up there on Friday? Friday's only the twenty-eighth. Do your patients know you'll be leaving so early?"

"Effectively, Friday's the end of the month."

"No, the end of the month is next *Monday*. The end of the month is the thirty-*first*, that's when the end of the month is."

"I know, but . . ."

"I'm glad you're not *my* shrink, David, I have to tell you. Ducking out before the month even ends. By the way, I've planned a big surprise for your birthday, so I hope you're not planning to run up to the Vineyard even *earlier* than you . . ."

"No, I won't be going up till . . ."

"Good. My place at eight then. We're dark on Thursday nights, so I won't have to worry about getting to the theater, will I?"

"Kate, I think we . . ."

"Wait'll you see what I got you."

"I hope you didn't spe—"

"You'll love it. Will you have *another* birthday party when you go up to the Vineyard?"

"Yes."

"When?"

"Friday night."

"Is that why you're going up so early?"

"I'm not going up early. My patients . . ."

"Ducking out three days before the month ends," she says, and turns fully toward him now, swinging around in a dancer's position or perhaps a yoga position, he doesn't know which, bringing the soles of her feet together, holding them together with her hands, sitting quite erect, her knees wide, the black shorts rising higher on her thighs so that he can now see the edge of her panties beneath them, white like the ones she was wearing in the park that day long ago, the side-slit in the very short green nylon running shorts exposing a hint of white cotton panties beneath, strengthening the image of youth, white like the ones she was wearing yet longer ago when one day at the beginning of September with russet leaves drifting onto the parking lot she unzipped her cutoffs for him and removed them and lowered her panties and sat on his desk and spread herself wide to him.

"My patients *know* when I'm leaving," he says. "We've talked about nothing else for the past three weeks."

But this isn't quite true.

They've talked about other things as well.

And all at once it was dark, and in the dark she could have been anyone, in the dark she was opening her robe and spreading her legs, warm and wet and pulling me into her.

"Kate," he says, "what I think we should do . . ."

"What *I* think we should do is get a bit more *comfortable* here, don't you think?" she says, and rises suddenly from whatever odd position it was, dance, yoga, exercise, whatever, rises with arms extended for balance, rises slowly like a swimmer coming up out of icy blue water, stands barefoot on the cushioned blue couch for only a moment, and then springs to the white-carpeted floor with a single catlike leap, yanking shorts and panties down over her knees at once. Delicately, she steps out of them, lifting one long dancer's leg, and then the other, and then tosses them over her shoulder. Smiling, she takes a step toward him, and then another, dancer's steps, knee coming up high, toes pointed, foot slowly descending flat to the carpet, slow-motion steps, moving closer and closer, like a cat stalking its prey, but there's a smile on her face.

"Would you like to fuck me now?" she asks, and falls to her knees in a dancer's soft collapse. "Say," she says, and unzips his fly, and whips him free of his trousers and his underwear, gripping him tightly in her fist. She looks up into his face. Her eyes hold his in an innocent green gaze. Her eyebrows are raised. Well? her expression is saying. "Or would you rather stick this big beautiful thing in my mouth?" she asks, and smiles radiantly.

He throws his head back and stares up into the blinding light above the painting, lost in the glare of the light and the insistence of her relentless hand, the light radiating spikes of rapture, losing all resolve within seconds, lost within seconds in her youth, lost beyond recall in her incandescent passion, utterly bewilderingly ecstatically lost.

"Which?" she demands. *"Say!"*

On Monday morning, he calls Stanley Beckerman to say he'll go along with the August deception.

Everything in his life has a title now.

The August Deception.

As is usual at this time of the year, each of his patients comes up with different but not entirely original ways of coping with what they consider David's wanton neglect and lack of consideration. How *dare* he leave them for the entire month of August? *More* than that. Five weeks and four days if you count the days he'll be gone at the end of July and the days he'll be gone in September before he returns on the fifth. Five weeks and four days, never mind any goddamn *month*, who's kidding who here?

Arthur K's way of dealing with this abominable situation is to try to wrap up the analysis before the end of the month. Not merely put it on hold until after Labor Day, but wrap it up forever. *End* it. Which David knows from experience is not always a simple thing to do. But Arthur K—who's been telling him that the night on his sister's bed after the dance was the one and only time he'd ever touched her—seems eager to confess this Tuesday that he and his sister had been making love on and off, every now and then, ever since that night, even *after* they were both married . . .

"To other people, of course. She's my sister, marrying her would be incest."

. . . had been doing it *regularly*, in fact *incessantly* right up to the time of her death twelve years ago, when Arthur's phobic reaction to automobiles started. If David would like to *know*, in fact—and then perhaps they can put this thing to rest once and for all and bring this so-called *analysis* to its long-awaited conclusion—if David would like to know what *really* happened that day . . .

Veronica's husband, Manny, is off at work as usual, he owns a ladies' ready-to-wear store on Fourteenth Street, he sells mostly to Spanish people, yellow dresses, red dresses, the cheap gaudy shit they like to wear. His sister and Manny live up in Larchmont, which is where Arthur goes to see her at ten o'clock that Wednesday morning. Wednesday is when he goes to his chiropractor and then drives up afterward to see his sister. He does this every Wednesday. He does not think he can get through a week without seeing his sister, without doing to his sister what they started doing together all those years ago. He loves his sister more than anyone on earth.

"I was never ashamed of my love for her. I *still* love her, if you want to know."

On that fateful day that will mark the end of her life, she is wearing for him what she wears each and every time they make love, a blue robe not unlike the one she'd worn when she was fifteen and a virgin, and a laced pink nightgown, though shorter than the one back then.

"Veronica never had any children," Arthur K says. "She always kept her body nice. Same body she had when she was fifteen. Firm belly, breasts, everything, even though she was . . . what . . . fifty-*three* when she got killed in the accident?"

His voice catches.

David waits.

"I really want to *end* this fucking thing," he says.

Should David risk a prompt?

End *what?* he wonders. The belief that their transgression is what caused his sister's death?

Or the analysis?

He waits.

"She told me . . . she said she . . ."

David waits.

"She said she told Manny."

There is a long, shattering silence.

"I said . . . I . . . I was flabbergasted. I said *What?* You told Manny? I told Manny, she said. About us? I said. About us, she said. She said this would have to be the last time we ever, what we did, what we just finished doing. She said Manny never wanted to see me again, never wanted to talk to me again, never wanted to *hear* about me again, fucking my own sister, the shame, the *shame*. This is what Manny told her. Said I was fucking my own sister. We had just finished . . . she was sitting on the edge of the bed naked when she told me all this. This was afterwards. We always had a cigarette afterwards. We were sitting there smoking when she told me this. She was sitting on the edge of the bed, I was in this little easy chair she had with the gold fabric. We were both smoking. I said Veronica, how could you *tell* him this, are you crazy? She said she couldn't bear the guilt any longer, she had to tell him. I said *What* guilt, what are you talking about, guilt? We *love* each other, what guilt? How could you *do* this? She said I'm sorry, Arthur, I couldn't bear it anymore, the lying.

"I . . . I got on my knees in front of her, I took her hands in mine, her cigarette was in the ashtray, smoke was coming up. I said Veronica, you've got to tell him you were kidding, and she said Kidding? How can I tell him I was kidding? Who would kid about something like this, Arthur? I kissed her hands, I kept kissing her hands, I kept saying Please, Veronica, over and over again, and she said Arthur, you have to go now, I have a manicure appointment, I have to drive over to my manicurist, and I said Please, Veronica, I was crying now, I said Please don't leave me, and she said I have to, and I said Please please, Veronica, and she said Go now, Arthur, please, he'll kill me if he knows you were here, and I said I hope he does. She was crying when I left. Her Camaro was parked in the driveway outside the house."

She comes to his office on his lunch hour that Tuesday afternoon. She brings bagels and Nova and they make love on his couch afterward. She tastes of onions when he kisses her.

On Tuesdays, the show is dark.

He goes to her apartment again that night.

But he makes sure he is home again by ten so that he can call Helen before she goes to sleep.

He calls Menemsha again at seven the next morning, and tells Helen he'll be leaving for the office early, lots to do before he comes up there on Friday. She asks him what he'll be doing on his birthday tomorrow. He tells her he may go to a movie. She says he ought to go celebrate with Stanley Beckerman. He tells her he'll think about it.

"Anyway, we'll be talking again before then," he says.

Today is Wednesday.

Matinee day.

But not in his office. No matinee on the black leather couch today because Kate must be at the theater by twelve-thirty for a *real* matinee at two. The moment he puts the receiver back on the cradle he runs downstairs and catches a cab to her apartment.

At ten that night, he calls Massachusetts again and tells Helen he's going down for a walk and a cup of cappuccino at that place on Seventieth Street. She advises him to be careful, and he tells her he'll call again in the morning. As soon as he hangs up, he heads for the theater. The stage door is on Seventh Avenue. He gets there just as the cast is coming out. She takes him by the arm.

"Hi," she says and reaches up to kiss him on the cheek.

"Goodnight, Kate," one of the girls calls.

"Goodnight!" another one calls, waving.

They have cappuccino together in a place on Sixth Avenue. He kisses her frequently and openly as they sit holding hands at a corner table. Later, they go to her apartment where they make love frantically and hastily. He does not get home until midnight, and is relieved to see that there are no messages from Helen on the answering machine.

Alex J has his own way of dealing with the imminent month-long hiatus. Month and *more*, don't forget. Alex J clams up. He has been silent all this week. Today is Thursday, and the hour is ticking away, and he is still silent. This is his way of punishing David. You want to go to wherever you're going and leave me flat? Okay, I'll pretend you're *already* gone, how's that? And if you're already gone, I don't have to talk to you. I can just lie here and look up at the ceiling, okay?

"Yes?" David asks, as if reading his mind.

"What?" Alex J says with a start.

"I thought you were about to say something."

"Why would I be about to say anything?" Alex J says curtly.

"Sorry. I thought you were."

There is another long silence. David wonders what sort of a surprise Kate has cooked up for his birthday tonight. She keeps calling it a "party," but he hopes she hasn't been foolish enough to have planned a *real* party, with guests other than themselves. He recognizes that over the past week he's become if not entirely reckless then certainly somewhat less than cautious. He hopes she hasn't taken this as a signal to . . .

". . . weather will be hottest," Alex J is saying.

"Yes?"

"Were you asleep?" he asks.

"No, no."

"Then what did I just say?"

"You said the weather will be hottest," David says, and takes a wild guess. "While I'm away. In August."

"Yes. How often do you fall asleep when I'm talking?"

"Never."

"I'll just bet."

"You'd lose."

"When the dresses are thinnest," Alex J says. "These flimsy little dresses they wear."

David says nothing.

He waits.

"When the weather is hot, I mean," Alex J says. "Did you ever read that story by Irwin Shaw?"

"Which one is that?"

" 'The Girls in Their Summer Dresses'?"

"Yes?"

"That's what it is, you know. The way they dress in the summertime. I wouldn't be doing this if it was the winter. Following them home, I mean. It's just because it's . . ."

What? David thinks.

". . . the summer. These skimpy little dresses they wear."

Following them *home?* David thinks.

Alex J is a thirty-seven-year-old stockbroker who commutes all the way from West Ninety-third to Wall Street by subway every weekday and sometimes on weekends as well. He is married and has three children, and the reason he's been coming to see David for the past year now is that a month before he sought help a woman he was rubbing himself against on the subway suddenly jabbed her elbow into his gut and yelled, "Get the hell *away* from me!" To Alex J, this was the equivalent of finding snakes in his bed. Fearful he would be arrested the next time he rubbed up against someone, or inadvertently *touched* someone, God forbid, Alex J came to David to confess his irresistible urges.

Alex J is what is known in the trade as a *frotteur*, from the French word for "a rubber," he who rubs. In Alex's case, "he who rubs" does so against thinly clad women in the subway, a crime defined as submitting another person to sexual contact without the latter's consent, or—as David had reason to look up seven years ago when he was treating another such patient—"any touching of the sexual or other intimate parts of a person not married to the actor for the purpose of gratifying the sexual desire of either party, whether directly or through clothing." In other words, if Alex J gets *caught* doing what he's been doing (for the past six *years*, it turns out, and not for just the six months prior to his subway epiphany a year ago this July) he is in danger of spending anywhere from three months to a year in jail—small potatoes unless you happen to have a wife and three kiddies at home, hmm, dollink?

David is not here to keep Alex J out of jail, though this in itself is not a minor consideration. He is here to lead Alex J to a discovery of the root causes underlying his behavior, so that he may better understand it, and control it. But *now* . . .

And perhaps this is simply a ruse, perhaps Alex J is merely telling him all this as a way of making sure David is really listening. Think you can go away for the whole month of August, huh? Okay, now hear *this*, Doctor!

What David *now* hears is that Alex J, in addition to deliberately seeking out on train platforms any woman or girl of any age who seems clothed in what he calls "a flimsy provocative dress," and following her from the platform onto the rush-hour train, and allowing himself to be pushed against her by the rush-hour crowd, positioning himself strategically behind her, and rubbing himself against her until he achieves erection and on at least one occasion orgasm . . .

What David *now* hears is that Alex J has in recent

weeks developed an alarming new symptom that could land him behind bars for a very long time. Perhaps because he is afraid that his antisocial underground behavior will indeed lead to arrest and incarceration should he one day mistakenly rub up against a female detective third grade in a gossamer summer frock, he has taken to following women he feels certain are *not* cops and who, he feels equally certain, will not resist his advances when he makes his desires known. In short, he is on the edge of committing rape.

This is what he begins talking about ten minutes before his hour ends on this Thursday before David leaves for the entire month of August. This is how he has captured David's full and complete attention. He is no longer talking about subterranean ladies in flimsy provocative dresses. With the clock ticking rapidly to meltdown, he is talking about the provocative *above*ground ladies he's been following home from work, one of them all the way to a Spanish section of Queens.

"She knows I've got my eye on her. She knows I'll make my move soon. She wants me to," he says, and nods contentedly.

David carefully advises him not to do anything stupid—he actually uses that word—until they have a chance to discuss this more fully in September.

"Oh, sure, Doc," Alex J says cheerfully. "Have a nice summer."

That night, when David rings the bell outside her apartment, she opens the door a crack, stands out of sight behind it, and whispers, "Close your eyes."

He hopes she hasn't assembled a cast of characters who will yell *"Surprise!"* the moment he steps into the apartment. Dutifully, but feeling utterly foolish, he closes his eyes.

"Are they closed?" she whispers from behind the door.

"They're closed," he whispers back.

He hears the door opening.

"Come in," she says.

He steps inside, and smells at once the pungent scent of incense burning, mingled with the scent of her own heady perfume, subtler than the incense, underscoring it like a leitmotif. His eyes are still closed. He hears the sound of the door easing shut behind him, the familiar oiled click of tumblers falling as she bolts both locks. There is music coming from across the room where he knows her audio equipment is stacked against the wall. The music sounds vaguely familiar, a symphonic swelling of strings and woodwinds, surely he knows what it is, surely he has heard this poignant melody before. Something lush and sensual, it oozes softly from the speakers, an insinuating strain that murmurs of distant exotic places, faraway caravans, shifting sands . . .

"You can open your eyes now," she says.

She is standing some four feet back from him, entirely naked under sheer black harem pants that flare to her ankles, where she is wearing thick golden bands that look like restraining cuffs. An ornately brocaded red silk vest threaded with gold is open over her naked breasts. She is wearing red high-heeled pumps that match the vest and add at least two inches to her height. She stands before him shyly, her gaze averted, her wrists and neck festooned with golden bangles and chains, the fingers of both hands encircled with thick heavy rings set with bright colored stones. Her hair is piled upon her head in shimmering copper masses held by a metallic gold ribbon that glimmers in the pale light. She is an Occidental slave girl transported here to the sybaritic East—for now he sees what she has done to the apartment and recognizes the motif.

The lamps have been dimmed but they are also draped with gossamer silken scarves, black and red and gold to complement her costume. Thick candles in the same colors flicker in brass holders everywhere around the room, and scrolled brass pots of incense smolder on the coffee table. The door to the bedroom is open just a crack. Red light suffuses the wedge and spills like blood onto the living room carpet. The music swells. It is Rimsky-Korsakov, and she is his birthday Scheherazade, here to tell him rapturous tales of perfumed ecstasy.

"Do you like it?" she asks.

"Very much."

"Give me your glasses. I'm going to blindfold you."

She takes his glasses, steps behind him, loops over his head a black silk strip of fabric—a scarf, a piece of lingerie? He cannot tell because he is instantly sightless. With his eyes closed, and the blindfold knotted at the back of his head, what had earlier been merely semidarkness now assumes the magnitude of utter blackness.

"Give me your hand," she says.

He feels her hand taking his, her ringed fingers closing gently around his. He cannot recall her ever wearing a ring before.

"Can you see anything?" she asks.

"No," he says.

"Promise?"

"Yes."

Not a suggestion of light filters around the blindfold. She leads him in absolute darkness around obstacles he knows are there, the coffee table in front of the couch, an ottoman, remembered pieces of furniture she avoids as she guides him across the room to what he surmises is the bedroom door now spilling unseen red light. He hears the door swinging gently open before them. She leads him into the room.

"Stand right here," she says.

There is the smell of incense burning here, too.

He hears the door closing behind him.

The sound of *Scheherazade* is gone.

There is only silence now.

"I'm going to kiss you now," she whispers. "Keep your hands at your sides, I don't want you to touch me."

He feels her moving closer to him, leaning into him. Her lips find his. She kisses him openmouthed, her tongue searching. In the dark, her mouth is wet and demanding, her lips thick with lust. He feels himself responding at once. She removes her mouth from his instantly, takes a quick step back. Her voice whispers out of the darkness again.

"Did you like that?"

"Yes."

"Would you like me to kiss you again?"

"Yes."

"Bet you'd like to touch me, too, wouldn't you?"
"Yes."
"Oh, but you can't."

Her voice retreats. Her lips suddenly find his again.
Her hand glides lightly over the front of his trousers,
lingers there, begins stroking him through the fabric
while her tongue insistently probes. He feels his zipper
being lowered. She slides her lips from his, and steps
back again, out of reach.

"What would you like me to do?" she whispers. "Say."
"Whatever you want to do."
"Kiss you again?"
"Yes."
"Oh yes. Take that thing out of your pants?"
"Yes."
"Oh, I'll bet."

He waits in the expectant dark. There is movement.
She is kneeling before him, her hands seeking, and suddenly he is free, and her mouth claims him, wet and
determined. Each time he tries to touch her face, her
hair, she pulls away, only to return inexorably a moment
later. And then, as if sensing he is dangerously close, she
vanishes entirely. Her voice floats from somewhere out
of the darkness.

"Did you like that?"
"Yes."
"Would you like more?"
"Yes."

"Of course," she says and her voice fades, and all at
once she is upon him again, ravenously drawing him
into her mouth. His hands reach for her face, but she

quickly moves away from his touch, and he hears her voice hanging disembodied someplace, "No, baby, not yet," and in the silence that follows, there is only the rustle of silk and the faint metallic clink of bracelets and chains and the mixed aroma of incense and a thousand perfumes. He stands waiting, trembling. Where is she?

"Would you like me to take off the blindfold now?" she whispers.

"Yes."

"Maybe I will. Let you see what I'm doing to you."

"Yes."

"You'd like that, wouldn't you?"

"I would."

"I'll bet you would," she says, and steps behind him.

He feels her fingers at the back of his head, struggling with the knot. The black silk falls free. He opens his eyes.

"This is Gloria," Kate says.

Gloria is black and Gloria is long and supple and Gloria has sloe eyes and a voluptuous mouth and Gloria is wearing nothing but high-heeled shoes and a gold chain that is wrapped around her waist several times.

"Happy birthday," she says, and smiles.

"She's your present," Kate says.

He remembers all at once the soft thick lips that possessed him while he was blindfolded. A red lamp is burning on the bedside table. It tints the room red. It tints Gloria's full-breasted body red. It tints Kate's nipples red in the open red vest.

"Did you enjoy it?" she asks.

David is trembling again.

"Say."

"Yes," he says. "I enjoyed it."

"Then come to me, baby," Gloria says, and extends her hands to him.

He takes them.

In the hallucinatory movie that plays that night— for surely this is a waking dream, this scene can't *really* be unreeling here in Kate's bedroom on Kate's familiar bed—he learns that the long-legged black woman with the sloe eyes and voluptuous mouth is a dancer like Kate . . .

"We met during *Les Miz* . . ."

. . . although this is the first time they've ever done anything like this together.

"Right, Gloria?"

"Umm," Gloria murmurs, her mouth tirelessly work- ing, Kate simultaneously smothering David's lips with kisses and whispering words of encouragement to her dear old friend.

This is surely a film he saw on Times Square, a film he is *starring* in on Times Square, for without question he is the leading man in this vehicle titled **Birthday Boy Bonanza!**, the object of all this rampant, sweaty passion here on Kate's bed in Kate's room, where now Gloria's lips are on his, claiming his mouth again, tongue flicking his tongue while Kate's own tongue teases and tempts below, refusing to let go of him, the red light beside the bed casting tall dark shadows on the ceiling and walls.

Gloria swings one long leg over his face, and lowers herself onto him. Amazingly, he accepts her without hesitation, this woman he has met for the first time tonight, albeit intimately, this passionate creature with whom he is now starring in a multimillion-dollar production titled **MUFF DIVER!** while below Kate is starring in her own intensely intimate and private film tentatively titled *The Flautist*, ad-libbing lines the screenwriter never wrote but which the director, *herself*, likes to encourage among her actors and actresses. David and Gloria, the only other performers in this double feature—or perhaps triple feature, it is difficult to know who is in charge here anymore—seem to have had their earlier speaking roles reduced to a series of sighs, cries, moans and groans while Kate, speaking directly from either the heart or the id, keeps murmuring an incessant litany of cocks and cunts and gutter fucking, and then suddenly abandons both improvisational dialogue and glistening anticipatory flute to slide up onto the pillows, roll over on her back, and open herself wide to Gloria, red light washing with a redder glow her crisp pubic hair and pink interior. Long naked legs spread, she says "Do *me* now, Glo," which gentle suggestion Gloria obeys with amazing alacrity, demonstrating a versatility that had not been immediately apparent in the rushes.

It is as if they have been doing this forever, the three of them. It is as if the movie formerly titled **Folie à Deux** has been given an expanded budget and cast and retitled **Ménage à Trois**, starring the inimitable threesome that brought you . . .

But, no, the stars here are neither the Andrews Sisters nor the Three Stooges nor the Nairobi Trio nor even Athos, Portos and Aramis, however dexterous and accomplished they may seem, however well they work together in triplicate. For despite the fact that Gloria has her head buried between Kate's spread legs, and despite the fact that David has mounted Gloria and is plunging repeatedly into her from behind, it is Kate who is the conduit here, Kate through whom their separate energies and passions flow. The true star here, the *only* star here, the ringmaster who urges and cajoles this inverted Oreo performance is Kate alone, encouraging, commanding, and finally deciding upon the exact moment of their concerted release, screaming "Oh *Jesus*, I'm coming!" just as Gloria shouts, "Oh Jesus, me *too!*" and David closes his eyes and silently, seemingly, empties himself into *both* women quaking beneath him.

As they lie side by side afterward, sweaty and spent on tangled sheets and sodden pillows stained red by the bedside lamp, David between them, Gloria and Kate holding hands across his wet belly, Kate sighs contentedly and whispers, "When you marry me, we can do this all the time."

"Let's do it again *now*," Gloria suggests.

He has set the alarm for seven A.M.

He showers and shaves and then goes back to where the two women are sleeping side by side in each other's arms. He gently nudges Gloria awake.

"What time is it?" she asks at once.

"Seven-thirty."

"Okay," she says, and swings her long legs over the side of the bed and rushes into the bathroom. He hears her showering as he dresses in the early morning light sifting around the edges of the blinds. Kate is still dead asleep.

Gloria comes out of the bathroom wrapped in a towel.

"What time is your plane?" she whispers.

"I don't go till this afternoon. But I have patients to see first."

"Where do you fly from?"

"Newark this time."

She goes to the dresser, picks up her watch, squints at it in the light spilling through the open bathroom door.

"Malik's supposed to be here at eight," she says, and straps on the watch.

David does not know who Malik is. Nor does he ask. He does not know where Gloria and this man might be going at seven in the morning. He does not ask that, either. He recognizes all at once that he knows virtually nothing about her. She stubs her toe on something in the dim light. "Shit," she says. She sits on the edge of the bed, pulls on a pair of panties, stands, leans into a bra, cups herself, clasps herself. He watches her dress. Skirt and blouse. Sandals. She is beginning to look like a person. I don't even know her, he thinks. She goes back into the bathroom, begins applying lipstick. He watches her, fascinated. He doesn't even know her. She catches him in the mirror, winks.

"That was good last night, wasn't it?" she whispers.

"Yes."

"When are you coming down again?"

"On the fifteenth."

This is the Tuesday night he and Stanley have chosen for the start of the imaginary lectures.

"Will I see you?" Gloria asks.

"Oh sure."

"Good," she says.

He is wondering if he *will* ever see her again.

"Would you like some orange juice?" he asks.

"Mmm, yes," she says, and turns from the mirror. "How do I look?"

"Good," he says.

"Only good?"

"Beautiful," he says.

"Better," she says, and snaps out the bathroom light.

In the kitchen, they stand at the kitchen counter together, drinking orange juice. The sun is up. Light spills around the drawn shade over the air-shaft window.

"Malik drives a Jag," Gloria says, "he'll be downstairs at eight sharp." She looks at her watch again. "What time will you be leaving?"

"Little after that."

"For your office?"

"Yes."

"I'd better get out of here," she says, and goes into the bedroom for her bag. When she comes back, she says, "I kissed her goodbye, but she's asleep." She raises one eyebrow. "How about you?" she asks. "You asleep, baby?"

She steps up close to him. Tilts her crotch gently into him. Touches her glossy lips to his, lightly.

"Again later," she says, and moves away from him.

He hears the apartment door opening and then closing behind her. The apartment is utterly still.

He looks at his watch.

Three minutes to eight.

In the bedroom, Kate is still asleep. He touches her shoulder. She stirs beneath his hand.

"Kate?" he says.

"Mmmm?"

"Kate, I have to go now."

"Are you leaving?"

"In a few minutes. Sleep, honey."

"Honey, yes," she says.

She closes her eyes. He sits on the edge of the bed, watching her.

Her eyes open again.

She looks up into his face.

"You know, don't you?" she says.

"Know what?"

"You know."

"I don't."

"A shrink," she says, "you probably know," and closes her eyes again. She is silent for a moment. Then, in a very small voice, she asks, "Are you leaving me?"

"Yes, I . . ."

"I mean *leaving* me," she says.

"No. I'm not leaving you."

"Come back, David."

"I will."

"Do you love me, David?"

"I love you, Kate."

"I know you do."

"Goodbye, Kate," he says, and kisses her.

"I'll see you on the fifteenth," she says.

He kisses her again.

Her mouth is so goddamn sweet.

Susan M has come to her last session with a list of clothing changes that will take her through Labor Day. As she explains to David in great detail, the problem is she doesn't have enough clothes to accommodate a change every day for thirty-nine days, which is exactly how many days it will be between today and September fifth when she'll see him again.

"That *is* when I'll see you again, right?" she asks. "September fifth?"

"Yes," David says.

"Same time, right?"

"Same time," he says.

"Let me tell you how I've figured this out," she says, and takes from her tote bag her Month-At-A-Glance calendar. "Tomorrow's Saturday," she says, flipping rapidly to the facing pages for July, "so I'll be wearing something simple but sexy, you remember we went over that two weeks ago. The white A-line mini and a cropped mesh top, but I'll be wearing it with a white bra, the top, because otherwise hoo boy! Strapless, though. And white sandals and panties, of course. On Sunday, I'm having brunch with my friend from Omaha when I used to live out there, she's here in town and we'll be going to the Plaza, so I thought I'd wear . . . I know I told you I'd be wearing the boxy wheat jacket and cream-colored pants with the white suspenders, remember? But that was before I knew Marcy was flying in, so I thought for the Plaza the shaped jacket and pleated skirt in the windowpane plaid, with the white tank and black shoes and that little black hat with the gray feather. White panties and bra. Then on Monday . . .”

The scheme she's worked out is one that takes into account laundering and dry-cleaning time, which makes it virtually impossible to simply begin a recycling process two weeks from tomorrow but which requires instead a complicated balanced pattern of substitution and duplication. Not only does Susan M display her charts and lists, but she also details the number of days it will take to have a silk blouse dry-cleaned, for example, or a man's tailored shirt laundered so that she'll be able to wear one or the other of them in the rotating wheel she's designed.

As she explains all this to him, displaying the charts and the lists and the days on her calendar, she constantly checks her watch, fearful that her hour will run out before she completes the recitation and demonstration, thereby placing her mother in Omaha in extreme danger of decapitation or defenestration or any of a hundred other dire possibilities. It is with enormous relief—which David incidentally shares, so high is the level of anxiety in this office—that she is able to tell him in the remaining few minutes what she'll be wearing to her session on the day after Labor Day. “The man-tailored pinstriped suit,” she says, “with black heels, black shirt and white-scarf tie, and black undies and panty hose, phew!” Before she leaves the office, she ascertains once again the date and time of their next session, and then holds out her hand like an embarrassed little girl, smiles shyly, and says, "Have a nice summer, Dr. Chapman."

He shakes her hand.

"You, too, Susan," he says.

When he steps out of his office building at ten minutes to two, a long black limo is waiting at the curb. The rear window instantly rolls down, and Kate's head appears. She says nothing, merely smiles. He walks immediately to the car.

"Hi," she says. "Want a lift?"

He looks at her in wonder, slowly shaking his head from side to side in pleased amazement. "Where'd you get this?" he asks.

"I ordered it, where do you think I got it? Get in."

He gets into the car. It smells of rich black leather and polished walnut panels. A bottle of iced champagne sits in a silver bucket on the side console. The driver turns to her.

"Is it Newark, miss?" he asks.

"It's Newark," she says.

She is wearing what looks like a tennis skirt, short and white and flirty, topped with a sheer pink tank and a white cotton jacket. On her feet, she wears white strappy heels and shocking-pink anklets to match the top. Her fingernails are painted the same outrageous pink. Her legs are bare.

"Why don't you open the champagne?" she suggests.

He fiddles with the wire, unwraps the foil, pops the cork. Foam overspills the slender dark neck of the bottle.

He pours into two glasses from the side console, hands one to her, replaces the bottle, and then lifts his own glass in a toast.

"To the fifteenth," he says.

"To *us*," she corrects.

"To us *and* the fifteenth."

"Four whole nights together," she says.

"Yes."

"I'll invite Gloria," she whispers, and turns her head toward him. Her eyes meet his.

"Just for one of the nights," he says.

"Whatever you want."

"I want *you*."

"You'd better," she says. "But I know you liked Gloria, too, didn't you?"

They are still whispering. He glances at the rearview mirror on the windshield above the driver's head. The driver's eyes seem fastened to the road.

"Yes, of *course* I liked her, but . . ."

"I'll get her again, she's very sexy. Didn't you think she was sexy?"

"Very," he says, and glances into the rearview mirror again. The driver's eyes are still on the road.

"Very, yes, right," Kate whispers. "Or I can find someone else, if that's what you'd prefer."

"I told you, all I want . . ."

"Yes, but you're lying. Last night you wanted Gloria, too. I'll get her for you again. Maybe before you go back up again. On your last night here maybe. Like this time."

"If that's what you want."

"It's what *you* want," she whispers sharply, and begins furiously jiggling one sandaled foot.

The big car rolls steadily downtown toward the tunnel. Holding hands, they sip champagne. She keeps jiggling her foot. He glances at her bare legs. Without looking at him, she tosses the switch that rolls up the glass privacy panel, and stretches one leg onto the folding seat in front of her.

By the time they reach the airport, his lips are raw, his trousers stained. She gets out of the car after him, and throws her arms around his neck, and kisses him stickily, fiercely, in plain view of the passengers moving in and out of the terminal. Looking directly into his face, her eyes locked on his, her lips not inches from his mouth, she says, "You'd better not forget me."

"I won't."

"You'd better not," she warns.

That evening before curtain time, a dozen red roses are delivered to her dressing room.

The enclosed handwritten card reads:

I love you, Kathryn.

"Of course you do," she says aloud.

3: *saturday, july 29–monday, august 14*

On Saturday evening, another dozen roses are delivered to the dressing room. Like the roses that arrived last night and again this afternoon before the matinee performance, they are long-stemmed and blood-red, nesting on a bosky glen of fern and baby's breath, wrapped in green tissue paper in a long white box. The enclosed card again reads *I love you, Kathryn*. But each of the three bouquets—now arranged in vases that crowd virtually everything else off Kate's makeup table—are from different florists, and the handwriting is different on each card. Which of course means that David called the orders in before he left and dictated the message for each card. *I love you, Kathryn*. Written in a different florist's hand each time.

The only performers with private dressing rooms are

the five principals in the show—what Actors Equity calls white contracts—and only one of these is a woman, Grizabella. The rest of the cast are all so-called pink contracts and share dressing rooms to a greater or lesser extent. Kate shares *her* dressing room with eight other dancers and two booth-singer swings. In a so-called dancing show like this one, most of the performers have at one time or another gone on for anyone who is sick or merely "indisposed," as the expression has it, or responding to a "family obligation." The dancers who share this room are interchangeable cogs in a choreographic machine; on stage, under all that heavy makeup and furry attire, they even look alike.

Now, as they paint on their cat faces and squeeze into their cat costumes, even their voices begin to sound alike, their conversation echoing a thousand backstage dialogues Kate has heard in dozens of other dressing rooms. Tonight—as is almost invariably the case—the talk is of men. Or, to be more exact, the talk is of a *specific* man, Kate's "Secret Admirer" or—as she is surprised to hear him called by dancers even younger than she is—her "Stage Door Johnny" or "Sugar Daddy," expressions that went out of fashion long before any of them were born.

"Roses don't come cheap these days," Rumpleteazer says.

"Marla Trump better watch out," Sillabub says.

"Is this the guy who picked you up earlier this week?" Jennyanydots asks.

"When *was* that?" Demeter asks. "Wednesday?"

"The tall gangly guy with the glasses?"

Wait'll he hears *that* description, Kate thinks. But she is secretly pleased that David's extravagance has caused her to become the center of attention here in a room she shares with women she secretly believes are much better performers than she is. The other "kids." All of whom can sing and dance rings around her.

"Oh, *I* get it," one of the dancer-swings says. "Some *girl* named Kathryn is sending you flowers with I-love-you notes."

"This is beginning to get ridiculous," Bombalurina says.

"Yeah, who died?" one of the singer-swings asks.

"I *hate* the smell of roses."

"I hate the smell of *all* flowers."

"Some flowers have no scent at *all*," Jellylorum says. "Did you know that?"

"Good."

"How many does this make, four?"

"Three."

"In sequence though."

"Five dollars a rose, they get nowadays," the other singer-swing says.

"Four."

"Not in Grand Central."

"Long-stemmed roses? *Five* dollars. Grand Central, wherever."

"Who *is* this guy, anyway?"

"A friend," Kate says shyly.

"Meaning he's married."

"Sounds possessed. Three performances in a *row?*"

Across the room, one of the dancers throws an ankle

up onto her dressing table. Bending from the waist, leaning into the leg, stretching, she says, "I heard the kids in *Oh! Calcutta!* used to get all *kinds* of expensive gifts."

"That was centuries ago."

"Also, they were dancing nude."

"That was during the days of the Holy Roman Empire."

"The Pilobolus company *still* dances nude."

"So does the Netherlands."

"Maguy Marin, too."

"It wasn't just the nudity. *Calcutta* was a dirty show."

"It was even dirtier when it first opened."

"How would you know?"

"My mother told me. They had a scene where one of the girls goes down on a flashlight."

"Your *mother* told you that?"

"Well, I think she put it a little differently."

"*My* mother thinks fellatio is a little town in Italy."

"That's not how the joke goes."

"How does it go?"

"I'm not sure, but that's not it."

"Does this guy come to every show?"

"No," Kate says.

"Just sends flowers, huh?"

"Every performance of *Calcutta*, there used to be a dozen bald heads in the third row. Same guys every show."

"It's two *Japanese* towns. The joke."

"I heard it with an Italian town."

"Fucking and Sucking. The woman in the joke thinks they're two Japanese *cities*, that's it."

"Used to send all kinds of expensive presents back."

"Has he seen the show at *all?*"

"Oh yes."

"How many times?"

"Once."

"How'd he like *me?*" Jennyanydots asks, and shakes her fanny and switches her tail.

"These bald guys. All kinds of expensive presents."

"She's a Jewish American Princess. The woman in the joke."

"I like it better with an Italian town."

"Does he live here in the city?"

"Or is he some big Texas oilman?"

"He lives here," Kate says.

She is enjoying all this talk about David. Well, not *really* about David because he is, after all, married and she must be careful. But *almost* about him. Just talking *almost* about him is somehow exciting. And somehow, it adds *permanance* to their . . . affair, she supposes you could call it.

A knock sounds on the door.

"Half-hour," the stage manager calls.

When her phone rings at ten o'clock on Sunday morning, she thinks it's David calling from the Vineyard, and immediately snatches the receiver from its cradle.

"Hello?" she says.

"Katie?"

Her mother.

"Yes, Mom."

"Has he called you yet?"

For a moment, Kate believes her mother is prescient.

How else could she know about David? How else could dear Fiona McIntyre, who's been using her maiden name ever since the divorce nine years ago . . .

"Has he?" she asks again.

Fiona's voice, as always, is a subtle cross between an ambulance siren and marmalade. Kate cannot understand how she manages to sound both strident and plaintive at one and the same time, an acquired skill she envies not in the slightest.

"Who do you mean?" she asks cautiously.

"Your father," Fiona says.

This is the man who used to be "Dad" or "Daddy" until he left his wife and family when Kate was eighteen and Bess was sixteen, running off to Dallas, Texas, from Westport, Connecticut, at which time he became in Fiona's lexicon "your father," the unspoken words "the bastard" or "the son of a bitch" tacitly implied by the sneer in her alarmingly honeyed voice.

"Why should he call me?" Kate asks.

"He's in New York," Fiona says.

Oh shit, Kate thinks.

"How do you know?" she asks.

Fiona knows because her closest friend on earth, a woman named Jill Harrington who lives at the Lombardy on East Sixty-first Street and who visits Fiona whenever she goes to La Costa, called last night to say she'd run into him at Le Cirque . . .

"Of *course* Le Cirque," Fiona sneers in her jellyhorn voice . . .

. . . with a blonde who was definitely *not* the horse-faced bitch he ran off to Texas with, lo those many moons ago, gone but not forgotten, as the saying goes.

"My guess is he'll be contacting his darling little girl . . ."

His darling little girl, Kate thinks.

". . . the moment he gets a few drinks in him. You always *were* his favorite," Fiona says thoughtfully, as if she hasn't said this a hundred times before, always thoughtfully, always as if in discovery.

Most often in the presence of poor dear Bess.

Your sister *was always your father's favorite, you know.* Thoughtfully.

"I just thought I'd warn you," Fiona says now.

"Thanks," Kate says.

"How's everything otherwise?"

"Fine."

"Are you still in that show?"

She's been in *Cats*, on and off, for the past ten years now, but her mother still calls it "that show." Well, this is understandable. Difficult title like *Cats*. Be different if it were something simpler. Then you could *blame* her for not taking the trouble to learn the fucking name of the show her daughter is dancing in. Or for having known it and forgotten it.

"Yes, I'm still in it."

Cats, she thinks. It's called *Cats*, Mom. C-A . . .

"What time is it out there, anyway?" she asks.

"Seven."

"Isn't that early for you?"

"I had a bad night."

I don't want to hear it, Kate thinks.

"Whenever I remember what that son of a bitch did to us," Fiona starts, and the recitation begins yet another time, a conversation Fiona believes is privileged and therefore welcomed, a conversation Kate knows to be hurtful and therefore loathsome. It took Kate six years in analysis with Dr. Jacqueline Hicks, her dear Jacqueline, to stop hating her father for what he did, though it's not what her mother *thinks* he did. Six years to stop hating her mother as well, for constantly *reminding* Kate of what he did—though, again, it's not what she *thinks* he did. But each time Fiona hops on the goddamn *treadmill* again, Kate starts hating both of them all over again, something she is supposed to have *stopped* doing a year ago come October.

One would think that her mother's so-called friends would refrain from telling her they just ran into Neil Duggan at Le Cirque or McDonald's or wher*ever* the hell, but no, they keep feeding her rumors like Romans tossing Christians to the lions, delighting in her initial inquisitive reaction and her subsequent tearful tirades— though it is most often Kate who gets the waterworks, as she is getting them now on a Sunday morning when David might be trying to call her collect, as they'd agreed he should do whenever a phone booth presented an opportunity. Why don't you go cry in *church?* she thinks. Don't they have any *churches* in San Diego? Doesn't the very *name* of the town suggest Spanish missions all over the place? Why cry all over *me*, Mom?

But lest the world forget that she is the only woman

in history whose husband left her for another woman, Fiona is relating yet again how Kate's "father" (the son of a bitch) ruined her life, which makes Kate desperately hungry for a cigarette, as seems always to be the case whenever her mother traps her in one of these labyrinthine monologues. Before Kate started going to Jacqueline, she smoked incessantly, a suicidal habit for *anyone*, never mind a dancer. Now, listening to her mother, she wants a cigarette again. She wants a whole *pack* of cigarettes. She wants a whole pack of *Camels*. She wants to *eat* a whole pack of Camels.

". . . destroyed all our lives," Fiona is saying, which of course her father didn't do. He didn't destroy her mother's life, and he didn't destroy Kate's, either—even though Kate was his favorite, as if anybody *cared* who his favorite was, as if anybody *now* cares who his goddamn favorite *is!* The promise of him calling, the *threat* of him calling is enough to cause Kate to break out in a cold sweat, her mother's earlier words hovering like a swinging scimitar over her head, *My guess is he'll be contacting his darling little girl the moment he gets a few drinks in him. You always* were *his favorite*, her mother's monologue grinding relentlessly onward . . .

". . . humiliated me in front of the entire town, Westport was practically a *village* nine years ago, everyone knew everyone else, especially in our circle, running off with a woman every man in town had known before him, your *wonderful* father, did he have to pick *her*, the town *slut?* Forgive me, Katie, I know you *adored* him, but what's right is right, as God is my witness he didn't have to do it so cruelly, so thoughtlessly, I've always tried to be a kind and thoughtful person, he didn't have to be so *mean* to us, he didn't have to *abandon* us . . ."

Her mother goes on for at least half an hour.

By the end of that time, Kate is ready to jump out the window.

"Mom," she says, "I have to pee. Can we finish this some other time?"

"Sure, some other time," her mother says, weeping.

"I'll call you soon."

"Sure," her mother says.

"G'bye, Mom. Enjoy the rest of the weekend."

"Sure."

Kate hangs up.

Her heart is beating very fast.

He's in New York, she thinks.

And goes into the bathroom to wash her face.

The phone rings again at a quarter past eleven, just as she's about to leave the apartment. Her mother consistently tells her she dresses too provocatively, but she doesn't care what her mother says, she dresses for comfort and she dresses to look attractive, yes, *and* sexy, yes. She's an American girl, right? A *dancer!* Today, because she doesn't have to be at the theater till one-thirty for the three o'clock show, she plans to check out some of the galleries in SoHo, and is wearing for her outing a short white cotton crochet-knit dress and laced white leather Docksiders. Her immediate thought is that it's her mother calling back to weep a little more. Her next thought is that it's her father, God forbid. A minute more and I'd have been out of here, she thinks. Safe, she thinks. But the phone is still ringing. Get out anyway, she thinks. She picks up the receiver.

"Hello?"

"You have a collect call . . ." a recorded voice says.

"Yes," she says at once.

"From . . ."

And then *his* recorded voice, announcing *his* name, "David . . ."

"Yes," she says.

"Will you accept charges?"

"I will. Yes, yes, yes, yes, yes."

"Thank you for using AT&T," the recorded voice persists, seemingly unwilling to get off the line.

"David?"

"Yes, hi, how are you?"

"Why don't you come make love to me?" she asks.

"I wish I could."

"Where are you?"

"In a drugstore. I tried to get you earlier . . ."

Damn her, Kate thinks.

". . . but the line was busy. Are you all right?"

"I'm fine. I miss you."

"I miss you, too."

"I'm counting the days."

"Me, too."

"Seventeen, counting today."

"I know."

"I'm marking them on my calendar. You *are* coming, aren't you?"

"Oh yes."

"Good. I can't wait. Is there any chance you can come down on the fourteenth instead? Because . . ."

"I really don't . . ."

". . . we're dark on Tuesdays, you know . . ."

"Yes, but . . ."

". . . and that would give us the whole day together."

"Well, the way Stanley and I have it worked out . . ."

"I wish you . . ."

". . . we'll have the whole day, anyway. Because we're saying the lectures *start* that Tuesday night, you see . . ."

"Wonderful!"

"So I'll be taking a plane down that morning . . ."

"I'll meet you at the airport."

"That would be great."

"With a limo again, if you like."

She hears a sharp intake of breath. There is a sudden silence on the line.

"Kate," he says abruptly, "I have to . . ."

"No, please, not yet."

"I see the kids coming. Really, I have to . . ."

"I love you, I love you, I *love* you," she shouts.

"I love you, too. I'll call again. I really have to . . ."

"*Wait!* Thanks for all the *flowers!* They're *beautiful!*"

"What flowers?" he asks.

Before the evening performance on Monday night, the last day of July, a long white box is delivered initially to the Seventh Avenue stage door of the Winter Garden and then to the dressing room two and a half floors above street level. The night-shift doorman breezily walks into a roomful of women in various stages of undress, but he has worked many a Broadway show, m'little darlings, and has seen it all and heard it all. He scarcely bats an eyelash when Kate—in the midst of applying white makeup, a towel over her shoulders, her leotard top lowered to the waist—accepts the box and begins opening it.

They are roses, of course.

But instead of the now-familiar card, there is a sealed envelope in the box. The stock is heavy, it feels expensive, like something she'd find at Tiffany's or Bergdorf's. A cream-colored envelope, her name handwritten in purple ink across the face of it.

Miss Kathryn Duggan

She had thought at first, when David told her *he* hadn't sent the flowers, that perhaps her father was the secret admirer the kids were speculating about. But the handwriting doesn't appear to be his. She tears open the flap of the envelope. The page inside is of the same color. The same thick stock. The same handwriting in the same purple ink.

My dearest Kathryn,
I hope you're enjoying these small tokens of my deep affection, I cannot tell you how much I admire your beauty and talent, If you can find it in your heart to single me out with a smile, a wink, a touch tonight as you flit by, I would be most appreciative.
Your one true love.

Well, not dear Daddy, that's for sure.

The flowers have stopped.
Now there are the letters.
Three of them are waiting for her at the theater when she gets there on Wednesday night. The same cream-colored stationery. The same purple ink. The same hand.

Miss Kathryn Duggan
Winter Garden Theater
1634 Broadway
New York, New York 10019

The postmarks all read *New York, New York, August 1.*

Today is the second day of August.

The envelopes are marked sequentially, the handwritten numerals **1, 2,** and **3** on their separate faces. She feels an odd sense of dread as she starts opening the first envelope. Someone across the room—Kate's head is bent as she tears open the flap of the envelope, and she can't be sure who it is—*someone* calls, "No flowers today, Kate?"

The letter reads:

My dearest Kathryn,
Did you like the roses?
I kept waiting for some
acknowledgment Monday

194

night, but you never once looked at me. You are the prettiest Kitty in the show. I never tire of watching you. Please favor me with a smile or even a glance.

Your one true love.

She resists the urge to crumple both letter and envelope, understanding at once and with a sharp clarity that this letter, *these* letters must be saved. These letters are evidence. *Evidence?* she thinks. And her hand starts shaking as she opens the second envelope.

Darling Kitty-Kat,
I dream of you day and night, all dressed in white like a pussycat bride. You are so smooth in your satin and silk with your lovely Kitty-whiskered face! Won't you look at me so I'll know you know I _exist_ *?*

Your one true love.

She does not want to open the third envelope, but she does. Sitting at the dressing table covered with brushes and liners and jars of makeup, she reads it silently:

Or perhaps I should call you Victoria? My darling dearest Victoria—cat who stalks the stage so slinkily, but never once looks at me? Did the flowers displease my sweet Victoria-cat? How can I make amends? Please, please smile at me or I shall perish.
Your one true soul.

There are more letters waiting before Friday night's performance. Four more letters delivered in the mail that afternoon. Each marked sequentially with the hand-written numerals **4, 5, 6** and **7**. The postmarks all read *New York, New York, August 3.* Which means they were mailed yesterday sometime. She stuffs them into her handbag and does not open them until she gets home that night.

Sitting at her kitchen table, sipping a glass of milk, eating a ham sandwich she bought in the all-night deli on Second Avenue, she cold-bloodedly slits open the first of them with a sharp paring knife.

It reads:

What is wrong with you, sweet Victoria Puss? Have I done something to annoy you? I keep begging for a mere glance but you favor other men in the audience instead. Why is this? Don't you know how much I love my sweet Victoria? How much I love my pussy whose coat is so warm?
      Your one true love.

She puts the note on the table alongside the first one, and then slits open the next envelope. The letter inside reads:

Darling Victoria Puss,
Did someone in the audience bother you on Wednesday night? I thought I detected you frowning. Did someone try to touch you? You didn't let anyone touch you, did you? You know that you are mine, I hope, and that no one else is permitted to touch you. I truly hope you know that. Give me a smile to let me know, or put your hand on my shoulder as you glide by. A touch. A glance for . . .
      Your one true love and master.

How come the quantum leap? she wonders. How'd my adoring supplicant all at once turn into my one true lord and master? Is there something transitional in this letter, something that bridges the gap between the letter preceding it and the one I haven't yet opened? There must be. Otherwise, why has he bothered to number them? If there isn't a continuity, a sequence, then why the orderly progression? Tell me *that*, my lord and master.

Calmly, she slits the envelope marked with the number six. Calmly, she unfolds the thick sheet of cream-colored stationery. Calmly, she reads the next note:

Okay, Miss Puss,
Now I mean this. I don't want to be ignored a moment longer. I can't afford expensive flowers every goddamn night of the week, if that's what you're looking for. The ticket alone is exorbitant, they should be ashamed to charge such prices! You should be ashamed, too, Victoria, parading around in that skintight costume and showing yourself to all the men in the audience, exposing yourself, letting them touch you as you go by I'll bet. I'll be there watching you as always, so you better be careful. And you better dance nice for...
   Your one true lord and master —

Still oddly calm, she picks up the last of that day's envelopes. Looks at the handwritten words spelling out her name and the address of the theater. Looks at the numeral **7**. Studies her name again. The purple ink lends urgency. The handwriting seems suddenly frantic, almost frenzied. She is tearing open the flap when the telephone rings.

It is one of those odd coincidental occurrences, two separate unlinked events happening simultaneously, as if one has triggered the other, the tearing of the flap seeming to activate the ringing of the phone and causing her to drop the envelope at once, as if it has just burst into flames. The phone is still ringing. She looks at the clock on the kitchen wall. It is almost one A.M. The phone persists. She goes to the window and draws the shade, as if suddenly certain she is being observed, as if knowing without question that her one true lord and master is watching her as she moves to the counter and snatches the receiver from the wall phone.

"Hullo?" she says.

Cautiously.

"Katie?"

She is almost relieved.

But not quite.

"Hi, Dad," she says.

"Hello, darlin," he says. "How are you?"

Enter Neil Duggan. Yet another time, folks. A curtain call for the very same charmer who ran off with a blond, lanky (horse-faced, her mother insists) woman thirteen years his junior nine years ago, but who's counting? His sweet lilting voice a bit mellow at a little past one in the morning and a little past six or seven drinks, she guesses. But that's the only time he *ever* calls, really. In the middle of the night when he's had too much to drink. To tell his darlin little girl how much he loves her. Let's hear it for him, folks.

"How've you been doin, Katie?"

"Fine, Dad," she says.

She does not ask him why he's in New York, does not ask him how long he's been here, does not inquire after *his* health because frankly, my dear, she does not give a damn. She waits for him to speak next. She stands beside the counter with the phone to her ear, waiting.

"Are you still dancin, Katie?"

"Yes, Dad."

And waits.

On the kitchen table, the last envelope is also waiting. She dreads opening it, but she would rather do that— would rather walk on a bed of coals in *Bombay*, for that matter—than spend another minute on the phone with Neil Duggan, her *wonderful* father. Another *second*, for that matter.

The silence lengthens.

"I just thought I'd see how you were doing," he says.

"I'm doing fine, Dad."

"Well, I'm happy to hear that."

Silence again.

"Have you seen your sister lately?"

"I visit her every month," Kate says.

Her voice catches. There are sudden tears in her eyes, sharp, burning.

"How is she? How is my dear Bessie?"

"Your dear Bessie is just fine," she says, unable to keep the caustic edge out of her voice.

"Now, now," he says.

"Dad . . ." she says.

And catches herself.

What good is the anger?

What does the anger accomplish?

"Dad, it was nice of you to call," she says. "But I've got two performances tomorrow, and I really need to get some sleep. So if you don't mind . . ."

"I'll let you go then," he says.

The words seem peculiar, all things considered.

"Thank you," she says. "Goodnight, Dad."

"Goodnight, Katie."

There is a click on the line. She replaces the receiver on its cradle, hesitates a moment, and then goes back to the table and the envelope with her name on it. Boldly, she tears open the flap. This time, the phone doesn't ring. Calmly, she unfolds the note. It reads:

All right, Miss Open Pussy, what the hell do you want from me? Do you want me to get down on my knees in front of you? Is that what you'd really like your master to do? Humiliate himself before you and the entire audience? All right, fine,

Say the word and I'll do it.
Wink at me as you go by, and I'll
know that's a signal. Just don't
fucking ignore me anymore!
Kneel beside me and let me touch
you fur. Crouch at your
master's feet!
    I mean it.

"Oh sure, master," she says aloud.

But her hand is trembling again as she slides the letter back into its envelope. She scoops up all four envelopes and carries them into the bedroom. The letters she received on Wednesday are in the top drawer of her dresser, on a stack of leg warmers. She adds these to the pile. Closing the drawer, she goes immediately to the windows and pulls the blinds shut.

Tomorrow will be almost a week since last she heard from David.

He could be anyone in this Saturday matinee audience.

Where before now her concentration has always been entirely on her performance—focusing on how to move like a cat, look like a cat, think like a cat, *become* a cat—she now scans the spectators in their seats, wondering which of the men is the one who sent her the roses and is now sending her the letters.

Her part requires her to go into the audience.

She wonders where he is sitting.

PRIVILEGED CONVERSATION

Who out there is waiting for her to smile at him, wink at him, glance at him?

Who out there might misinterpret any innocent move she makes?

Any innocent look that crosses her face.

She is happy for the white makeup.

It hides her from him.

She feels naked in the tight white costume.

Who out there will try to touch her?

Who out there is the one who thinks he *owns* her?

You know that you are mine, I hope . . .

Who out there is waiting for her to crouch at his feet?

Kneel beside me and let me touch your fur.

There is a moment in the show when she comes down off the stage—during the "Macavity" number—comes swiftly down the side ramp on the right of the theater, crawls through the wide space in front of row K, and then crouches alongside the aisle seat, sits up, seemingly detecting a human presence, seemingly startled, jerks her head around and looks directly into the face of whoever is sitting in that seat, her green eyes wide. The moment is literally that. An actor's moment, but an actual moment as well. She is off again at once, scampering onto the stage again, gray-white tail twitching.

But today she glimpses from the corner of her eye the face of the man sitting in that aisle seat. It is a thin pale face, the deep-set eyes a dark glowering black.

After the show, she asks the dance captain if it would be okay for her to stay out of the audience for a while.

"What do you mean?" he asks.

"Not go down in the audience."

"Why?"

"Somebody's bothering me out there," she says.

"What do you mean, bothering you?"

"Some creep."

"Bothering you? *How?*"

"I've been getting letters," she says. "Can't we just work around it? Nobody'll miss me out there, believe me."

"Change the choreography? How can I . . . ?"

"Please," she says. "I'm asking you. Please."

The dance captain looks deep into her eyes.

"Sure," he says.

That night, from where she is standing stage left, waiting for a music cue, she locates the aisle seat.

A fat woman in a bright purple dress is sitting in it.

The letter is delivered on Tuesday morning.

Well, well, well.
I see little Kathryn is trying to avoid me. Now why should that be, Miss Duggan? Do you consider yourself unworthy of my attentions? Did you think I wouldn't notice the glimmer in your eyes as you skittered past your master this afternoon? Please don't try to be coy, little kitten, I don't like playing games. You're mine and you know it, so let's quit the

cocktease poze, shall we? you know
you want ites much ae I do, And
now I know where to get it.
Your only lord and master.

The letter is delivered to her home address.

She desperately wishes she could talk to David.

But it is nine days since he last called, and he won't
be back in New York till next week—*if* he'll be back
in New York—and a lunatic now has her home address.

She wishes next that she could talk to Jacqueline Hicks,
but of course this is the month of August and every
fucking psychiatrist in the city of New York is away at
the beach or in the mountains.

This is *Lost Weekend*.

This is Ray Milland in the reruns she's seen on television, frantically trying to find an open pawnshop on
Yom Kippur.

She goes to an open bike shop instead.

Rickie Diaz is changing a tire when she gets there,
wearing much the same outfit he had on when she
bought the bike. Red nylon shorts with a white nylon
tank top this time, the same numeral 69 on the front of
it. In blue this time. Same bulging pectorals, biceps and
triceps, same tattooed head of an Indian chief in full
feathered headdress on the biceps of his left arm. *Plus ça
change*, Kate thinks, perhaps because she, too, is wearing
the same outfit she'd worn that day David came here

with her to help pick out the bike. Green shorts and orange shirt, white socks and Nikes, *plus c'est la même chose*. Rickie's shiny black hair is pulled to the back of his head in a ponytail and held there with the same little beaded band he was wearing the last time she saw him, and took his number, and told him she might give him a call someday. Because a girl seeing a married man never knows *how* long it might last, right, David? Where the hell *are* you, David?

"Well, well, well," Rickie says, "look who's here," and rises from his squatting position to shake hands with her.

Well, well, well.

I see little Kathryn is trying to avoid me.

"Can I take you to lunch?" she asks.

"Let me lock up," he says at once.

He reads the letters silently and thoughtfully.

"Your lord and master, huh?" he says.

"Yeah," she says.

"Where'd he get *that* idea?"

"A weirdo," she says, and shrugs.

"Must be," Rickie says, and continues reading. "Who's Victoria, anyway?"

"That's my name in the show. The character I play."

"Darling Victoria Puss," Rickie says, and nods.

"No, just Victoria."

"I mean, that's what he calls you here."

"Yeah."

"And *Sweet* Victoria Puss."

"Yeah."

"Whose coat is so warm."

"Yes."

"Miss *Open* Pussy."

Kate nods.

"I guess he likes that word, huh?" Rickie says.

"Well, it's . . . *Cats*, you know. The show."

"Oh, sure, I realize."

He keeps reading through the letters.

"This guy ought to have his mouth washed out with soap."

"Tell me about it."

"Cock-tease, wow."

"Well, he's nuts, you know."

"Sure sounds that way."

"Well, obviously."

"This kind of thing ever happen to you before?"

"Never."

"Boy."

"What scares me . . ."

"Sure, he knows where you live."

"Exactly."

"Must've followed you home or something."

"That's what I figure."

"Have you gone to the police?"

"No."

"Why not?"

"Well, for one, I don't know who he is."

"But that's *their* job, isn't it? Finding *out* who he is?"

"I guess so."

"But you don't think so."

"I just don't know if they'd even *bother* with something like this. It isn't as if he's *threatening* me or anything."

"It isn't as if he's exactly stable, either."

"He does sound a little nuts, doesn't he?"

"A little?"

"I guess I will call them. If he doesn't quit."

"What makes you think he'll quit?"

"Well . . . I have this idea."

"Yeah?"

Rickie Diaz has been cleared with the night-shift doorman and when he asks for Kate Duggan after the Wednesday night show, he is immediately allowed entrance to the theater and told where her dressing room is. He stands looking somewhat embarrassed and awed as she introduces him to the other kids, all in various stages of feline undress, using his full proud Puerto Rican name, Ricardo Alvaredo Diaz, as she learned it yesterday while outlining her brilliant plan to him. Rickie has now seen the show from a house seat provided and paid for by Kate, from which sixth-row-center vantage point he alternately watched the prowling cats on stage and checked the house for any male who seemed *too* interested in the particular cat in the white costume. As they come out of the Seventh Avenue stage door at ten-fifty that Wednesday night, hand in hand and trying to look very lovey-dovey, Kate scans the men waiting on the sidewalk for the performers to come out. Most of them are holding autograph books. One of them is carrying a flash camera.

PRIVILEGED CONVERSATION

Rickie is wearing jeans and a long-sleeved white shirt detailed with an embroidered parrot in red, yellow, orange, and green, a gift from his uncle in Mayagüez, he tells her later. Kate has asked him to look casual tonight because she herself is wearing what she customarily wears to and from the theater in the summertime, just jeans and a T-shirt, sometimes with a sweater if it's cool, which this summer shows no sign of becoming. So she's pleased that Rickie looks not like a theatergoer but like someone who might just possibly be her big, tattooed, longhaired, bulging-muscled boyfriend, which is just what he's supposed to look like. To reinforce this notion, she reaches up to touch his cheek the moment they step out onto the sidewalk, kisses him quickly, says, "I'm starved, honey," and loops her arm through his as they begin walking uptown.

She hopes they are being followed.

She hopes he is watching.

The idea is to have him think she's truly involved with this powerful-looking stud. Get him to believe this is not some defenseless little girl dancing her heart out on the stage of the Winter Garden, but is instead a grown woman clever enough to have chosen Arnold Schwarzenegger as her boyfriend. So watch your fuckin onions, my one true lord and master. Hang up your expensive stationery or Arnie here will break you into tiny little pieces.

The choice for a crowded delicatessen where he will be able to see them holding hands across their hot pastrami sandwiches and ostentatiously billing and cooing is the Carnegie on Fifty-fifth and Seventh or the Stage between Fifty-third and -fourth. They choose the Carnegie because it allows a slightly longer walk from the theater, with him in close pursuit, they hope. Neither of them appears particularly nervous or suspicious or watchful as they wander hand in hand up Seventh Avenue. The idea is to make this seem entirely natural and unplanned, something that happens all the time, no matter *who's* watching them. This isn't a show here, this is two people madly in love with each other and one of them happens to be six feet two inches tall and by the way tips the scales at two-twenty, get the message?

Rickie turns out to be a pretty good actor, leaning over the table toward her and taking both her hands in his while they're waiting for their orders to come, talking earnestly—and somewhat touchingly—of his early youth in a South Bronx barrio where he spent most of his time trying to avoid recruitment by a gang called Los Hermanos Locos, "which means 'The Crazy Brothers,' I guess you know." Steadfastly refusing their admonitions, exhortations, and eventual daily beatings designed to encourage and persuade, he took up bodybuilding as a means of self-defense, hoping to cope effectively with these jackasses unless one day they decided to shoot him, which they didn't do after he'd gained fifty pounds of muscle and busted a few heads and they lost interest. He tells her all this with a proud look on his fiercely handsome Conquistador face with its high cheekbones and aristocratic nose, tossing his ponytail in utter disdain. Kate is thinking This is someone who can *really* break someone in half if he so chooses.

PRIVILEGED CONVERSATION

The Indian tattoo, he tells her, has nothing at all to do with his Latino heritage—"My family doesn't go back to any Indian tribe or anything, though there used to be some tribes in Puerto Rico," rolling the name of the island on his tongue, Pware-toe *Ree*-coe—the tattoo was just something he decided to have done one night when he was a little drunk.

"The feathers in the headband ripple when I flex," he tells her, "I'll show you later," which means, she realizes with something of a start, that he later plans to take off the long-sleeved shirt and flex his biceps for her, let the feathers ripple for her, a performance above and beyond the call of duty. But she does nothing at the moment to correct his mistaken assumption, satisfied that whoever may be watching in this noisy, crowded place should be utterly convinced that they are indeed girl-and-boy. She allows herself a few discreet glances around the room, green eyes sidling from patron to patron, idly seeking the pale thin man with the dark brooding eyes, but she sees no one who even vaguely fits that description.

They have ordered not the pastrami but the hot roast beef sandwiches instead, served with creamy mounds of mashed potatoes and brown gravy and a bucket of sour pickles and cream soda the likes of which she hasn't tasted since the time some boy, she forgets who, took her to Coney Island shortly after she joined the cast of *Cats* the first time around. The show has been such an integral part of her life that what's happening with this lunatic seems almost ironic. The idea that he *saw* her in the show, knew how to get to her *because* of the show, knew *where* to send the flowers and the notes, knew *when* she'd be coming out of the theater after each performance, knew that all he had to do was *follow* her to find out where she lived, all of this is very frightening, hey, no kidding?

But it's also somewhat *eerie*, you know? As if everything was somehow *preordained*. Everything that happened to her *before* she got into *Cats* was leading up to the actual moment she first stepped on the stage of the Winter Garden as part of the two-boy, two-girl, so-called "Cats Chorus." But more than that, she now has the creepy feeling that everything *since* then has been leading up to *now*, this very *instant*, sitting here in a restaurant with a handsome twenty-year-old Puerto Rican who's here to protect her because her lover—who hasn't called her in more than a week—is up there in Massachusetts making love to his goddamn *wife*.

The idea galls.

She eats voraciously, as she does after each performance, her hands obligingly freed by her make-believe lover who is telling her about his ambition to own his own fitness studio one day. Working in the bicycle shop is just one of *three* jobs he has, how about that! He also drives a limo part-time for a company in Queens, and he works weekends in the produce department at Gristede's. Meanwhile, he's going to NYU at night to study business administration so he'll know what he's doing when he opens his own place after he's saved enough money to do it. "Start with a small studio uptown someplace, expand to a whole *chain* of them, I have big ideas, Kate. Lots of the guys in Los Hermanos are either dead or in jail now, can you imagine what *I* could've turned into if I let them talk me into mugging people, or selling dope or whatever the hell?" Listening to him, Kate is secretly hoping the lunatic out there *will* actually make his move so Rickie can stomp him into the pavement and end his career. In fact, she's beginning to wonder if maybe they shouldn't *walk* home after they get out of here, but it's a long way to Tipperary and also to Ninety-first and First. So when at last they've finished their coffee and Rickie has paid the bill . . .

She whispers, "I'll settle with you later," but he pulls a macho face and says, "Hey, come on, willya?"

. . . they step out onto Seventh Avenue on a night so torrid they could just as easily be in Mayagüez, and then walk up to Fifty-seventh, again hoping he's following. In any case, he knows where she lives. If he wants to take a cab and be waiting for them there, that's fine with Kate. All she wants is for him to get the message. The message is blazing in lights a mile high:

LEAVE ME ALONE!
I HAVE A BIG JEALOUS
BOYFRIEND!

The crosstown bus runs over to First, where they transfer to a bus running uptown. They get off at Ninety-first Street and begin walking toward her apartment on streets rather dark and deserted at this hour of the night. They get there at a little before midnight, and she is surprised to find the doorman actually *there* at his post instead of out buying himself a hamburger or catching forty winks in the storeroom near the switchboard. He greets her with a cheery "Evening, Miss Duggan," and she says, "Hi, Domingo," at which point Rickie bursts into a stream of rapid-fire Spanish, which Domingo answers and they machine-gun it back and forth as if reciting in tandem the history of Queen Isabella and the Spanish Armada while Kate debates whether she should simply shake hands with Rickie or kiss him on the cheek in case *he's* someplace watching.

"Goodnight, Rickie," she says at last, and reaches up to kiss him, but he turns his head slightly at the very last moment, either by accident or design, and their lips meet. His tongue is in her mouth in an instant, a hot Latin tongue that sends sparks clear down to where she doesn't want to be feeling anything of the sort. She draws away, and looks at him in surprise, and then says, "Goodnight" again, and goes into the building. He stands on the sidewalk watching her for a moment, and then he shrugs and walks away. Domingo looks a little puzzled, too.

She has lived in New York long enough to know that a spring latch is worthless on the door to an apartment. Her top lock is a Medeco and the one under that is a dead bolt. She double-locks the door, and then draws all the blinds, the ones on the windows facing the street, and the ones covering the single window opening on the air shaft. "Yes, Hannah," she says, "hello, sweetie, how are you?" and then goes into the bedroom and slips out of her jeans and T-shirt. She leaves her panties on like an old maid afraid to look under the bed, and takes from the closet a silk kimono Ron bought for her in Fort Lauderdale when they were touring *Miss Saigon*. The kimono is very long, with a sash that belts at the waist. Its predominant color is a sort of saffron, printed with these huge olive-colored tendrils. It feels soft and smooth and slippery against her skin.

Barefoot, she starts back into the living room, and, as she invariably does, stops to look at the corridor wall hung with framed photographs. The picture of the Palace Theatre in London, where she played in *Les Miz*, shows the big marquee on Shaftesbury Avenue, and hanging under that a photo of the stage door around the corner with its stone lintel and chiseled words shamelessly proclaiming:

PALACE THEATRE ••• STAGE ENTRANCE THE WORLD'S GREATEST ARTISTES HAVE PASSED AND WILL PASS THROUGH THESE DOORS

Artistes, she thinks and smiles.

There's a framed photo of the Operettenhaus in Hamburg, where she played in, guess what, *Cats*, and all around that are pictures of the various theaters in Denver, Minneapolis, Fort Lauderdale, Washington, and Detroit, from when she was touring *Miss Saigon* with Ron. The biggest picture on the wall is a framed color photograph of Bess. Her sister is nine in the picture, and she looks happy and beautiful in a yellow sundress, but of course that was before she got so terribly sick.

She stares at the photo for a long time, and then she sighs heavily and goes into the living room and over to the wall where her stereo equipment is stacked. From one of the metal shelves there, she takes down a bottle of Beefeater's gin that was a gift from the stage manager last Christmas, and she pours a hefty two fingers into a fat solid-feeling glass she bought at Pottery Barn.

She carries the glass into the kitchen, cracks a tray of cubes, and drops two of them into the drink. "Cheers," she says aloud to no one, and takes a good swallow. "Mm, good," she says, and goes back into the living room and searches through her CDs till she finds Handel's *Water Music*, to which she once danced in a recital in Miss Davenport's dance class in Westport, Connecticut. But that was when you and I were young, Bessie. That was before the *Incident*, as Jacqueline and I took to calling it after hours of skirting it, and circling it, and finally dealing with it and putting it to rest.

Maybe.

Or alternately, the *Bathroom* Incident, delicately avoiding the more emotionally laden term *Trauma*.

The Handel is soft and soothing and suited to the hour, which she knows is late. She lowers the volume. Drains her glass. While she's standing there, she pours herself another one. Standing there with the drink in her hand, she visualizes herself as a skinny twelve-year-old in leotard and tights, drifting across the large open room that was Miss Davenport's second-floor studio, mirrors lining one entire wall, windows on the other, flowing, floating to the sound of Handel's violins, richly romantic when she was twelve, but sounding somewhat stout and stately now. She sips at her fresh drink. Twelve years old. A spring recital. Faint breezes wafting through the open windows. Sweaty little girls drifting. Everything so beautiful at the ballet, "Thank you, *Chorus Line*," she says, and raises her glass in a toast, and sips at it again. Everything so beautiful. But that was before the summer of our discontent, wasn't it?

The telephone rings.

Don't be my fucking father, she thinks.

She goes into the bedroom and picks up the phone on the bedside table.

"Hello?"

"Hi. It's me."

"Rickie," she says, relieved, "hi."

"I just got home. Is everything okay?"

"Yes, fine."

"No trouble from the nut?"

"Not yet."

"Maybe we scared him off, huh?"

"I hope so," she says, and sits on the edge of the bed, and takes another sip of the gin. "That was very kind of you," she says. "What you did tonight."

"I just hope it worked."

"We'll find out, I guess."

"Oh sure. By the way," he says, "we were so busy trying to fool him, I never got to tell you how much I liked the show."

"Thank you."

"You really *are* the prettiest cat in it. Whatever it was he said in his letter."

"Prettiest *kitty*," she says. "Thank you."

"You're also a very good dancer," he says.

"Thank you."

"I'll bet he sees every performance, don't you think? Judging from the letters?"

"Probably."

"Probably standing downstairs right this minute. Looking up at your window."

"Well, I hope not."

"Probably jacking off in some doorway," he says. "Where do these nuts come from, anyway?"

The Incident is suddenly upon her full-blown.

"There used to be a kid lived in my building," Rickie says, "he used to throw bricks down from the roof. Just at anybody passing by. My uncle comes to visit us one day, this crazy bastard on the roof throws a brick down at him. He runs up the roof, my uncle . . ."

A hot summer night at the beginning of August.

A Sunday night.

Thirteen-year-old Kate is standing in front of the misted bathroom mirror, drying herself in a large white puffy towel.

". . . gave me the shirt, by the way."

"What?"

"My uncle in Mayagüez. The one who told the kid to stop throwing bricks off the roof or he'd throw *him* off the roof. He's the one sent me the shirt I was wearing tonight. With the parrot on it. Did you like it?"

"Yes, it was very nice."

"Yeah, it's cool."

Eleven-year-old Bess is submerged in the tub in a sea of white suds.

"He used to be a doorman on East Seventieth, he

retired last October, went back to the island. He's got a house down there, a pool, anything a person . . ."

Downstairs in the living room, her father is listening to his records.

Gently . . .

Sweetly . . .

Ever so . . .

Discreetly . . .

Her hand suddenly begins shaking.

"Rickie," she says, "excuse me, but I have to go now."

"Is something wrong?"

"No, nothing, I'm all right."

Her hand is shaking so hard she's spilling gin all over the front of the kimono.

Open . . .

Secret . . .

Doors.

"Kate?" he says.

She can see her sister in the tub, precociously budding, thin and tan and supple, her sweet dear innocent Bess.

"Kate?"

You always *were* his favorite.

"I'm okay," she says.

She can't stop trembling.

"There's nobody *there*, is there?"

Yes, there's *everybody* here, she thinks.

"No, I'm just very tired."

"I can imagine. I'll let you go then."

Her father's words.

But he doesn't.

Ever.

"Can I call you again sometime?"

"Yes, fine," she says.

No, don't, she thinks.

"Goodnight then."

"Goodnight," she says, and hangs up, and drains the glass, and goes back into the living room to refill it. The orchestra is into the "Hornpipe" section. She turns off the stereo. The apartment goes suddenly still.

If David were here, she thinks, he would know how to deal with this, right? A fucking shrink? But David isn't here. If Jacqeline were here, she too would know how to deal with this. She dealt with it ad infinitum and ad nauseam over the years, didn't she, so she would certainly know what to say now to soothe the savage beast, something Handel's venerable music apparently did not have the charms to accomplish.

Listen, she thinks, let's either do the mantra or go hide the silverware, okay?

She swallows a goodly amount of gin, which burns on the way down, strengthening her sense of resolve. Through Understanding, Peace, she thinks. So leave us understand.

I was not responsible for what happened.

I know I wasn't.

I was not to blame.

I know.

I didn't need to go fuck poor Charlie.

Daddy's dearest friend.

I didn't need to pursue him like a lioness after a

warthog, chasing him into his underground hole, yanking him out by his tail, forcing him to relive with me . . .

Stay away from the Incident, she thinks.

I felt no guilt over what happened.

The blame was all my father's.

I felt only shame.

Because I wasn't able to stop it.

Isn't that why you make it happen again and again?

But I don't.

Without Bess each time?

My poor darling Bess.

It's what you do, Kate.

Is *that* it?

Oh, yes, that is most definitely it.

Over and over and over again.

Thank you, Dr. Hicks.

She puts down her glass. Deliberately, she goes into the bathroom and runs a hot tub. She pours in a generous amount of bath oil. She slides out of the kimono and steps into the foaming suds.

Take off the curse, she thinks.

Take off the curse.

It was all that kid's fault in the park, she thinks.

If he hadn't stolen my bike, we wouldn't have met.

Gloria's eyelids are shaded with a blue that complements her pale scoop-necked blouse and somewhat darker mini. Her narrow face, the eyes as dark as loam and somewhat slanted, the nose as exquisitely sculpted as Nefertiti's, today possesses a curiously vulpine look that seems to say *I want a part and I will* kill *for it*—but perhaps that's because she's just come from an audition. Her mouth is a voluptuous contradiction to the wolf metaphor, Bugs Bunny transplanted onto Brer Fox, its upper lip flaring imperceptibly to reveal a minuscule wedge of faintly bucked teeth, exceedingly white against her chocolate complexion.

"The show is set in the year 3706," she's telling Kate, "in a sort of striated—is that the right word?—society where the robots are in charge and they're chasing humans. Oh, *I* get it, it's *Blade Runner*, right? Only Daryl Hannah's Basic Pleasure Model is a Belgian nun, right? Anyway, the humans still wear clothes but the robots wear only body makeup. Which is understandable, since if you're made of metal, why would you need clothes? The producer asked me if I'd be willing to be a dancing robot who wears just body makeup and these metallic stiletto-heeled pumps. I told him that could get awfully chilly in the wintertime. You know what *he* said?"

"What'd he say?" Kate asks.

"He said, 'Yeah, well this is still August, honey.'"

"He wanted you to undress for him, is what *that* was."

"Oh, tell me about it," Gloria says.

"Did you?"

"No, I told him I wasn't looking for *that* kind of dancing role. He said 'Too bad, it's a featured role.' I told him 'Yeah, too bad.' Who needs that kind of shit?"

"Really," Kate says.

The two women are in a cappuccino joint in the Village. Kate has already told her about the guy who's been writing letters to her, and how last night she tried to scare him off, which is probably why Gloria went into the long story about the producer wanting her to take off her clothes. Now she tells Kate that she once had a guy phoning her day and night, but this was somebody she knew. Kate tells her, "No, this isn't anything like that, this is some nut." She keeps looking around the coffeehouse. Trying to spot anyone paying excessive attention to her. She is uncomfortable out in the city, out of her apartment. He has done that to her. Made her feel that any one of the people here in this place might be watching her as she sips at her *latte*.

"Have you told David about it?" Gloria asks.

"No. Not yet."

"Is he still coming in next Tuesday?"

"I don't know."

"Because he told me he'd be back again on the fifteenth."

"I haven't heard from him."

Gloria says nothing for a moment.

She sips at her espresso and then looks across the table with those coal-black eyes of hers and says, "That's too bad. I was hoping to see him again."

Me too, Kate thinks.

Because, yes, now that this lunatic has entered her life she is finding it more and more difficult to suppress what happened during that summer long ago. Which is why she supposes she couldn't fall asleep last night, even *after* the hot tub, even *after*, in fact, she masturbated under the suds.

You're right, she thinks, I'm a whore.

Was that the word he'd used?

Whore?

Or was it slut?

Which?

But, yes, if David does by some miracle come in next week, she *would* like Gloria to be with them because if there's one thing she's learned over the years, it's how to restage the Bloody Fucking *Incident* in a variety of inventive ways. With a bit more practice she guesses she might even be able to forget entirely what happened back there in the Westport house on that August night fourteen years ago. *Aluvai*, as they say in the trade. But then she might start stuttering again. Or worse. Again.

But that's all behind you now.

Sure, Jacqueline, thank you very much.

And I certainly hope so, Ollie.

Still and all, she *would* like to be together with both of them again.

You always *do this.*

You're right, she thinks, I'm a *cunt*, okay?

Yes.

Le mot juste.

Exactly what was said.

"So call me," Gloria says. "If you hear from him."

"I will."

"Because I'd really like to do it, you know?"

At eight minutes before curtain on Friday night, the doorman announces over the P.A. system that she's wanted on the telephone. It is David calling from Menemsha to tell her how much he loves her and to assure her that he'll be there on Tuesday, as he'd promised, will she be coming to the airport to meet him?

"Yes," she says, "I'll be there."

"My plane gets in at seven thirty-eight," he says.

"La Guardia or Newark?"

"Newark."

"I'll be there. I love you."

"I love you, too."

"Why haven't you called?"

"There's only one car. We go every place together. I just haven't been *alone*. There's always someone with me."

"Where are you now?"

"Home. The house. They all went . . ."

"Isn't that dangerous?"

"Yes."

"I don't want anything to happen to us."

"Neither do I."

"I don't want to lose you."

"Don't worry."

"Five," the stage manager warns.

"I love you, David. Please hurry before . . ."

She stops herself dead.

"I love you, too," he says.

"Tuesday," she says.

"Tuesday," he repeats.

And is gone.

The letter is waiting in her mailbox when she comes down to the lobby on Saturday morning.

It reads:

How dare you, Puss!

Who is the monkey with the Parrot? Does he realize how much trouble he's making for himself? If he so much as breathes on you again, he's asking for more misery than he's ever known in his life. Get rid of him! Don't irritate me, Kate! I'm watching all the time. Remember that. I own you!

The detective is the same one who ran the lineup for her and David back in July. His name is Clancy . . .

"No relation," he says at once, though Kate doesn't understand the reference . . .

. . . and he seems happy to see her again, happy to be of assistance to "one of the tribe" as he puts it. Kate has never thought of herself as being particularly Irish, except for her looks, but she's grateful for the ties that seemingly bind. Clancy could not look less Irish. He has brown hair and brown eyes and a mouth that seems perpetually set in a skeptical sneer. He also needs a shave. She suspects he had a tough Friday night here in the big bad city.

The letters she has collected as evidence of whatever crime the lunatic is committing are now on Clancy's desk, bathed in sunshine on this hot, sticky, what-else-is-new, late Saturday morning. Clancy is sitting in shirt-sleeves, the better to promote the image of hardworking cop. A pistol is holstered at his waist on the right-hand side of his belt. He is smoking, of course. He looks like a cop on a television show. Except for the fact that they don't smoke on television these days. To Kate's enormous surprise, he opens the top drawer of his desk, and removes from it a pair of white cotton gloves. He pulls on the gloves. They give him a somewhat comical appearance, like a vagabond at a society tea.

"Has anyone but you handled these?" he asks.

"Well . . . yes. I showed them to a friend."

"His name?"

"Rickie Diaz."

"How do you spell the first name?" Clancy asks, and opens a thick black notebook.

"With an 'i-e.' "

Clancy scribbles the name into his book.

"Anyone else?"

"No."

"O-kay," he says, and opens the first of the envelopes.

He reads the letters in sequence.

He looks up every now and then and nods across the desk to her.

At last, he sighs heavily, lights a fresh cigarette, and says simply, "Yeah."

She wonders Yeah *what?*

She waits.

"Your typical nut," he says.

But *this* she already knows.

"Nine times out of ten, they're harmless," he says.

Which is reassuring.

"But this *is* a crime," he says.

Good, she thinks.

"What's the crime?"

"Aggravated Harassment."

She nods.

He opens the top drawer of his desk again, takes out a paperback book with a blue and black cover. Upside down, she reads the title of the book:

GOULD'S
CRIMINAL LAW
HANDBOOK
OF NEW YORK

Clancy opens the book, begins leafing through it.

"I think it's two-thirty," he says idly, though the clock on the wall behind his desk reads eleven twenty-seven.

He keeps leafing through the book.

"No, it's two-forty point three-oh," he says, and turns the book toward her. "This is the Penal Law," he says.

She reads:

• §240.30. Aggravated harassment in the second degree.

A person is guilty of aggravated harassment in the second degree when, with intent to harass, annoy, threaten or alarm, he or *she*:

1. Communicates or causes a communication to be initiated by mechanical or electronic means or otherwise, by telephone, or by telegraph, mail or any other form of written communication, in a manner likely to cause annoyance or alarm; *or*

2. Makes a telephone call, whether or not a conversation . . .

"He hasn't called me," she says, looking up sharply.

"Not *yet*," Clancy says.

Which is somewhat less than reassuring.

. . . whether or not a conversation ensues, with no purpose of legitimate communication; *or*

3. Strikes, shoves, kicks or otherwise . . .

"The rest doesn't apply," Clancy says.

Thank God, she thinks.

"What's Aggravated Harassment in the *first* degree?" she asks.

"Has to do with race, color, religion and so on. *That's* a felony. Second degree is just an A-mis."

"What's that?"

"A class-A misdemeanor."

"Like stealing my *bike*, right?"

"Well . . . yeah."

"Then this isn't a very important crime, right?"

"I would say harassing someone is important."

"Important enough for anyone to pay attention?"

"Oh, sure."

"So how do I stop him?"

"You file a complaint. There's not much to go on here, but hopefully we can find him."

"How?"

"Well, there may be latents on the letters here. He may have a record, or he may have been in the service, or in government employment, there are fingerprint records we can look at. If we locate him, we check his handwriting against what we have here. Then there are two ways we can go."

Kate waited.

"We can have somebody talk to him, we've got . . ."

"*Talk* to him?"

"Yeah, we've got people here who are very good at this. Take the guy aside, tell him Listen, you want to go to jail, or you want to be reasonable here? Leave the girl alone, don't bother her no more, that's the end of it, you don't hear from us again. But you try to contact her, you write to her, you phone her . . ."

"He hasn't . . ."

"I know, I'm just saying. You phone her, you go near her building, you even walk on her *block*, we're gonna come after you and put you away. Lots of times, they listen."

She is thinking This guy isn't going to listen to anybody talking to him. This guy is *nuts*.

"What if he *doesn't* listen?" she asks.

"You let us know he's still bothering you, and we arrest him and charge him with the A-mis."

She is thinking What if he kills me between the time you talk to him and the time I tell you he's still bothering me?

"Each letter he sent constitutes one count of the crime, you see. What've we got here, eight, nine letters?"

"Ten."

"Okay, that's ten counts of Aggravated Harassment. But the most he can get is two years in jail, even though technically there are ten counts of the crime. It's complicated. If he gets off with *less* than the max . . ."

She is thinking What happens when he gets *out* of jail?

". . . the judge can grant an order of protection, which

if he comes near you again is contempt of court and yet *another* crime."

"I'm very afraid this person will try to hurt me," she says levelly, trying to keep the quaver out of her voice.

"I realize that. But what I'm trying to tell you, Miss Duggan, you're not entirely helpless in this matter. We can look into it for you, if you want to file a complaint, or there're people in the D.A.'s Office you can talk to, if you prefer that, the Sex Crimes Unit down there."

She is thinking Jesus, what am I getting into here?

"Do they ever just *stop?*" she asks. "On their own?"

"Sometimes. Sometimes, if you ignore them, they . . ."

"I *am* ignoring him."

"I know that. What I'm saying, sometimes they just get bored or whatever and go away."

"He doesn't seem to be getting bored."

"No, he doesn't, but sometimes they just quit all of a sudden. There are lots of women out there, you know."

"Yes," she says, and nods thoughtfully.

"So how would you like to proceed?"

"What I'm afraid of, you see, is if somebody goes to talk to him, he'll come after *me.*"

"Well . . . I really think that's a very remote possibility."

"But a possibility, right?"

"Anything's possible, Miss Duggan. The roof of this building could fall in on us right this minute. That's a possibility, but a very remote one. I really don't think this person would try to harm you after somebody from the police talked to him."

"But he might."

"There's no telling *what* crazy people will do, but in my experience . . ."

"I'd like to give it some further thought," she says.

"Entirely up to you," Clancy says, with what she detects as a slight dismissive shrug. He opens the top drawer of his desk again, takes from it a large manila envelope printed with the words POLICE DEPART-MENT—CITY OF NEW YORK and below that the bolder word **EVIDENCE**.

Evidence, she thinks.

He turns down the flap of the envelope. There are two little red cardboard buttons on the envelope, a red string dangling from the one on the flap. He wraps the string around the lower button.

"You'd better hang on to these," he says. "Case you decide."

David calls collect on Monday evening.

He reminds her that his plane will arrive in Newark at seven thirty-eight tomorrow morning.

"I'll be there," she says.

Hurry, she thinks.

Please hurry.

And closes the blinds against the encroaching dusk.

4: *tuesday, august 15–saturday, august 19*

David knows at once that something is wrong.

She stands just past the security gate waiting for him, a black umbrella in her hand, her red hair pulled up under a man's gray fedora that hides it completely, a black raincoat buttoned to her throat, jeans and yellow rain boots showing below the hem. She looks as if she's been crying.

"What's wrong?" he asks.

"Lots," she says, and kisses him swiftly on the cheek.

It is pouring outside the terminal. Kate has borrowed a car from one of the "kids" in the show, and it is tiny and cramped, and there is a faint whiff of stale sweat wafting from the backseat, which is littered with leg warmers, leotards, tights, socks, panties, bras and a tangled assortment of unidentifiable soiled or stained garments waiting to be transported to the Laundromat. Or the city dump.

She begins crying the moment she pulls the car out of the airport parking lot.

"What *is* it?" he says.

In fits and starts and bits and pieces, like a patient dredging up a traumatic experience, she rambles tearfully through the events of the past two weeks and more, starting with the delivery of the first box of roses, "I thought they were from you, well, naturally, the card said I *love* you, Kathryn," and then the subsequent flowers, all of them sent to the theater and delivered to the dressing room, four boxes of roses altogether, long-stemmed roses, all with a different florist's card saying I love you, and then the letters started, ten letters in all, so far. She'll show him the letters when they get home, Clancy said it's a crime, the detective, remember? From that time with my bike? I went to see him Saturday. Each letter constitutes a separate count of Aggravated Harassment, but he can only get two years in aggregate, whatever that means, I've been so frightened.

Bursting into tears again, trying to choke the tears back while David listens in amazement to the recited contents of the letters as she's memorized them, the voice of a man obsessed if ever he's heard one, and he most certainly has heard plenty of them. Once again, he listens to the familiar symptoms, altered to accommodate the scenario with Kate, the expected shift from reality to fantasy, Kathryn becoming Victoria, Victoria becoming a kitten and then a pussy, the repetitive fixation on the slang expression for the vagina, the slavish supplication, the reversal of roles so that he now becomes lord and master, the possessiveness and jealous rage, the abusive language and escalating obscenity, the initially veiled threats, the later open sexual invitation-cum-threat, the final threat against Rickie . . .

"Rickie?" he says. "Who's Rickie?"

"The kid from the bike shop," she says.

How'd *he* get into this? David wonders.

"How'd *he* get into this?" he asks aloud, and turns to her in puzzlement, his knees banging against the dash-board in this goddamn toy car. He should be listening to this in the limo she promised, he should be holding her in his arms while somebody else drives, telling her he's here, assuring her that everything will be all right.

Well, she goes on to explain, crying more fiercely now, frightening him because it's raining very hard and there's quite a bit of traffic heading into the city at this hour of the morning, and he doesn't want her to run into one of the trucks rolling ponderously toward the George Washington Bridge, but how can she *see* through this driving rain and her own veil of tears, her vale of tears? Well, she says, I got very scared when he sent the letter to my building because that meant he'd followed me from the theater and he knew where I lived, and it sounded very threatening, the business about my wanting it as much as he did and now he knew where to get it and all, it sounded like somebody getting ready to *rape* me, for Christ's sake! And you were *away*, David, don't forget that, *you* weren't here, you hadn't even *called*, where the hell *were* you?

She is beginning to sound hysterical, he has dealt with

235

hysteria before. "Honey," he says, "calm down, I'm here now," but she keeps ranting about how she had to go to *someone* and the only one she could think of was Rickie, the kid from the bike shop, who was kind enough and brave enough to take her for something to eat after the show, and walk her home afterward, so that fucking *lunatic* would think he was her boyfriend and get scared off.

"Kate, watch the road," he warns.

"It isn't as if I have a brother or a *father* I can turn to," she says, "and my sister is helpless, of course, and even if my mother *wasn't* in San Diego, she wouldn't give a damn if an *ax* murderer was following me. You don't know what she's like, David . . . "

And now he listens to a furious recitation that truly could come from any one of his patients, a conversation so privileged that it transforms this teeny-weeny car into a psychiatrist's cubicle, or, more accurately, a priest's confessional. Patiently, he listens. This is the woman he loves, and she is in serious trouble. As the windshield wipers snick at the incessant rain, he listens.

The fury she expends on her mother has one dubious side effect in that it stanches the flow of tears and forces a hunched-over-the-wheel concentration on the road, as if Kate is driving this tiny car not only through the fiercely slanting rain but also, like a sharpened stake, directly into her mother's heart. Her mother's name is Fiona, but it could just as easily be Shirley, or Rhoda or Marie or Lila, who are the respective reviled mothers of Arthur K, Alex J, Susan M and Michael D, or for that matter David's own mother Ruth before he went through the extensive analysis that put his hatred for her to rest. (A father named Neil lurks in the background of Kate's fiery recitation, somewhat like a shadow lingering offstage, a fact that brings him immediately to prominence in David's trained analytical mind.) But her rage seems exclusively directed toward Fiona as the car approaches the bridge in a similarly raging storm that buffets it with wind and water. Everywhere around them, rumbling trucks lumber like dinosaurs.

According to Kate, her mother was—and *is*—a demanding, ungiving, unforgiving bitch who would rather kick a cripple than light a candle in church. "We used to call her Fee the *Fair*," she says, virtually grinding the words out through essentially clenched teeth . . .

. . . not only because she was an extravagantly beautiful woman, but also because she was so fucking *un*fair with the girls, and even with their father (Neil still skulks in the shadows, a figure reluctant to take his proper place on the stage of Kate's mind), accusing them of plots to thwart her will or topple her carefully organized plans. Bess was the *true* beauty in the family—with their mother's red hair and green eyes, of course, which both of them had inherited—but also with a rare sort of radiant inner beauty that shone on her face like something beatific. Maybe this was why Fiona tended to pick on her more often than she did Kate, who, to tell the truth, was a scrawny, skinny kid who looked more like a boy than the girl she was supposed to be . . . well, he knows that, she's already told him what she looked like at thirteen. Even so, Kate really *was* her father's favorite, as her mother never failed to point out to poor Bess (Neil taking a step closer, into the spotlight, and then retreating swiftly into the shadows again).

"Here, I've got it," David says, and hands her the change for the toll.

Kate rolls down the window, hands the coins over to the collector, and quickly rolls it up again before they both drown. The brief interruption serves as an end to the first act. But when the curtain goes up again after intermission, it is on another scene entirely, perhaps another *play* entirely.

David wishes they were someplace else, *anywhere* else, anywhere but inside this claustrophobic car hurtling through the rain. He longs to hold her, kiss the drying tears from her face, comfort her and console her, tell her how much he loves her, promise he will be here to take care of her, she has nothing to worry about, he's *here* now. Somehow they make it over the bridge and are heading downtown on the Harlem River Drive. Out on the river tugboats move listlessly through the shifting mist on the water. As Kate sifts sobbingly through the tattered tissue of her memory, the windshield wipers swipe ceaselessly and ineffectively at the rain. He is truly afraid she will crash the car into any one of the vehicles everywhere around them, certain tomorrow's headline in the *Daily News* will read **LOVERS PERISH IN FLAMES.**

Flames.

Flames have suddenly become the thesis of this large-screen, full-color extravaganza. Flames are what now envelop Kate's sister on a night in August long ago, everything seems to happen to Kate in August, wasn't it a wet and steamy day in August when she was just thirteen—yes, the theater's business manager, or accountant, or whatever the hell he was, his small office, yes, her blatant, brazen seduction of her father's best friend. But the fire is . . . *what?* Three years later? And flames are consuming her fourteen-year-old sister as she runs out of the burning house she herself has set on fire. Flames are everywhere, the house, Bess's gown, her hair, red as fire anyway, redder now with flames that lick and bite at curling crackling strands. Flames are the theme, flames are the plot, flames are the horror. In hot and almost comic pursuit, like a small band of inept Keystone Kops chasing a human torch, Fiona and a shrieking Kate come running across the lawn after her. Bess is yelling, "Let me die, let me burn in hell!" Kate can hardly breathe. Her father suddenly rushes out of the house with a wet sheet trailing from his hand. He chases his younger daughter, tackles her, brings her to the ground, her nightgown in flames, her hair on *fire*, Jesus, oh *Jesus*, holds her pinned to the ground as Kate screams "Leave her *alone*, you son of a bitch!" and Fiona, all wide-eyed and shocked, stands by appalled as Bess repeats over and over again, "Bless me, Father, for I have sinned . . . bless me, Father, for I have sinned . . . bless me . . . " He wraps her in the cool wet sheets, the sheets beginning to steam around her, the smell of her scorched and smoldering hair stinking up the August night, the sheets steaming on the humid August night, everything happens in August, August is the cruelest month.

"I almost told Rickie last Wednesday," she says.

"Told him what?"

"All of it."

And now young Ricardo Alvaredo Diaz boldly takes the stage, suddenly stepping out to tumultuous applause, grinning at the audience and flexing his muscles, the feathers rippling on the tattooed Indian's headdress as Kate steers the car off the drive and onto East Ninety-sixth Street.

"Where were *you*, David?" she asks, turning sharply from the wheel. "Where the hell were *you* last Wednesday? Doing it to *Julia* up there on the Vineyard? When you should have been doing it to *me?*"

How did this get to be *this?* he wonders.

All I wanted to do was kiss you.

And who the hell is Julia?

"If you'd been here," she says, "I wouldn't have let him," and suddenly yanks the car over to the curb and throws her arms on the steering wheel, and lowers her head onto them, and begins sobbing uncontrollably.

It is now almost ten A.M. Across the room, Kate is on the couch, the little girl on the *Les Miz* poster staring sorrowfully into the room from the wall behind her. She has stopped crying. She has taken off the black raincoat and the yellow rain boots, and she is sitting cross-legged in jeans, a white cotton T-shirt, and white socks, the man's gray fedora still pulled down over her hair. It occurs to him that she covered her hair so that it wouldn't signal blatantly to the man stalking her. But they are now in her apartment, where she is safe, so why is she still wearing the dumb hat?

He is inordinately, and unprofessionally, angry with her. He is supposed to be a psychiatrist, trained and caring and concerned, but instead he is reacting like a jealous schoolboy. After all she told him in the car, and knowing now the very real trouble this son of a bitch letter-writer has been causing, all he can think of is that last Wednesday she *let* that kid from the bike shop . . . the very word infuriates him. *Let* him. Like kids on a goddamn rooftop. Will you *let* me, Katie? Sure, Rickie, just let me take off my panties, dear. The *Miss Saigon* helicopter is waiting to take him out of here, perhaps back to the Vineyard. The cats in the apartment—the real one nuzzling his leg, and the yellow-eyed one in the poster above the sofa, and the green-eyed one sitting on the sofa opposite him, still wearing the goddamn *hat*—are all waiting for his next move. He's thinking if she doesn't give him the right answers, he just might . . .

The problem is he wants to hold her.

Touch her.

Kiss her.

The problem is he has missed her desperately.

"All right," he says, "tell me what happened last Wednesday."

"I don't wish to discuss it further," she says.

Then go to hell, he thinks.

"Then why'd you bring it up?" he says.

"Because I wanted to get it out in the open."

"It's not in the open yet. Not until I know what happened."

"What do you think happened?" she asks.

"Just tell me, okay? Was Gloria here, too?"

"No. How'd *Gloria* get into this?"

"How'd *Rickie* get into it, is what *I* want to know."

"Then why'd you mention Gloria? Can't you wait to get at her again?"

"Look, Kate, don't try to shift the goddamn *guilt* here . . ."

"I'm not trying to shift any guilt. I don't *feel* any guilt."

"Then why were you bawling in the car?"

"Not because I was feeling guilt. Don't give me guilt, okay? I had *enough* guilt with Jacqueline. I've been through guilt and *back* again, David, okay? I'm fine now, okay, so don't . . ."

"Why'd you go to bed with him?"

"Go to *bed* with him? Are you dreaming?"

"You said . . ."

"I said . . ."

"You said if I'd been here, you wouldn't have let him."

"That's right."

"Let him *what?*"

"*Kiss* me, for Christ's sake! Anyway, are *you* so celibate up there on the Vineyard?"

"You know I'm married."

"Yes, and you know I'm single."

"What is that supposed to be? A license to kill?"

"Nobody killed anybody, David."

"Oh, I'm sure of that."

"Anyway, we've been through this before."

"I don't think so."

"I *told* you he'd asked me out."

"You also told me you didn't give him your number."

"I didn't. Not then. I went to *see* him right after the letter was delivered here. *That's* when I gave him my number. He was *helping* me, David. Anyway, we're not married, you know."

"So I'm beginning to understand."

"You make love to *her*, you know. So you can't . . . "

"That's something altogether . . . "

"Don't you?"

"Yes, I do."

"So you have no right . . . "

"That's right, I don't. So I guess if there's nothing further to discuss, I'll just . . . "

"We're having another fight, you know. About Rickie again."

"With a *difference* this time."

"What's the difference?"

"Last time, you hadn't kissed him."

"It didn't mean anything."

"I can't believe you just said that."

"What's wrong with it?"

"It's the cliché of all time. If it didn't mean any-thing . . ."

"It didn't."

"Then why the hell did you *do* it?"

"To thank him."

"For what?"

"For helping me. For *being* here! Where the hell were *you*, David?"

"Look, what's the sense of this?"

"None. Not if you want to keep on fighting."

But she seems delighted that they *are* fighting. He

senses the argument adds a dimension of domesticity to
their tottering romance, perhaps provides it with the
promise of longevity as well. After all, if they're having
their *second* fight, and if they survive it, the implication
is there'll be a third fight and a fourth and a fifth ad
infinitum. Just like Mum and Dad, kiddies. Having their
cute little fight, so they can kiss and make up afterward.
Except that he has no intention of kissing her now, not
after she kissed her young toreador last Wednesday night.
And God knows how many times since.

"Have you seen him since?" he asks.

"No."

"Has he called you?"

"Yes."

"I'll bet. Give them a taste of honey . . . "

"Stop it, David! I'm not a whore!"

"Who said you were?"

"I'm *not* a whore!"

He has not even *mentioned* this word, and he wonders
where it comes from now. A whore? Simply because
she kissed . . .

"What kind of kiss?"

"What do you mean?"

"A friendly kiss, a brotherly kiss, a paternal . . . "

"A goddamn *soul* kiss!" she says angrily.

The room goes silent.

"I thought you loved me," he says.

"I do."

"In your fashion."

"No. Completely and utterly."

He looks at her.

He wishes he could believe her, but then why the Wednesday night Latino? Besides, she's correct in maintaining there are no strings on her, mister, she is as free as a bird and entitled to kiss whomever the hell she chooses. The thing is . . . he thought . . . he assumed . . . mistakenly, it now turns out . . . but nonetheless . . .

"Do you plan on seeing him again?" he asks.

"Not if you don't want me to."

"Never mind what *I* want!" he shouts. "What the fuck do *you* want?"

"I want you."

"Then why . . . ?"

"I want only you."

"Then . . ."

"I want you to love me."

"Kate, why don't we just . . . ?"

"Don't say it!"

"I think we should just . . ."

"Don't *say* it!"

She is staring at him now, looking small and vulnerable and tired and pale in the blue jeans and white cotton shirt and adorable gray fedora, hands folded in her lap, green eyes wide and beseeching. He does not want her to cry again, he does not believe he can bear it if she starts crying again. She sits there on the very edge of dissolution, the tears standing in her eyes but not spilling over, and in a barely audible voice, she says, "Don't leave me, David."

He stands watching her.

"Please," she says. "I beg of you."

He takes a step toward her.

"Love me," she says. "Just keep loving me."

He calls Stanley Beckerman at a little before eleven.

"Boy, thank God," Stanley says. "I thought you weren't coming."

"There was a lot of traffic," David says. "The rain."

"The sun was shining in Hatteras," Stanley says.

"The Vineyard, too."

"Any trouble getting away?" Stanley asks, lowering his voice though David suspects he is alone in his office. Or perhaps his little nineteen-year-old bimbo has already joined him. Perhaps she is already sitting on his couch like Sharon Stone, legs wide open, no panties.

"No trouble at all," David says.

Stanley believes that he alone is the one who needs protection and cover in the days ahead, and David doesn't plan to disabuse him of the notion. Therefore, the responsibility of working out a series of fictitious lectures and whatnot has fallen to Stanley as presumed solitary philanderer and liar in this four-day subterfuge. David has given Helen only the scant information Stanley provided in his one invitational call to Menemsha two weeks ago. Now he listens carefully, eager to protect his own ass, but playing to the hilt the role of Stanley's beard.

"I'd like to fax this to you, hmm?" Stanley says. "Do you have a fax in your office?"

"No," David says.

"Well, can I leave it with your doorman then?"

"Where?"

"The office, the apartment, wherever."

"The office would be better," David says.

"I'll drop it off later. Meanwhile, can we go over it on the phone?"

"Yes, let's."

"I really don't want any contradictions here, Dave. This is too important for either of us to be saying something the other one contradicts. What'd you tell Helen?"

"That Syd Markland . . . "

"With a 'y,' right?"

"Yes."

"Syd with a 'y.' "

"Yes, had put together the program and invited all the guests."

"Yes."

"That's the name you gave me . . . "

"Yes, he doesn't exist."

"Good."

"Did you say the APA was sponsoring it?"

"Yes."

"Good. That's what I told Gerry. Did she question any of this? Helen?"

"No."

"Good. What I've tried to do, Dave, is set up a practically morning-to-night round of talks, meetings, panel discussions . . . I'm sorry to do this to you, I know you'll just be killing time here in the city . . . "

"I have work to do, don't worry."

"I truly appreciate this, Dave."

"Don't mention it."

"I just want to seem busy and *involved* all day long, hmm?" Stanley says. "That's why I'd like you to look over the schedule carefully, so in case Helen asks where you're going to be on such and such a night . . . "

"She probably will."

"Why?" Stanley asks at once. "She doesn't *suspect* anything, does she?"

"No, no."

"You didn't *tell* her about me and Cindy, did you?"

"Of course not."

"Then why would she want to know where you're going to be? Gerry never asks where *I'm* going to be."

"It's the sort of information we normally exchange," David says.

"Why? Doesn't she trust you?"

"Yes, she trusts me."

"Well, Gerry certainly trusts *me*. Which is why she never asks."

"Then why'd you work out such a complicated schedule?"

"In *case* she asks. Besides, it isn't complicated."

"You said panels, meetings, lectures . . . "

"Yes, but scattered throughout the day, hmm? It isn't complicated. Besides, I didn't leave her a copy of it. But in *case* she asks what's happening tonight, for example, I can tell her I'll . . . where the hell is it? Here. Dr. Gianfranco Donato from Milan will be giving a talk on Learning and Motor Skill Disorders."

"Okay."

"At the Lotos Club."

"Okay."

"Five East Sixty-sixth."

"Got it."

"You don't have to write this down, I'll be dropping the schedule off. Are you at the office now?"

"No."

"Where are you?"

"In a coffee shop. A phone booth in a coffee shop."

"Shall I bring it to you there?"

"No, just drop it at the office. I'll pick it up later."

"Are you sure? Suppose Helen calls you ten minutes from now?"

"Stanley . . . "

"All right, all right. But you can't blame me for wanting to be careful, Dave. You have nothing to lose here. I realize the favor you're doing, but even so, please try to understand my caution, hmm?"

"I understand completely."

"When will you be at the office?"

"I'm not sure."

"I'm just afraid you'll talk to Helen before you get the schedule, and you won't know where the hell we're supposed to *be* all day."

"I won't be talking to Helen until later tonight."

"How do you know?"

"Because that's what we arranged."

"Doesn't she trust you?"

"Stanley, we've been over that."

"I mean, calling on *schedule*, that sounds like a woman who doesn't trust you." His voice lowers. "Cindy's with me now," he says. "You should see her."

"Stanley, I have to go now."

"No, wait. *Wait!* Let me read this to you. At least, this afternoon's meetings and tonight's schedule. In case you talk to her."

"I won't be . . . "

"In *case*, okay? In fact, you'd better write it down, after all. Have you got a pencil?"

David sighs.

"All the lectures are at the Lotos Club," Stanley says, "but I've put the panels and meetings at different places, in case anyone tries to get to us. By the way, I'd appreciate it if you didn't give all of this to Helen. I mean, if she *asks*, you can tell her where you'll be at any given point in time, but I wouldn't volunteer the *entire* schedule."

"I wouldn't do that, anyway."

"That's in case she talks to Gerry. Though I can't see *why* they'd be talking in the next few days, can you?"

"No, I can't imagine that happening."

"Neither can I. But just in case. Okay, this afternoon at two, there'll be a panel discussion on Mood Disorders, chaired by Dr. Phyllis Cagney who'll also be doing the one on Eating Disorders tomorrow afternoon. She doesn't exist, either. I've got those at a meeting room at the Brewster, that's a small hotel on Eighty-sixth off Fifth, this isn't supposed to be a huge *convention* or anything, you know."

"Yes, I know."

"I've already given you Dr. Donato at the Lotos Club tonight . . . "

"Yes, what time?"

"Eight. I told Gerry you and I would be having dinner together first, hmm?"

"Where?"

"Bertinelli's. On Madison and Sixty-fifth. Actually, I'll be taking Cindy there," he says, his voice lowering again on her name. "I'll put it on my credit card, and say it was you."

"Fine. I'll do the same."

"I didn't tell her where. That's just in case she asks later. I didn't think we have to give them any restaurant names in advance. Unless they ask."

"Okay."

"Will Helen ask?"

"I'm sure she will."

"So where do you want to say?"

"Well, *not* Bertinelli's. If you'll be there with her."

"Cindy."

"Yes."

"You should see her. So where *will* you say?"

"I don't know yet."

"Well, *pick* something, just in case Gerry . . . "

"You can tell Gerry it was Bertinelli's, I'm sure Helen won't be calling her. I'll tell Helen whatever. Wherever I finally end up tonight. I'll let you know in the morning where it was."

"But not too early, hmm?" Stanley says.

He has never before used the call-forwarding feature on the telephone in their apartment, but when he goes there late that morning he first calls the Vineyard to tell Helen he's arrived safely, and then he consults the manual. The manual says:

- **Call Forwarding Works Like This**

TO USE CALL FORWARDING, DIAL: 7 4 #
**LISTEN FOR A DIAL TONE. THEN DIAL THE TELEPHONE
NUMBER YOU WANT YOUR CALLS TO BE FORWARDED
TO. LISTEN FOR TONE(S) FOLLOWED BY RINGING.
CALL FORWARDING WILL BE ESTABLISHED WHEN
SOMEONE ANSWERS. TELL THE PERSON WHO
ANSWERS TO EXPECT YOUR CALLS.**

He reads the instructions yet another time. He keeps the manual open before him as he punches out 7, 4, #. He listens for the dial tone. He dials Kate's number. He hears a beep and then her phone begins ringing.

"Hello?" she says.

"It's me," he says.

He feels like a spy.

Later that afternoon, he records an outgoing message on Kate's answering machine, and then, from a pay phone on the corner, he dials his own number. There is a single ring, and then an almost imperceptible click, and then another ring, and another, and another, and Kate's machine kicks in, *not* with her familiar, "Hi, at the beep, please," but instead with David's recorded voice: "Hello, no one can answer your call just now, but if you leave a message at the beep, someone will get back to you as soon as possible."

Aside from that tiny click—which could, after all, have been the answering machine switching modes— there is no way that anyone on earth can know that the call is not being answered in the Chapman apartment. If Helen calls from the Vineyard, she will have no way of knowing his voice is coming from Kate's machine rather than their own. She will have no way of knowing that her husband is a lying cheat.

"Does it work?" Kate asks.

"Yes," he says.

Smiling, she takes his arm.

After dinner that night, they go back to her apartment.

He feels relatively safe.

Sort of.

"Your boyfriend's on the phone," Mistoffelees says.

Already in costume for the Wednesday matinee performance, he comes bouncing down the hall as part of his warm-up exercises, a virtual jack-in-the-box in black, springing up and down and up again as he gestures toward the wall phone and leaps away out of sight.

The receiver is hanging from its cord.

She picks it up.

"Hi, darling," she says.

"Well," he says approvingly, "that's better."

A chill races up her back.

"Who is this?" she asks at once.

"Who do you think it is, Puss?"

"Go away," she says.

"Don't hang up," he warns.

She stands transfixed, a barrage of thoughts bombarding her mind. This number is unlisted, how did he get it? Does he know someone in the show? Is he an investor? Is he an actor who once worked the Winter Garden? Has he dated one of the . . . ?

"How are you?" he asks pleasantly.

"I'm going to hang up."

"No, I don't think so."

"What do you want from me?"

"Obedience," he says.

"Leave me alone. I'll go to the police again."

"*What* did you say?"

"Nothing."

"Have you gone to the police?"

"No. But I will if you don't . . . "

"*Have* you?"

"I *will* go. I said I *will*."

"No, you said *again*."

"No. But I will."

"I wouldn't."

"I will."

Her voice weakening.

"I'm watching you, Puss."

"Please. You have to stop . . ."

"I'll be there tonight."

"No. Please."

"Watching. Dance nice."

"No. Don't come. Please. I don't want you to come."

"You don't want me to *come*, darling?" he says, and begins laughing.

She hangs up at once. She is shaking violently. She stands by the phone, her open hand pressed to her pounding heart.

"You okay?" someone asks.

She looks up.

Rum Tum Tugger.

"Yes, fine," she says.

But immediately following the performance that afternoon, she limps over to the stage manager and tells him she thinks she sprained her ankle during the "Growltiger" number.

"I want to check with my doctor," she lies. "But meanwhile I wouldn't count on me for tonight."

David has chosen a place he's read about in *New York*, a dim, wood-paneled, clubby sort of dinner-dancing spot in the Village. "The steaks are terrific," wrote the magazine's restaurant critic, "and the eight-piece band plays much *bigger*-band music." The tunes these musicians are playing now are hardly reminiscent of those David grew up with. Starting with when he was twelve or thirteen and first beginning to notice girls, the doo-wop songs he favored seemed to reflect his every adolescent mood and emotional shift, ranging from Brenda Lee's "All Alone Am I" to "So Much in Love" by the Tymes, and all the other hanging-out, malt-shop, jukebox tunes that dominated the radio waves.

When he was fourteen or fifteen the charts exploded with "I Want to Hold Your Hand" and "Can't Buy Me Love" and "I Feel Fine" and "She Loves You," and more Beatles tunes than he could count, all of them an integral part of his tumultuous adolescence—when you were in love, the whole damn *world* was Paul, John, Ringo and George. And then when he was sixteen, the song that possibly best expressed his own inner turmoil, the song that seemed to speak directly to him, was the Rolling Stones' "Satisfaction," of which he, too, couldn't seem to get none nohow. Oddly, when he was seventeen and his taste began to change somewhat, he played Frank

Sinatra's "Strangers in the Night" day and night, longing for that stranger in the night who would fill his arms one day. Or night. Or anytime, for that matter.

When he got out of high school and decided early on in college that he wanted to be a doctor, his musical taste took a more serious turn. "Ode to Billie Joe" was perhaps his favorite song that year, all haunting and solemn with ominous cello passages and dark hints of abortion or infanticide or both. When he turned nineteen, pop music seemed to go out of his life completely. The future was looming. "Mrs. Robinson" perhaps best exemplified for him the turn from a silly childish past to a mature responsible future. He was, after all, twenty-six and already a doctor when he first met young Helen Barrister on the bank of the Charles.

Tonight, much older but perhaps no wiser, he holds in his arms a radiant twenty-seven-year-old who floats with him to the strains of "Moonlight Serenade" and "You Made Me Love You," rendered as Glenn Miller and Harry James must have done them back in the dim, dark forties before either he or Kate was born. He knows how foolhardy it was for a clumsy oaf like himself to have asked a dancer, a professional *dancer*, to go dancing with him, but here they are and she makes him feel like Fred Astaire in *Top Hat*, makes him feel like Gene Kelly in *Singin' in the Rain*, makes him feel light-footed and light-hearted and light-headed as he glides her airily about the floor to these Golden Oldies neither he nor she recalls. To David, a Golden Oldie is Elvis Presley's "Surrender." To Kate, a Golden Oldie is Styx's "Too Much Time on My Hands."

Most of the patrons here have come to dance. Many of the women are wearing ballroom gowns, although this is a mere Wednesday night. One dark-haired woman in a long red gown is even wearing a tiara. The couples drift about the floor like so many versions of Velez and Yolanda, showing off their ballroom training in whirls and dips and fancy turns—but their brilliance kneels to Kate's luster. *You have witchcraft in your lips, Kate*, he thinks out of nowhere, and wonders again about the wisdom of bringing her here to a place where he can be seen dancing with her in public.

She is wearing black tonight.

He is beginning to think that *any* color is her color, but she wears black superbly, her fingernails painted not to match the sleeveless, V-necked mini she is wearing, thank God, but echoing instead the carnivorous red lipstick on her mouth and the dangling red earrings on her ears. She has left a sheer, black, long-sleeved jacket over the back of her chair, and she steps out now in just the short flirty dress, piped in white at the hem and neck, flaring out dramatically over long legs sheathed in black. Her hair is swept up and away from her face, ribboned with the same piped fabric entwined around a fake white carnation tilted recklessly onto her elegant brow. Black high-heeled strapped sandals designed for a runway rather than a dance floor add several inches to her already spectacular height.

She is leading him, he realizes.

But perhaps she's been leading him from the start.

He suddenly remembers her seduction of poor hapless Charlie. And wonders why she did that. And wonders again why she soul-kissed that kid from the bicycle shop. But the frown that creases his forehead is only momentary. He is lost in the scent of her perfume, lost in the dazzle of her flying feet, lost in the silken feel of her in the gossamer gown.

But perhaps, too, he was lost from the very start.

He has developed the philanderer's habit of checking out a room the moment he enters it, reconnoitering it further as the evening progresses, wanting to be prepared for any unexpected contingency that will force him to explain, plausibly he hopes, what he is doing here with this young and beautiful dancer. As they come off the floor now . . .

The bandleader has announced something called "Elk's Parade" which turns out to be a jumpy tune David has never heard in his life, and something neither he nor Kate would care to dance to, though he's sure she can dance to *anything* and make it look spectacular . . .

. . . as they come off the floor, he scans the room again, checking out the diners, checking out the men and women moving off the floor or onto it, even searching the faces of the waiters and busboys to make sure there are no surprises lurking in the shadows here. He has thought of how he might introduce Kate if he ran into anyone he knows, but he has not come up with anything that would sound even remotely plausible. This is a psychiatrist from Seattle, we're attending the same seminar. Nice try, David. This is a student of mine at Mount Sinai, I'm instructing her in Dance Therapy as a course of treatment for premenstrual dysphoric disorder. Oh yes, completely believable, David. Hi, this is my daughter's first-grade teacher, I'm filling her in on Annie's feats and foibles. Sure, David. Nudge in the ribs, accompanied by sly conspiratorial wink. The vast Brotherhood of Philanderers. Or, as it is known in the profession, the Order of Priapic Disorder Victims. Just kidding, folks. But he finds none of this funny.

The steaks *are* good.

He doesn't very often eat red meat because he is a physician and well aware of the fact that his father suffered a serious heart attack when he was only fifty-seven, eleven years from now on David's personal calendar. Moreover, until six years ago, he was smoking two packs of cigarettes a day—Marlboros, no less—and he knows his former habit increases his relatively high genetic risk. No need, therefore, to increase the old cholesterol intake, hmm? No need either, he supposes, to take this risk tonight, perhaps far more dangerous to his health than any tiny little cholesters, as he thinks of them, swimming around and clogging his arteries.

They are on coffee and dessert when Kate asks whether it might be possible for them to get out of the city for the next two nights, maybe find a little country inn . . .

"Well, I . . . "

" . . . someplace, figure out something . . . "

"I'd have to talk to Stanley first," he says. "Make sure he can justify . . . "

"You can say one of the lecturers lives out of town."

"That's a possibility."

"And can't travel because he broke his leg or something."

"Like you."

259

"God forbid. All I told him was that I sprained my ankle. Which leaves me free, you see. That's why I thought . . . "

"I guess there's nothing *really* tying us to the city, is there?"

"Not until my ankle heals."

"Where'd you have in mind?"

"Not Massachusetts. Too close to her."

"Connecticut then?"

"Too close to *her.*"

He looks at her, puzzled.

"I was thinking maybe New Hope," she says. "Have you ever been to New Hope?"

"Once. Long ago."

"With her?"

"With Helen, yes."

But why does she think *Connecticut* is close to Martha's Vineyard? Or has he misunderstood her?

"I'll talk to Stanley," he says. "See what he thinks."

"Don't leave the thinking to Stanley. Stanley sounds like a jackass."

"He is."

"Then tell him what *you'd* like to do . . . "

"Well, I can't . . . "

"Not about *me*, of course. Just say you're finding it very dreary, hanging around all alone in the city, and you'd like to get out of town, and you've figured out a way to make it sound plausible."

"Yes, what's the way?"

"I don't know. You're the married one. I don't have to make excuses."

"You've already made one to your stage manager."

"Yes, but not because I wanted to get out of town."

The band is playing something he recognizes, but it's something *everyone* recognizes, Artie Shaw's arrangement of "Stardust." The dance floor is suddenly filled again with stiletto-thin men and women, gliding, floating, drifting to the sound of the soaring clarinet. He tells her about the time he was in Liberty Music on Madison Avenue and Artie Shaw was in there buying records. This was around Christmastime, oh, ten, twelve years ago . . .

"I was fifteen," she says.

"Well, yes, I suppose you were. Shaw was buying dozens of albums as gifts. He told the clerk he had a charge at the store, and the clerk said, 'Yes, sir, may I have your name, please?' And Shaw said, 'Artie Shaw,' and the clerk said 'Is that S-H-O-R-E, sir?' "

"You're kidding."

"I'm serious. A *music* store."

"Didn't know Artie Shaw."

"Incredible."

"*Everybody* knows Artie Shaw."

"*Sic transit gloria mundi,*" David says.

"*Our* Gloria?" Kate asks, and they both laugh.

"Why *did* you tell him you sprained your ankle? I thought it was because . . . "

"He called me."

"Who? Your stage manager?"

"No, Artie Shaw."

"Really, who . . . ?"

"The nut who sent me the flowers and . . . "

"Called . . . ?"

" . . . the letters. Yes."

"Where?"

"Backstage."

"At the *theater?*"

"Yes."

"Aren't those numbers unlisted?"

"Yes."

"Then how . . . ?"

"I don't know. David, I'm very frightened. That's why I want to leave the city. That's the *real* reason."

"Kate," he says, "you have to go to the police again."

"No, I can't. He warned me not to."

"Then *call* Clancy. Ask him to come see you. I'm sure he'd be willing to . . . "

"Sure, in New York? Anyway, how *can* I call him?"

"Why not?"

"He'd find out."

"How can he possibly . . . ?"

"He knows everything I *do!*"

"How can he hear a phone call you make from your own . . . ?"

"How do I know? How'd he get the number at the theater?"

"Are you sure it was him?"

"Of course. Who do you *think* it was?"

"Maybe someone you know. Maybe someone playing a . . . "

"I don't have friends who kid around that way. Besides he called me Puss, of *course* it was him."

"You didn't give *Rickie* either of those numbers, did you?"

"No."

"Who else has them?"

"Everybody in the show."

"I mean, who'd *you* give them to?"

"My agent, of course. And my mother. A few friends . . ."

"How about your sister?"

"My sister doesn't make phone calls."

"What do you mean?"

"My sister is in Whiting."

"Whiting?"

"The Whiting Forensic Institute. In Middletown, Connecticut."

The band is playing "Gently, Sweetly." A male vocalist croons into the microphone. A mirrored globe rotates over the dance floor. Spotlights strike its myriad facets and beam splinters of reflected light to every corner of the room. Across the table, Kate's face seems shattered with light.

"It's a maximum security hospital," she says.

"Gently . . ."

"For the criminally insane."

"Sweetly . . ."

"Burning down the house was just the start."

"More and more . . ."

"Completely . . ."

"She tried to kill my father."

"Take me . . ."

"Make me . . ."

"Yours."

The band's saxophone section—two altos and two tenors—modulates from the singer's key to a somewhat higher one that lends a soaring semblance to the next chorus.

David is staring at her now.

"Yes," she says, and nods in dismissal.

The song ends.

They order coffee.

They hold hands across the table.

They dance some more.

She doesn't wish to discuss her sister further at this present time, thank you.

He respects her wishes.

Frankly, he doesn't want to open *that* can of worms, anyway.

When she excuses herself to go to the ladies' room, he tells her he'll meet her near the coat check at the front door, and then pays the check and goes to the men's room.

Dr. Chris Fielding is pissing in the urinal alongside his.

"David!" he says, cock in hand, "how *are* you?"

"Fine, fine, Chris, and you?" David says, unzipping his fly, thinking Jesus, did he spot us on the dance floor, does he know I'm here with, Jesus, Helen *knows* him, Helen knows his *wife*, Jesus *Christ!*

Side by side, they urinate.

"How do you like this place?" Chris asks.

"Great, great."

"What does Helen think?"

Helen?

Helen thinks I'm listening to Dr. Gianfranco Donato giving a talk on Learning and Motor Skill Disorders at the Lotos Club, is what *Helen* thinks, he thinks, and immediately says, "I'm here alone. Helen's on the Vineyard."

"Oh?" Chris says.

"I love listening to these old songs," David says. "It's a great band. Sounds much bigger than it is," he says, quoting *New York* magazine. "And the steaks are terrific."

"So they are, so they are," Chris says, a trifle in his cups, giving his cock a little shake with each repetitive observation.

But Kate is waiting at the coat check.

No one *needs* coats in this sweltering August, but she is waiting there nonetheless, looking eminently gorgeous in her little black Fuck Me dress and strapped high-heeled Fuck Me shoes and sheer black Fuck Me jacket. And as fate would have it, as fate always fucking *does*, mousy Melanie Fielding is *also* waiting at the coat check as Chris Fielding—Question: What do you call the guy who ranked last in his class in medical school? Answer: Doctor—Dr. Chris Fielding, then, staggers his way toward his wife with David close behind him, trying to catch Kate's eye, but she seems thoroughly absorbed in reading the framed reviews of the place hanging on the entrance wall, her back to him, "David, *hello*, what are *you* doing here?"

This from Melanie Fielding, who spots him now and

quickly looks past him to see where Helen might be. For this is a place where couples come to *dance*, no? What then . . . ?

Kate has turned.

Please, he thinks. Be smart.

You're smart.

Be smart.

"Hi, Melanie," he says, and takes her hand, and leans into her, and kisses the air beside her cheek, and says, "I *love* this big-band stuff, Helen's on the Vineyard . . . "

"She's on the Vineyard," Chris says blearily.

" . . . and the steaks are terrific."

"Oh, what a shame," Melanie says.

Kate is walking out the door.

"Give her my love, won't you?" Melanie says.

"I'll be talking to her in . . . "

David looks at his watch.

" . . . a half hour."

"Give her my love."

"I will."

"Mine, too," Chris says.

There is only one message on her answering machine when they get back to her apartment at eleven that Wednesday night. It is from Rickie Diaz.

"Hi, Kate," he says, "who's that answering your machine?"

"None of your business," she says.

"I was hoping I could see you this Friday night. I

have tickets for the Mets game, and I thought you might like to go with me."

"Nope," Kate says.

"I don't know if you like baseball or not . . . "

"I hate baseball."

" . . . but let me know either way, okay? You have the number, give me a call. Thanks."

"Friday night, I'll be down in New Hope," Kate says, and tosses the gossamer jacket over the back of a chair.

"I have to call Helen," David says.

"Sure," she answers. "I'll go hide in the bathroom."

She blows a kiss at him, and goes into the bathroom, closing the door behind her. As he dials the number in Menemsha, he hears the water running. He is on the phone with Helen for perhaps five minutes, telling her he went to this place in the Village, highly recommended by *New York* magazine, where he had a steak and, oh, guess what, he ran into Chris and Melanie Fielding, they both send their love. Annie gets on the phone, wanting to know when he'll be coming home—both girls already think of the Menemsha cottage as home—and he tells them he'll be up on Saturday morning, and she tells him she caught a frog and she has him in a jar and his name is Kermit. In the background, David hears Jenny say, "How original." He speaks to her for a few minutes, and then Helen gets back on the line and they talk for a few minutes more before they say goodnight.

A narrow line of light is showing under the bathroom door.

The water is still running.

"Kate?" he calls softly.

The air conditioner is clattering noisily.

"Kate?"

He walks to the bathroom door and knocks gently.

"Yes?"

"Are you all right?"

"Of course. Come in."

The bathroom is full of steam. She is lying in the tub under a mountain of bubbles. Her hair is wrapped in a white towel, a single red tendril curling on her forehead like a tiny wet serpent. Her arm comes out of the water. She turns off the faucet, and then pats the rim of the tub. "Come sit," she says.

Soapsuds cling to her fingers.

There is an odd little smile on her face.

He sits on the edge of the tub.

She slides deeper under the suds, closes her eyes, rests the back of her head on the white porcelain rim. "Do you remember the movie *1984?*" she asks.

"Yes?"

"Where the thing he fears most, the hero, I forget his name . . ."

"Smith."

"Yes, he fears rats more than anything in the world. And what they do to him, what Richard *Burton* does to him, is put this cage over his face where there's a rat in one end of it, but the rat can't get at his face because there's a sort of partition that keeps him away. What Burton is trying to do is get John Hurt . . . that's who played the hero . . . to betray his girlfriend, her name is Julia. So he starts opening this little partition that separates

Hurt's face from the rat, this little sort of gate that pulls up, or to the side, I forget which, and as it's starting to open Hurt yells, 'Do it to Julia!' I was thinking of that before you knocked on the door," she says.

"Why?"

"I don't know. Richard Burton opening the gate. I just happened to think of it."

"Who's Julia?" he asks.

"The girl in the movie."

"Yes, but you mentioned her once before."

"I don't know anyone named Julia."

"But don't you remember saying . . . ?"

"Even when I read the *book*, I found that scene frightening."

"When was that?"

"The summer I worked at the Playhouse."

"The summer you were thirteen?"

"Yes. But, listen, David, if you're going to play shrink, I've been over this a hundred times already, really. I don't enjoy . . . "

"Over what?"

"What happened. I was in analysis for six *years*, you know. Jacqueline and I . . . "

"What do you mean, what happened?"

"What *happened*."

"At the theater? With Charlie?"

"No. I don't want to talk about this."

"What happened, Kate?"

"I've talked about it enough. I'm sick of talking about it. I'm sick of my goddamn sister and her goddamn prob—"

"Did it have something to do with your sister?"

"No."

"You told me she set the house on fire . . . "

"That was three years later. I *also* told you I don't want to *talk* about it!"

"Who's Julia?"

"Nobody."

"Don't you remember saying something about my doing it to *Julia* . . . "

"No."

" . . . on the Vineyard . . . "

"No."

" . . . when I should have been doing it to *you?*"

"I never said anything like that."

"Yesterday morning. In the car."

"I know your wife's name is Helen. Anyway, let's not talk about her, either. And you'd better *not* be doing it to her."

"Why'd she try to kill your father?"

"Who, Helen?"

"Kate, you know who I'm . . . "

"Who, Julia?"

"Your *sister.* Who's in a maximum security hospital for the criminally . . . "

"Go ask *her*, you're so interested."

The room goes silent. She nods in curt dismissal. The mirror over the sink is dripping with mist. Everything looks slippery and wet.

"Put your hand in the water," she says.

The same little smile reappears on her face.

"No sharks in here," she says playfully.

Tilts her head to one side. Towel wrapped around it like a turban.

"Give me your hand, okay?" she says.

Smiling.

"Don't you want to?"

Lifting one eyebrow.

"Say."

Her voice turning suddenly harsh.

"*Do* it!"

He plunges his hand into the foam, wetting his sleeve to the elbow.

"Yes," she says.

And finds her.

"Yes."

"I want to get away for a few days," he hears himself telling Stanley. "Tonight and tomorrow night. Go down to New Hope maybe. Or someplace else in Pennsylvania. I'll fly back to the Vineyard on Saturday, from wherever I happen to be."

"Why?"

Careful, he thinks.

"I'm getting cabin fever," he says.

"But I'm not, Davey."

Davey? he thinks. When did I get to be Davey? Just when I was getting used to being Dave.

Stanley has taken the subway downtown to Fifty-ninth and Lex, and has met David outside Bloomingdale's, as arranged. Their Thursday morning stroll takes place on East Fifty-seventh Street as the two men saunter westward toward Victoria's Secret, where Stanley hopes to purchase lingerie suitable for his nineteen-year-old delight.

"I don't *want* to leave the city," he says. "I even hate having to go out for *food*. So why would I choose to go to *New* Hope, of all places? I'm perfectly happy doing just what I'm doing. Life is sweet, Davey, and time is short."

He is dressed for his lingerie-shopping expedition in clothes that look as if he's slept in them. Perhaps he has. Aside from Tuesday night's visit to Bertinelli's, he and Cindy have not budged from his office. His beard has grown several inches since the last time David saw him. He looks like a homeless person who hasn't shaved in a month. A derelict who sleeps on the sidewalk in a cardboard box or else on a black leather couch in some philandering psychiatrist's office. He can't wait to get back to his little Cindy. He wants to buy her some crotchless panties and a garter belt . . . .

"I don't think they sell crotchless panties," David says.

"Oh, of course they do."

"Victoria's Secret, I mean."

"Then I'll find them someplace else. You ought to buy some panties for Helen today," he suggests. "I certainly plan to buy some for Gerry."

"Stanley, let's get back to this, okay?"

"Davey, I do not want to leave the city."

"I do."

"Why are you so eager to get out of town?"

Their eyes meet.

He knows, David thinks.

"I'm bored," he says.

"So go eat your chocolates."

David doesn't get the reference. Nor does Stanley bother to explain it. They are approaching Victoria's Secret now. Stanley looks in the window. He doesn't see any crotchless panties, and he confesses that he's somewhat embarrassed to go inside and ask for them. Will *David* ask the salesclerk for a pair of crotchless panties, size five?

"They don't carry crotchless panties," David says.

"Would it hurt to ask?"

"I'll ask, but it'll be a waste of time."

"So will any story we give our wives about getting out of town."

David looks at him.

"I've been at this a long time, hmm?" Stanley says with his crooked little shark grin buried in his beard. "Not with a patient, that's a first. And never with a nineteen-year-old, *that's* a first, too. But a long time, Davey. A long long time. And I can tell you what a woman will buy and what a woman will not buy. And no woman's going to believe that thirty psychiatrists attending a conference in New York are going to shlepp all the way down to New Hope . . ."

"It doesn't have to be New Hope."

"*Wherever* the hell. It won't wash, Davey. They won't buy it. And if we try to *sell* it, we'd be jeopardizing everything we have going for us. So the answer is no."

"Stanley . . ."

"No," he says again.

And of course he's right.

And of course he knows.

273

★ ★ ★

Luis the doorman seems pleased to see him, and asks how Mrs. Chapman and the "leetle gorls" are enjoying the seashore. David tells him they're fine, thanks, just fine, and then goes to the lobby mailbox to see if anything has collected there. He is here at the building only to establish a pattern in the unlikely event Helen and Luis ever get into a conversation about his comings and goings. He goes upstairs as part of the deception. Ten minutes later, he is downstairs again and walking uptown to his office.

Gualterio, the doorman there, seems equally happy to see him and asks if he is already back at work again. David tells him he's here for some lectures and won't begin seeing patients again till the fifth of September, the day after Labor Day. Gualterio tells him to enjoy the rest of the summer, and then rushes to the curb when a taxi pulls up.

Again David is here only to establish a pattern; all is pattern, all is deceit. He checks for mail, goes into his office, sits behind his desk. Dust motes restlessly climb the shaft of sunshine slanting in through the blinds. On impulse, he looks through his Wheeldex for Jacqueline Hicks's office number, and then debates calling her.

But why would he want to?

And what will he say if he reaches her?

Hi, I'm having an affair with a former patient of yours, and I was wondering if you might be able to give me any insights into her behavior?

Absurd.

He dials the number, anyway.

PRIVILEGED CONVERSATION

An answering machine tells him Dr. Hicks is away for the summer.

Tonight, Kate is wearing an outfit designed to complement the setting she herself has chosen. For this is moonlight and roses, this is candlelight and wine, this is soft violins and soft-spoken waiters, this is cautious footfalls and discreet silences. To echo this faintly Mozartian locale, or perhaps to startle it into modernity, she has chosen to wear a very short double-layered silk organza dress, its bottom layer an apricot color, its top layer a gossamer tangerine—"They had it in blue and green," she says, "but Fee the Fair says blue and green should *never* be seen." She looks like a frothy double-flavored cotton-candy confection. Her long legs are bare, her feet slippered in high-heeled tangerine-colored patent-leather slides. A misty blue eye makeup causes her green eyes to snap and snarl.

He remembers the joke Stanley fumbled so badly this morning, and he tells it to Kate as they wait for their dinners to arrive. They are sipping champagne. He remembers the bottle of champagne in the limo. He remembers everything about her. It is almost as if she has been a part of his life forever.

It seems this little boy is sitting in his first-grade class with his hand in his lap when his teacher spots him. "What are you doing there?" she asks, and he tells her he's playing with his balls. "Why are you doing that?" she asks, and he tells her he's lonely. "Oh, you're *lonely*, are you?" she says, and she drags him down the hall to the principal's office, and whispers in his ear, and leaves the two of them alone. It isn't long before the kid's hand is in his lap again . . .

"I love it," Kate says.

. . . and the principal asks what he's doing there and he says he's playing with his balls and the principal asks why and the kid says because he's lonely and the principal sends for the kid's parents and they decide to remand the kid to a psychiatrist.

"Enter the shrink," Kate says.

"So they take the kid to a psychiatrist," David says, "and the two of them sit staring at each other for a little while until the kid's hand at last drops into his lap again, and the psychiatrist asks, 'Vot are you zoing dere?' Well, the kid tells him he's playing with his balls, and the psychiatrist asks, 'Vhy are you zoing dat?' And the kid tells him it's because he's lonely, and the psychiatrist says, 'Oh, come now, *lonely*. Vot are you, fife, zix years oldt? How can you bossibly be . . . ?' and the telephone rings on his desk. He picks it up, listens, says, 'Ja, hold on vun minute, please,' and excuses himself to go take the call in the other room. When he comes back to his office, he sits behind his desk and says, 'Zo tell me, how can a poy, fife, zix years . . . ' and stops dead and looks at his desk and says, 'Vhen I left zis office, dere vass a two-pound pox of chocolates on z'desk. Now z'chocolates are all gone. Zid *you* eat z'chocolates?' The kid tells him Yes, he ate the chocolates. 'Vhy zid you do dat?' the psychiatrist asks. 'I vass gone only fife minutes, you ate a whole two-pound pox of chocolates? *Vhy?*' The kid says, 'Because I was lonely.' And the psychiatrist says, 'Zo vhy didn't you play vid your palls?' "

Kate bursts out laughing.

"Stanley got it all wrong, though," David says. "He told me to go eat my chocolates. Anyway, he said no."

Her laughter trails.

She nods.

"So let's hope nothing happens," she says.

There are two messages on her machine.

The first is from Rickie Diaz.

"Hi, this is Rickie again," he says. "I'm wondering if you got my message about the Mets game. I don't want to rush you or anything, but I really would like to know if you think you can make it. Can you give me a call when you get a chance? The game is this Friday night . . . well, tomorrow night, in fact, I guess, so try to get back to me, okay? Thanks a lot, Kate. Talk to you soon. I hope."

Kate shrugs.

The second message is from Helen.

"David, where *are* you?" she says. "Can you please call me when you get in? There's something I forgot to mention when we spoke earlier. Love you. Bye."

David looks at his watch.

"I'd better call her," he says.

"Sure," Kate says, and goes across the room to sit on the sofa. She watches him as he dials.

"Hi, sweetie," he says.

"Hi, how'd the lecture go?"

"It was very good, in fact."

"Where'd you eat?"

"I grabbed a sandwich before it started."

"With Stanley?"

"No, alone."

"He's not so bad, is he?"

"He's awful."

Helen laughs.

On the sofa across the room, Kate watches and listens.

"Do you think you'll have time to do something for me tomorrow?" Helen asks. "Before you come up?"

"Well, I won't be coming up till Saturday, you know."

"Yes, I know."

"Saturday morning. I'll be on the . . . "

"I know. I didn't mean you'd be coming *up* tomorrow, I meant can you *do* something for me tomorrow."

"Sure, what is it, hon?"

Hon, he thinks. Sweetie, he thinks. Kate is hearing all this, he thinks. Cat-eyed, she watches him, her face expressionless.

"Do you know that little shop on Madison and I think it's Sixty-second or -third? I don't remember the name, but they sell all kinds of kooky handcrafted jewelry and things?"

"I think so, yes."

"Do you remember it? We bought Aunt Lily's Christmas gift there last year. The quilted cat."

"Is that the name?"

"No, that's what we bought her."

"Oh. Yes, I think I remember it."

"I don't know the name."

"Neither do I. But I'll find it. What did you want?"

"Can you see if they've got something really beautiful but not too expensive that would make a nice

birthday gift for Danielle? Harry's throwing a surprise
party for her on Saturday night, and I haven't been
able to find anything really nice up here. You know
how she dresses . . . "

"Yes."

"Very chic, very French. I thought something in that
oxidized metal, whatever it's called, eulithium, eulirium,
delirium . . . "

David laughs.

" . . . whatever, some nice dangling earrings maybe,
but not too expensive."

"How much is too expensive?"

"Anything over a hundred dollars."

"That sounds like a lot."

"Well, you can't get anything nice for *less* than a
hundred, but don't spend more than that."

"I'll go there first thing."

"I don't think they open till ten."

"I'll take care of it."

"When will you call again?"

"Tomorrow sometime? After the morning panel?"

"I miss you."

"I miss you, too."

"I love you, David."

"I love you, too."

"Good night, honey."

"Good night."

He puts the receiver down gently.

"You miss her so much, why don't you just go *up*
there?" Kate asks at once.

"Honey," he says, "I . . . "

"No, don't 'honey' *me*," she says. "*She's* your honey, don't give *me* any of that honey shit. You want her so much, just get out of here. Go do it to *her*, you want her so much."

And suddenly she's in tears.

He goes to the sofa and tries to take her in his arms, but she shrugs him away, telling him *she's* the one in danger here, *she's* the one getting phone calls at the theater from a lunatic, but instead *Helen's* the one who gets all his attention, *Helen* can feel free to call here at any hour of the day or night . . .

"Honey, the call was *forwa*—"

"I *told* you not to call me that. Don't you ever call me honey again, do you hear me? Call *her* honey if you want to call someone honey. But don't call *me* honey, not anymore, do you hear me?"

She is sitting in the center of the sofa in her misty little delicate apricot and tangerine dress. Tears are rolling down her face, hands clenched in her lap. He wonders why it has come to this again, Kate in tears. Where has his exciting young *mistress* gone? Who is this troubled *woman* in her place?

"Kate," he says, "I love you."

"Sure."

"You know that, Kate."

But he is wondering.

"Then why don't you *do* something?" she asks.

"What would you like me . . . ?"

"You can go shopping for *her* . . . "

"Kate, I'll do anything you . . . "

"But you can't do one simple fucking thing for *me*."

"What do you want me to do?"

"Take the letters to Clancy. I want to make sure they're safe in his hands. Tell him to come here. Tell him I want to press charges against this person who's ruining my life. I want this to *stop*, do you understand me?"

"Yes. But in all honesty, Kate, I think it would be more effective . . . "

"Is something *wrong* with you? I'm being *watched*, can't you understand that? Are you afraid to go, is that it?"

"I'm thinking of you, Kate. I'm trying to find the best way . . . "

"Are you afraid he'll find out you're fucking me?"

"Of course not!"

But he knows she's right.

"Are you afraid he'll tell Mama?"

"You know that's not . . . "

But it is.

"Tell *Helen* up there on the Vineyard? Give her a call and say, 'Hey, guess what, Mrs. Chapman, your husband's diddling a dancer in *Cats*, did you know that?' "

"I'm not afraid of anything like . . . "

But he is.

"Then why won't you take the letters to him?"

"I will. If that's what you want. That's . . . "

"I mean, I *realize* it'll be *difficult* for you, but at least nobody's about to *kill* you, is he?"

"Nobody's about to kill you, either."

"No? Then why is he hounding me?"

David sighs heavily. He knows her fear is appropriate;

there is, after all, a very real person out there threatening her. But her behavior of the moment seems somewhat irrational, no? A bit peculiar? A tad bizarre? A trifle off the fucking wall, vouldn't you zay, Doktor? He *is* an analyst, after all, and not a pig farmer, and he knows a fit of hysterics when it erupts in his presence. But he's not *her* analyst, is he? And besides, maybe he's wrong. After six years with Jackie—admittedly not the best in the business, but certainly capable enough—Kate may have entirely put to rest whatever was haunting her. Either way, it's not *his* problem, is it?

He wonders again where his sweet young mistress has gone. Will this ranting young woman on the couch—how appropriate that she's on a couch, he thinks—next confess that she has a weeping boil on her ass? Quite frankly, he doesn't want to hear about it. Until ten minutes ago, she was his lover. When did she get to be his patient? Tell it to Julia, he thinks.

Maybe he *is* a pig farmer, after all.

Maybe all he ever wanted from her was exactly what she'd provided all along. Maybe all he wanted was an eternal roll in the hay with a flaky twenty-seven-year-old dancer. Maybe the only difference between him and Stanley Beckerman, after all, was the eight-year age gap between their respective little roundheel darlings. Maybe if he grew an unsightly beard and dressed in clothes he found in a Dumpster, he'd be Stanley Beckerman exactly.

No, he is not Stanley Beckerman.

Nor was meant to be.

"Kate," he says patiently, soothingly, "the man is a classic . . . "

"Please don't give me any shrink bullshit, okay?" she says. "All I know is you won't take the letters to Clancy . . ."

"I just told you I would."

"When?"

"Tomorrow morning."

"Go now."

"Now? It's almost midnight."

"So? Don't cops work past midnight?"

"I'm sure it can wait till tomorrow morning."

"Sure. Let him come here tonight and kill *both* of us . . ."

"Nobody's coming here to . . ."

" . . . in our own fucking *bed!*"

"Kate, try to calm down, okay?"

"He knows where I live, he'll figure out a way to get in here. Even if we double-lock the door . . ."

"Kate, there's no way he can . . ."

"He knows how to *do* things!"

"You're not making sense."

"Is *he* making sense?"

"*He's* a fucking lunatic!"

"Exactly! Suppose he comes here tonight? Suppose . . . ?"

"I'm here tonight," he says simply.

She looks at him.

She nods.

"Then promise me you'll go first thing tomorrow."

"I promise you."

"Because I want this to end."

"I'll go tomorrow."

"It has to end, David."

"I know," he says.

It already has, he thinks.

Here in this office where he has helped so many other troubled people in the past, he sits behind his desk on Friday morning, and tries to determine how best he can help this troubled person who has been a part of his life for the past month and more. He has promised her he will go to the police, but he realizes the danger inherent in such an act. How can he explain that an encounter presumably ended after July's lineup has apparently blossomed by August into a relationship close enough for him to be running this errand for her?

Kate. From the park. The victim, remember?

He can visualize Clancy's cold blue eyes frisking him.

Just how well do you know this young girl, Dr. Chapman?

Well . . . ah . . . casually. This is a . . . ah . . . casual relationship.

The cold blue eyes mugging him.

And yet, it had to be done. David suspects that the man harassing Kate is as harmless as most of the obsessive stalkers out there, but the possibility that he might become truly dangerous makes it imperative that the police go to see her at once. The trick is to alert them without . . .

Are you afraid he'll find out you're fucking me?

Yes, he thinks.

The trick, then, is ending this honorably and decently without creating any problems for himself.

And, yes, of course, without causing unnecessary hurt

and additional damage to a person obviously traumatized sometime long ago. And still struggling—despite Jacqueline Hicks's treatment—to understand whatever the hell happened to her back then.

He looks up the number of the precinct.

He hesitates a moment, his hand resting on the receiver. Then he picks up the receiver and dials the number, and tells the sergeant who answers the phone that he would like to talk to Detective Clancy, please.

"Clancy's on vacation," the sergeant says.

"Can you tell me when he'll be back?"

"Monday morning, eight o'clock. One of the other detectives help you?"

He hesitates for merely the briefest tick of time.

"Thanks, I'll try him later," he says, and hangs up.

Reprieve, he thinks.

Oddly, his heart is beating very rapidly.

He sits quite motionless behind his desk.

He picks up the receiver again, dials another number.

"Hello?" Stanley says.

His voice sounds groggy but wary.

"Stanley, would you happen to know where Jacqueline Hicks goes on vacation?"

"Who is this?"

"David Chapman."

"What?"

"I need Jacqueline's . . . "

"Do you know what time it is, Davey?"

"Yes, it's ten o'clock."

"Yes, exactly. We're still asleep, Davey."

"This is urgent," David says.

Urgent? he thinks.

Stanley sighs in exasperation. In the background, David hears a very young voice asking, "Who is it, Stan?"

"A colleague," Stanley answers gruffly. "Just a second," he says into the phone. David hears muted voices in the background, and then what sounds like drawers opening and slamming shut. He visualizes young Cindy on the black leather couch, watching her analyst stamping around his office naked. He wonders how Stanley is explaining to his wife the peculiar habit he has developed of sleeping at the office these days. He guesses Stanley has never heard of call forwarding. Or perhaps young Cindy Harris doesn't have her own apartment. Perhaps she still lives with her parents.

"This is two years old," Stanley says into the phone.

Like your little playmate, David thinks.

"Jackie used to go to East Hampton. I don't know if she still does."

"Could I have the number, please?"

Stanley reads it off to him. David writes it down on the phone pad and then draws a picture of the sun shining over it.

"Thank you, Stanley," he says. "I really apprec—"

"I'll see you at the *lecture* tonight," Stanley says, hitting the word so hard that anyone listening would immediately know there *is* no lecture. "And, Davey . . . don't call me at the crack of dawn anymore, hmm?" he says, and hangs up.

David looks at the East Hampton number with the sun shining benevolently above it.

What am I doing? he wonders.

He dials the number.

A man's voice on the answering machine says, "No one is here to take your call just now. Please leave your name and number when you hear the tone. Thank you."

David wonders if everyone in the world has Call Forwarding.

He does not leave a message.

The office seems inordinately silent. For a moment, he wishes for the voices of Arthur K, Susan M, Alex J, resonating against the tin ceiling of the room. He wishes for all the great motion pictures of the past.

He shakes the letters out of Clancy's manila evidence envelope.

They sit on his desk in slanting sunlight, the thick cream-colored envelopes, the lurid purple ink. He must deliver these letters. He has promised to deliver these letters. But Clancy is away and won't be back till Monday.

He takes a piece of stationery from the top drawer of his desk. His name and office address are across the top of it. He rolls the sheet of paper into his typewriter and begins typing:

Dear Detective Clancy:

You will remember me from the lineup you arranged for Miss Kathryn Duggan back in July. She's the young lady whose bike was stolen in Central Park. She was sufficiently troubled and frightened by the enclosed letters to contact me quite unexpectedly and ask that I deliver them to you. She is afraid of going to the police herself because she knows she is being watched. She is further fearful that somehow her telephone conversations will be overheard.

Do you think you could possibly visit her in person at the home address on the last two letters? She tells me she is home most mornings and would be most appreciative of your time. I feel certain you will recognize the seriousness of the situation and contact her as soon as you can.

Sincerely,

Dr. David Chapman

He rereads the letter, and signs it in the space above his typed name, and reads it again, and reads it yet another time and another time after that. He thinks he has covered everything. More important, he thinks he has covered *himself.*

In the stillness of his office, he nods, convinced that he is doing the right thing, pleased that he is doing it in a way that will help Kate and not cause any problems for himself. He opens the lower right-hand drawer of his desk and takes from it the NYNEX Yellow Pages for Manhattan. He finds the number he is looking for— 777–6500—dials it, and asks for the location of the branch office closest to Ninety-sixth and Madison. He is told there's one at 208 East Eighty-sixth Street, between Second and Third. He looks at his watch. It is almost eleven o'clock. He makes a Xerox copy of his letter and then calls Kate's apartment and asks her if she can meet him for lunch in an hour.

"Did you take the letters to Clancy?" she asks.

"No."

"No? Why not? You prom—"

"He's on vacation."

"When will he be back?"

"Monday. He'll have them by then, don't worry."

"You won't be here Monday."

"I know. But he'll have them."

"But you won't be here."

"I know that, honey."

Honey, he thinks.

"Then how can . . . ?"

"I'll tell you when I see you," he says. "You'll be pleased."

"Okay," she says, sounding suddenly relieved. "Where shall I meet you?"

Before he leaves the office, he tries Jacqueline Hicks's number again, and once again gets her goddamn answering machine.

Over lunch, he shows Kate the Xerox copy of his letter, and tells her he sent the package by Federal Express from their office on Eighty-sixth. Although he could have opted for delivery tomorrow morning, he knew Clancy wouldn't be back by then, so he'd settled on Monday morning delivery instead.

This doesn't seem to please her.

She asks why he didn't just go to the police station and give the letters to some other detective.

"I thought Clancy would pay closer attention to them."

A lie.

Now he is even lying to *her*.

"Him knowing you, I mean."

Embroidering the lie.

"You mean you didn't want to get involved, isn't that what you mean?"

"Well, no . . . "

"Well, yes," she says. "But that's okay. I know you're married, listen. I just hope the letters don't get lost."

"FedEx is very good."

"I hope so."

"What I thought I'd do, I'd follow up with a phone call from the Vineyard . . . "

"*Could* you do that?"

"Yes. Of course. Make sure Clancy got the package, make sure he plans to come see you."

"Oh, David, *thank* you," she says, and reaches across the table to take his hand between both hers. Her fingernails are painted to match her short, pale blue, pleated skirt and cotton top. She is wearing strappy low-heeled blue sandals. There is blue shadow over her sparkling green eyes. She seems happier now. She does not yet know he plans to end it this afternoon.

They walk in the park after lunch.

"This is where we met," she says.

"Yes."

"The last day of June," she says.

It is insufferably hot and clammy today. Waves of mist rise from the foliage on either side of them, drifting over the path so that it seems they are in a movie about Heaven, where clouds are billowing up underfoot as they walk.

"I spoke to Gloria this morning," she tells him, and glances sidelong at him. "She wants to join us tonight."

"I'd rather she didn't," he says.

"Oh come on, I know you'd like her there."

"No, really."

"Gloria? Come on."

"Really," he says.

"Well . . . that's very nice of you," she says, sounding pleasantly surprised.

He is wondering how he can tell her it's over.

"Of course, that's what Jacqueline would *love*," she says.

He turns to look at her, puzzled.

"No more Glorias," she says.

The mist shifts ceaselessly around them. They seem to be alone in the park. Alone in the world. Alone in the universe.

"No more Davids, in fact," she says.

He wonders for a moment if *she* is about to tell *him* she wants to end it. But that would be too ironic. Letting him off the hook that way.

"But, of course, I love you," she says.

He says nothing.

"So how can there be no more Davids?"

He's not sure what she means. He remains silent.

"Jackie says I've mastered the art of restaging the *Incident*, you see . . . "

"The what?"

"The terrible *trauma* of my youth . . . "

Joking about it. But he's too smart for that, he's an analyst.

" . . . so that each time it's *performed*, so to speak, *I'm* the one in control. Like a director shooting through a lens smeared with Vaseline, do you know?"

"I'm sorry, I don't."

"Softening the outlines. The way the fog here in the park is softening everything. Blurring the edges of reality. So that everything is beautiful at the ballet again, nothing is threatening, all is serene."

Her voice itself sounds utterly serene, too, in sharp contrast to its hysterical stridency last night. He knows instinctively and at once that she is about to tell him something of vital importance, but he does not want to hear it, not now when he is on the edge of telling her something of vital importance to *himself*. Or rather, something of vital importance to David Chapman, Lover Boy, *erstwhile* Lover Boy, *former* Lover Boy who is about to lower the ax while *Dr.* David Chapman should be listening to what this troubled young woman is attempting to say. He remembers quite suddenly and with a pang of guilt, the oath he took once upon a time, when the world was young and covered with mist.

"Would you like to sit?" he asks.

The bench is green and flaking, it rises from the mist like a floating couch. In the mist, side by side, they sit silently on the bench. She is quiet for what seems a very long time, but he is accustomed to long silences and he waits. She keeps staring into the mist as if peering into a past too distant to fathom. He has been through this scene before. He waits. Patiently, silently, he waits.

"What I do, you see . . . "

She takes a deep breath.

He waits.

"I find a man old enough to be my father, some middle-aged man, you see, and I allow him, nay, *invite* him to do anything and everything he wishes to do to me. I guess you know that. I guess you know that's what I do. I keep looking for the Davids of the world, over and over again."

He says nothing.

"And then I . . . I bring in a Gloria, cast *her* in the leading role, a woman rather than a child, and transform her into a willing accomplice rather than a victim. Is what Jacqueline says I do. Over and over again. Because I'm just a cunt, you see."

"I can't believe Jacqueline said that," he says.

"No, not the cunt part. The cunt part came from a higher authority."

"Tell me," he says.

His soothing, analytical voice. Dr. David Chapman speaking. Who is still ready to end his romance with this beautiful young woman who sits on a green bench wearing pale blue that fades into a paler gray mist, but who listens, anyway. Her eyes, he sees, are brimming with tears.

"Oh dear," she says, and falls silent.

He is afraid he will lose her in the shifting mist. But no, she begins speaking again in a voice as soft as the fog itself, a rolling haze enveloping her as she sinks yet another time into an embracing cloud of memory. Now there is mist of quite another sort, a hot wet mist that fills a remembered steamy bathroom long ago . . .

"I'm wrapped in a big white towel in a room full of steam," she says.

. . . toweling herself dry before a mirror clouded with steam, wiping a portion of the mirror clear with one edge of the towel, seeing her own shining, thirteen-year-old reflection in the glass.

"Everything in the mirror, everything in the room is soft and hazy, and there's music playing somewhere far below, somewhere out of sight, drifting, floating. It's the beginning of August, and there's a full moon, and the night is soft and hot and misty . . . "

Eleven-year-old Bess is in the tub across the room, Kate can see her reflection in the big irregular circle she's cleared on the mirror. Her sister is smiling. Luxuriating in a sea of suds, only her face and her toes showing, upswept red hair spilling in ringlets onto her brow, she moves her head idly in time to the sweet strains of music floating upstairs from the living room below.

——*Gently* . . .
——*Sweetly* . . .

It is a Sunday night. The Playhouse is dark tonight, which is why Kate is home at ten o'clock, preparing for bed. Fee the Fair has gone to a movie with a woman the girls call the USS Hawaii because she weighs two thousand pounds and always wears muu muus. Kate's father is downstairs listening to his old records.

——*Ever so* . . .
——*Discreetly* . . .

The faucet over the sink needs a new washer. It drips intermittently against the white porcelain as counterpoint to the lovely lyrics flooding the house.

———*Open* . . .

———*Secret* . . .

———*Doors.*

Lean and bony Kate stands in front of the misted bathroom mirror, drying herself in the large white puffy towel. Bess, precociously budding at the age of eleven, sits up in the tub and begins soaping herself.

———*Gently* . . .

———*Sweetly* . . .

———*Ever so* . . .

The bathroom door opens.

———*Completely* . . .

Kate's father appears suddenly in the door frame, an odd little smile on his face. He is wearing a green robe over white pajamas, the robe belted at the waist, no slippers.

"Good evening, ladies," he says.

Bess says, "Oops!" and immediately slides under the suds, only her head showing from the neck up. Kate hugs the towel to her and says, "Daa-aad, we're *in* here."

"So I see, so I see," her father says.

Kate suddenly smells alcohol on his breath.

———*Tell me* . . .

———*I'll be*

———*Yours.*

"Come on, Dad," she says playfully, wondering what the hell's the *matter* with him, can't he see they're *in* here? But of course he can see they're in here, he knew they were in here when he opened the door and walked in. The funny little smile is still on his face.

"Just wanted to check," he says. "Make sure you

295

weren't drowning or anything. Hello, Bessie," he says, waggling his fingers at her. "How's my little darlin'?"

"Fine, Dad."

She, too, looks puzzled. She has sunk even lower under the suds. The water just covers her chin. Her green eyes are wide above the white foam.

"Dad, we have to get dressed now," Kate suggests gently.

"I used to change your diapers," he says. "Powdered your little behinds, too."

"Why don't you go down and listen to your music?" Kate suggests gently.

"No, I'll be going to sleep now," he says.

"Goodnight, Dad," Bess immediately chirps from the tub.

"Goodnight, Dad," Kate says at once.

"Where's my goodnight kiss?" he asks. "No goodnight kiss?" And takes a step toward her. She is still clutching the towel tightly to her, her knuckles just under her chin, the towel cascading to just below her knees.

———*Here with a kiss . . .*

———*In the mist, on the shore . . .*

He leans into her and cups her chin in his hand and kisses her full on the mouth.

———*Sip from my lips . . .*

———*And whisper . . .*

———*I adore you.*

And kisses her again.

Kate is terrified. But she is excited, too. She can feel her father's hardness under his robe and pajamas, feel him stiff and probing through the thick towel shaking in her hands. "So tender," he says, and reaches behind her and pulls her to him, and she feels his huge hand spread wide on one naked buttock and suddenly he yanks the towel away with his free hand and she is standing naked and trembling before him.

——*Gently* . . .

——*Sweetly* . . .

"Dad, no," she says, "please."

"Shhh, Katie, darlin'," he says.

——*More and more* . . .

——*Completely* . . .

"Please, no, Dad," she says, because now she can see him huge and purple and throbbing in the opening of the robe, "Shhh, Katie, shhh," and she tries to hold him away but he is pressing her naked against the sink, lunging at her below, until at last she turns sidewards to deflect his thrust with her hip, and slips out of his grasp.

——*Take me* . . .

——*Make me* . . .

——*Yours.*

Huddling against the wall with the narrow window high above it, moonlight yellow in the blackness outside, she cowers in fear against the towels on the rack below the window and all she can think to whisper into the suffocating steam-filled room is, "Do it to her."

Downstairs, the music in the living room soars to a crescendo and ends abruptly.

The house is still except for the dripping of the water faucet in the bathroom sink.

"As you wish, Katie," he says, absolving himself of all guilt, the dutiful father merely following his favorite daughter's instructions. He actually makes a courtly drunken bow to her, and then turns away and walks rather jauntily to where Bess lies wide-eyed in the tub. The suds are dissipating. Patches of her tanned body show through the tattering white.

"Any sharks in here?" he asks playfully. "Anything going to bite me in here?" and thrusts both hands into the water, reaching under the suds for her, soaking his robe to the elbows. She tries to slip away from him, darting like a fish as he searches for purchase under the foam, saying, "Daddy, please," and "Daddy, stop," water splashing everywhere until finally he gets a firm handhold between her legs and yanks her out of the suds slippery and wet and squirming and struggling and kicking and bursting into tears and sobbing, "Help me, Kate, don't *let* him!" but Kate does nothing.

She is the one, after all, who made the single wish impossible to retract, and he is doing now to Bessie what he would have done to Kate herself had she not suggested otherwise. As she watches in fear and loathing and shame and excitement, a thin trickle of urine runs down the inside of her leg.

In the mist, side by side, they sit silently on the bench. He puts his arm around her.

"It wasn't your fault," he says gently.

"So they keep telling me," she says.

"You weren't to blame," he says.

"I should have locked the door," she says, and turns her head into his shoulder and begins weeping bitterly.

★   ★   ★

PRIVILEGED CONVERSATION

In bed that night, she says, "Would you mind if we didn't make love tonight, David?"

No more Davids, he thinks.

"I'm simply exhausted," she says.

The alarm clock goes off at seven A.M.

"What time is your plane?" she whispers.

"Eight-thirty."

"Will you make it?"

"Oh sure."

"From where?"

"La Guardia this time."

"Mm," she says, and falls back asleep.

He considers this another good sign.

He is showered, shaved and dressed by seven-thirty. He goes back into the bedroom. She is still asleep. He debates waking her, decides against it.

He leaves the apartment without saying, "I love you," gently closing the door behind him for the very last time.

He is at La Guardia by eight-fifteen.

They are already boarding his flight.

He looks for the scrap of paper on which he wrote Jacqueline Hicks's number in East Hampton. The sun is still shining above it. He hesitates a moment, and then dials it. This time, she picks up. He apologizes for calling so early in the morning and then explains that a woman named Kathryn Duggan stopped by for a consultation while he was in the city this week . . .

"Is she all right?" Jacqueline asks at once.

"Yes, she's fine, fine. But she mentioned that you'd treated her . . ."

"Yes, I did," Jacqueline says.

"And since she's considering analysis again . . ."

"Oh?"

"Yes, I wondered if you could tell me a little about her."

"David, I have a houseful of people just now . . ."

"Yes, but . . ."

". . . and we're just sitting down to breakfast. Can you possibly call me . . . ?"

"Jackie . . ."

". . . after the weekend? On Monday? I'd be happy . . ."

"Can you just tell me . . . ?"

"Yes, but then I really must go, *really*. Call me Monday, okay? I love her, I'd be happy . . ."

"I will. What was the nature of . . . ?"

"She was suicidal."

"I'll call you Monday," he says.

He looks at his watch. Eight-twenty. He wonders if he has time to call Kate. He wants to warn her not to do anything foolish. He wants to assure her that he'll be contacting Clancy again on Monday. He wants to tell her everything'll work out all right for her.

But just then they announce final boarding for his flight.

And he hurries toward the gate.

Her telephone rings at twenty-five minutes past eight, awakening her.

David, she thinks. From the airport.

She fumbles for the receiver. Picks it up.

"Hullo?" she says.

A furious voice shouts, "Get him off your machine, *cunt!*"

There is a click on the line.

She slams down the receiver at once.

My home number! she thinks. He has my home number!

Naked, she pads into the living room, and stands trembling before the answering machine, obeying his command at once, pressing the ANNOUNCEMENT button, holding it down, "Hi," her voice quavering, "at the beep, please," removing David's offensive message from the tape. I have to get out of here, she thinks. He's too close. He has my number.

Hannah the cat rubs against her naked leg.

"Not now, Hannah," she says, and rushes back into the bedroom. She crosses to the dresser, fumbles open the top drawer, finds a pair of white cotton panties, steps into them, I'll go to Clancy, pulls them up over her thighs and her waist, I have to put an end to this, crosses to the closet, hurls open the door, we have to get him, takes a pair of blue jeans from a hanger, we have to stop him, and is about to put them on when all at once she wonders if the front door is locked.

Did David lock the door when he left?

But how? There isn't a spring latch, the door can't be locked by simply pulling it shut.

Then . . .

Did *she* get up to lock it?

She lets the jeans fall to the floor. Barefoot, wearing only the white panties, she runs out of the bedroom and toward the front door—"Not *now*, Hannah!"—feeling a sudden urgency to get to that door and *lock* it, he knows where she lives, he has her number, "Goddamn you, Hannah, not *now!*"

She is reaching for the thumb bolt on the top lock when the door opens, almost knocking her over. She backs away, and all at once he is in the room, the door slamming shut behind him.

"Hello, Puss," he says.

She has never seen this man before in her life.

He is a total stranger, a thin balding man wearing rimless eyeglasses, and blue jeans, and white sneakers, and the black "Cats" T-shirt with the yellow eyes on it, yellow against black, black dancers in the yellow eyes, she cannot breathe. He is holding in his right hand a two-foot section of wood cut from a green broom handle, its end splintered and jagged as though while sawing it off he'd lost patience with the task and simply ripped it free, the naked wood showing raw and white beneath the bilious green paint. Before she can scream, before she can beg him to leave her alone, before she can utter a single sound, the short green club lashes out and strikes her across the bridge of her nose. She feels only blinding pain at first, and then everything in her field of vision goes red.

His fury is monumental.

She cannot imagine what she has done to provoke such rage.

Hands flailing, she keeps backing away from him as

he strikes at her soundlessly, incessantly. Bleeding, trying to see through the blood, her eyes swollen, trying to speak, her lips swollen, she says, or thinks she says, Please, don't hurt me, please. But he has already hurt her, he has hurt her seriously, and he is still hurting her, and she knows he will hurt her even more severely than he already has, knows he will not stop hurting her till he has killed her.

Do it to her, she thinks.

"Do it to *her!*" she screams, or thinks she screams.

But there is only Hannah the cat in the blood-spattered room.

Wet with blood, slippery everywhere with blood, drifting in and out of whiteness, she knows he will kill her, knows he has already killed her, knows she is dead, knows she is not yet dead, knows she is dying, *hopes* he will kill her, has already killed her, but, no, she's still alive. And she thinks perhaps God, who knows how to get unlisted phone numbers, who knows how to get inside buildings and inside apartments, God in all His infinite mercy and splendor will spare her after all. In which case, why is He hurting her so?

And where is David, she wonders, why isn't David here to save me, where *are* you, David? And where's my vain and glorious mother on this blood-drenched night in this steamy bathroom, how was the fucking *movie*, Mom? Where's vainglorious Fee when there's *real* trouble? Do you know I'm dying, Mom, do you know I'm dead? I truly beg your pardon, but if I'm dead then please end the pain, please stop *hurting* me this way! I'm sorry I let him do it, really, I should have locked the door, I should have, I know I should have in some way, but you see, I'm sorry but I simply couldn't, I was just a *kid*, you see. So . . . so please . . . I . . . I . . . I beg you to . . . to . . . bess me . . . to bless me . . . to forgive me, truly, I'm *very* sorry, Bess, forgive me, Bessie, *please* forgive me, only stop it, just, please, *stop* it!

In the instant before she dies, she understands with blinding clarity that doors can't be locked against monsters.

5: *monday, august 21–monday, november 20*

David places his call at twelve noon that Monday.

He knows by then that Kate has been murdered. He has read about it in the *New York Times* and has also seen the news on local television and on CNN.

"I was just trying to locate you," Clancy says. "Where are you calling from?"

"Martha's Vineyard."

"I got the package. Thanks."

"Will they help?"

"Working on them now."

There is a silence on the line.

"How well did you know her?" Clancy asks.

"Just casually," David says.

"But well enough that she could ask you to send that stuff to me, huh?"

"Asked me to *take* it to you, actually. But you were away."

"Well enough for that, huh?"

"It wasn't much to ask."

"So you sent it FedEx. Cause I was away."

"Yes. I knew I wouldn't be in the city today."

"Right, you're up there."

"Yes."

"Have you got a number up there where I can reach you? If I need you?"

"Sure," David says, and reads the number from the little plate on the phone. Seven summers up here, still doesn't know the number by heart.

"And that's where?" Clancy asks.

"Menemsha. Martha's Vineyard."

"Might as well give me the address, too," Clancy says. "While we're at it."

They are not properly dressed for sunshine and sand. Detective Clancy is wearing a brown suit, a white shirt, a darker brown tie, and brown shoes and socks. The man walking beside him is wearing a blue suit, a white shirt, a red tie, and black shoes and socks. Like a mirage, they materialize out of glaring sunshine and ocean mist, and come trudging shimmeringly over the sand. It is the twenty-fourth day of August, a hot, sultry morning without a breeze stirring. Five days since Kate's murder, three days since he spoke to Clancy on the phone. These men are dressed for business.

"Dr. Chapman," Clancy says. "Nice seeing you again.

This is my partner Detective D'Angelico, is this your little girl?"

"How do you do?" David says, and shakes hands first with D'Angelico and then with Clancy. "This is my daughter, Annie, yes."

"Few questions we'd . . ."

Annie suddenly sticks out her hand, squinting up into the sun as she shakes hands with each of the men in turn. David wonders if they plan to question him in her presence. Annie is wearing a little green bikini. He is wearing blue trunks. All at once, he feels very vulnerable in swimming apparel, the two detectives standing there in business suits.

"Have you got anything yet?" he asks.

"Well, we've been trying to track down the wild prints on the envelopes."

"But no luck so far," D'Angelico says.

In contrast to the lean and wiry Clancy, he is short and rotund. Fat and Skinny, David thinks. Mutt and Jeff. Good Cop/Bad Cop. But Who will be playing Whom? Which one is which?

"We appreciate your sending the stuff, anyway," Clancy says.

"Are you *really* detectives?" Annie asks.

"Yes, honey," D'Angelico says.

"I want you to know," Clancy says, "that you're not a suspect in this case."

"Who, me?" Annie asks.

"Well, I should hope not," David says.

"Me, too," Annie says, nodding vigorously.

D'Angelico smiles indulgently.

"Although during the course of our initial investigation," Clancy says, "your name came up quite a few times."

"As you might imagine," D'Angelico says.

Bad Cop, David thinks.

"Why might I imagine anything of the sort?" he asks.

"Your knowing the dead girl and all," D'Angelico says.

"I knew her only casually," he says at once.

He does not want Annie to hear whatever he feels certain is coming next, but they are still at least a quarter of a mile from the house and he doesn't want her walking back alone, either. It occurs to him that this is a cheap NYPD ploy, questioning him with his daughter standing not a foot away. He wants to say something to them about it, but he thinks they *may* suspect him, after all, no matter what Clancy just said, and he's afraid he'll get deeper in trouble if he starts any kind of fuss here.

"In any case, we're not here to discuss your relationship with her," Clancy says.

Good Cop.

"What are you guys talking about, *anyway?*" Annie says, squinting up at them, her hands on her hips, her head cocked to one side.

"Whyn't you run on up the beach?" D'Angelico says.

"I like it here," Annie says.

"Whyn't you send your daughter up the beach?" D'Angelico suggests.

"Go ahead, Annie," David says. "Not too far ahead. Stay where I can see you. And don't go in the water."

"What do these guys want, *anyway?*" she asks, looking up into David's face now.

"Do you remember the girl whose bike got stolen?" David asks.

"Yeah?"

"Someone hurt her," David says. "They want to ask me some questions about it."

"Why?"

"Why, gentlemen?" David says, turning to Clancy.

"So your daddy can help us find who did it," Clancy says.

"He saved her life once," Annie says, nodding. "He's a psychiatrist."

"So run along now, okay, honey?" D'Angelico says.

"Okay," Annie says, and goes skipping off up the beach ahead of them.

"Nice kid," D'Angelico says unconvincingly. "She knows about the stolen bike, huh?"

"Yes, I told my family about it."

"Brave thing you did," D'Angelico says, again unconvincingly.

"Looks like an army handled those letters you sent us," Clancy says conversationally.

"Including the kid from the bike shop," D'Angelico says. "Who we talked to the minute the other girls in the show told us he was there with her one night."

"Alibi a mile long for the morning she got killed, though," Clancy says. "She ever mention anything to you about this guy?"

"I only knew her casually. I wouldn't know anything about anyone in a bicycle shop."

"Of course not. I meant the guy who was sending her the flowers and . . ."

"Or did *you* send the flowers?" D'Angelico asks.

"Me? Why would I . . . ?"

"Then you didn't, right?"

"Of course not. I hardly knew the girl."

"So *did* she mention anything about this guy?"

"She must've said *something* about him," D'Angelico says.

"As I told you in my letter . . ."

"Yeah, she contacted you quite unexpectedly, isn't that it? So what'd she say when she contacted you quite unexpectedly?"

"Just what I wrote in my letter."

"Nothing more."

"Nothing more."

"Guy's sending her flowers . . ." Clancy says.

"You see, we're trying to separate the fancy fucking from the killing here," D'Angelico says.

"I beg your pardon?"

"Don't beg our pardon, Dr. Chapman. We get people begging our pardon every day of the week. If you'd stop covering your ass here for a minute . . ."

"Hey, come on, Ralph," Clancy says.

"A guy's sending her flowers, writing letters to her, she never says a word about him to her goddamn *boyfriend?*"

"Her *boyfriend?*" David says. "What are you . . . ?"

"We know you were seeing her," Clancy says. "I'm sorry, Dr. Chapman."

"Well, you know nothing of the sort. How can you possibly . . . ?"

"We do, I'm sorry."

"I thought I wasn't a suspect here."

"You're not," Clancy says.

"Not anymore," D'Angelico says.

"But put yourself in our shoes."

"What shoes are those, Detective?"

"We had a lot of people placing you with her. Doormen here and there, the super at her building, other girls in the show, a lady in her elevator, the kid in the bike shop, and so on. We also have her phone bill with collect calls you made from up here. And the bike shop kid says your voice was on her machine the whole four days before she got killed. All of which seemed to add up to the fact that you would have known the girl pretty well for about seven weeks at the time of her murder, actually fifty-one days according to our calculations. So you'll forgive us for thinking you were maybe fucking her, huh?"

"If you think I killed her . . ."

"No we don't. Not anymore."

David looks puzzled.

"The coroner's report set the time of her death at around eight-thirty, nine o'clock in the morning," Clancy explains.

"You were on a plane coming up here at that time," D'Angelico says.

"We checked passenger lists," Clancy says, almost apologetically.

"Dr. Chapman," D'Angelico says, "your personal business is your personal business, and we're not interested in it, believe me."

David wishes he could.

"All we want to know is whether Miss Duggan ever said anything at all about this guy who was bothering her. Did she indicate he might be someone she knew, for example?"

David says nothing for a moment.

The detectives are waiting.

He takes a deep breath.

"No," he says at last. "She had no idea who he was."

"When did you first hear about him?"

"When I went down to New York on the fifteenth."

"Were you staying with her?"

He hesitates again.

"Dr. Chapman?"

"Yes," he says.

"In her apartment, right?"

"Yes."

"Did he ever phone her while you were there?"

"Not at the apartment."

"Then you wouldn't have spoken to him?"

"No."

"Wouldn't have heard his voice."

"No. He called her at the theater."

"When?"

"The Wednesday before her murder."

"The sixteenth," Clancy says.

"Yes. Just before the matinee performance."

"Did she actually speak to him?"

"Yes."

"Did she say what he sounded like?"

"No."

"Did he give her a name?"

"No."

"Any name at all?"

"No."

"What did he say?"

"Warned her not to go to the police. Which is why she asked *me* to get the letters to you."

"Make any threats?"

"No, I don't think so."

"Didn't say he was going to kill her or anything, did he?"

"No."

"Harm her in any way?"

"No, nothing like that."

"Any idea why she was out of the show the rest of that week?"

"Yes. She was scared."

"Then she didn't really have a sprained ankle, huh?"

"No. The phone call scared her."

"With good reason," D'Angelico says.

The men fall silent. Overhead, a flock of gulls wheels against an achingly blue sky, shrieking.

"Anything else, Ralph?" Clancy asks.

"No. You?"

"I don't think so. Dr. Chapman," he says, "here's my card, case you think of anything else."

"I'm sorry you had to come all the way up here . . ."

"Well, you were very helpful," D'Angelico says.

"Thanks a lot, we appreciate your time," Clancy says,

and extends his hand. David takes it. The gulls are shrieking again. In a grave voice, like an Irishman at a wake,
Clancy says, "I'm sorry for your trouble."

David realizes he's talking about Kate.

His eyes suddenly mist with tears.

Summer is dying.

August inches inexorably toward September and the
big Labor Day weekend that will signal its symbolic end.
The days are still hot, but at night there is a hint of
autumn briskness in the air, and in many of the houses
along the beach, smoke curls up from chimney pots. He
keeps reading the newspapers and watching television
for news that they have caught her killer, hoping that
in mysterious ways known only to policemen they have
somehow managed to locate the telephone from which
her unknown assailant made his call to the theater on
that Wednesday before her death. But there is nothing.

The days drift idly by.

He feels that he is watching the end titles of a movie.
Under the titles as they crawl past, he can see still photographs of scenes from the movie. The stills serve as a
reminder, a summary of what has gone by. It is a device
he has seen used by many directors.

The movie is titled **PROJECTION**, which he feels is
infinitely more commercial than **RATIONALIZATION**,
both of which are psychiatric terms appropriate to the
film since the male lead is a psychiatrist and the female
lead is a troubled young woman. In psychiatric terms,
projection and rationalization mean essentially the same
thing. Both are defense mechanisms designed to project

upon another person something that is emotionally unacceptable to the self.

PROJECTION is a very good movie title because of its double meaning. The movie, after all, is being *projected* on the screen of David's mind. Well, not the entire movie. Just the still photographs with the end titles running over them. Oddly, the titles do not list electricians or grips or best boys or other technical people, but instead seem to be snatches of dialogue with quotation marks around them, as if this is a silent movie, except that the dialogue appears *over* the photographs instead of on separate cards. The song "Gently, Sweetly," played by the London Philharmonic with lush strings and mournful woodwinds, accompanies these silent-film photographs and snatches of dialogue. And perhaps, psychologically speaking, the title **PROJECTION** may have a *triple* meaning, who knows? In that the word can also be used to describe an estimate of future prospects based on current tendencies. Who knows?

The first photograph shows Kate as she appears out of a shimmering haze. Where a moment ago the screen was empty, there is now a young girl on a bicycle, fifteen or sixteen years old, he guesses, sweaty and slender, wearing green nylon running shorts and an orange cotton tank top, tendrils of long reddish-gold hair drifting across her freckled face. She is smiling. The dialogue appears over her smiling face . . .

"Good morning, sir!"

. . . and is gone at once in a dazzle of sunlight.

But the shot clearly establishes that the girl in this movie, the woman actually, is the one who makes initial contact, an approach to which the man doesn't even respond. Moreover, as the parade of succeeding shots unfolds, it becomes more and more evident that the girl, the woman, is the aggressor, the pursuer, the ardent seductress . . . well, just *look* at the photographic evidence!

David is kneeling beside her. Dappled sunlight turns her eyes to glinting emeralds. Strands of golden-red hair drift across her face like fine threads in a silken curtain. The side-slit in the very short green nylon running shorts exposes a hint of white cotton panties beneath. The superimposed line of dialogue reads . . .

"It's beginning to swell."

. . . which is in itself suggestive, even when not coupled with the *next* line, which reads . . .

"Just what I need."

. . . indicating that what she needs is something that's beginning to swell, hmm, Doktor? Moreover, these blatant invitations run like a leitmotif throughout.

They are standing on Ninety-sixth Street, just outside the park. They have just exchanged addresses. They shake hands awkwardly. As he walks off:

"Hey! My name is Kate."

She comes down off the stage from the side ramp on the right of the theater, surprising him when she crawls through the wide space in front of row K, and then in her catlike way, sits up, seemingly detecting a human presence, seemingly startled, jerking her head around and looking directly into his face, her green eyes wide. The superimposed dialogue reads:

"Take me to lunch and flatter me."

316

PRIVILEGED CONVERSATION

The camera lingers on her green eyes. Green flecked with yellow. Sitting in slanting sunlight at a table just inside the window of the restaurant she's chosen for brunch on the West Side. Eyes glowing with sunlight:

"I dreamt you and I were making love in front of my mother's house in Westport."

The West Side restaurant dissolves to a Thai newcomer on the East Side, the strains of "Gently, Sweetly" rushing through beaded curtains, caressing, embracing them as they sit sipping their wine. The pale gold of the chardonnay echoes the outfit she is wearing this evening, a wheat-colored mesh linen vest with a sort of sarong skirt in crinkled silk with a sheer leaf print that matches the color of her nail polish.

"If I don't kiss you soon, I'll die."

On and on the titles come, relentlessly rolling upward on the screen of his mind, flashback and fast-forward combined, each successive photograph and remembered word fortifying the knowledge that the relationship was almost entirely a product of her own making, a reconstruction, a restaging, as she'd put it, of an unresolved childhood trauma.

"Kate. From the park. The victim, remember?"

But as he reviews, in effect, the story line of this film, as he plays the end titles over and over again in his mind, he realizes at last that perhaps *he* was the true victim here, that *any* red-blooded American male, for example, would have succumbed to the temptation of a young and beautiful redheaded dancer who supplied him with yet another eager young girl, woman, in her twenties . . .

317

Gloria is black and Gloria is long and supple and Gloria has sloe eyes and a voluptuous mouth and Gloria is wearing nothing but high-heeled shoes and a gold chain that is wrapped around her waist several times . . .

"Happy birthday."

. . . and promised him in the bargain even more opulently erotic adventures, perhaps even with *countless* other twentysomething *Asian* girls from *Miss Saigon* . . .

"Or I can find someone else, if that's what you'd prefer."

So who in this star-studded cast can cast the first stone, truly?

He *did* send those letters off, didn't he? A happily married man taking an enormous risk. Did in fact take the letters to the FedEx office on Eighty-sixth Street . . .

In one of the few end-title photographs of David alone, he is seen at the branch office counter, addressing the package and paying for its delivery in cash. Over the photograph of him looking intent and deliberate, the dialogue reads:

"But that's okay. I know you're married, listen."

The last photograph shows Kate and David sitting on a green park bench as mist rolls in off a narrow path. Her head is bent, she is weeping. He is sitting beside her attentively, the very image of a concerned physician. The superimposed dialogue reads:

"It wasn't your fault."

The music swells. The mist rises to envelop the bench and the figures sitting frozen in time upon it, obliterating them at last until the entire frame is a shifting swirl of pure, innocent, blameless white.

PRIVILEGED CONVERSATION

Take me . . .
Make me . . .
Yours.
And the movie ends.
And so does the summer.

Arthur K has bought a new automobile. He proudly describes it to David, even shows him pictures of it from the catalog. It is a Camaro like the one his sister was driving when she got killed, though not in the same color. He plans to go to the Motor Vehicle Bureau to apply for a new driver's license. He tells David that he has begun dating a young girl who looks a lot the way Veronica did when she was sixteen.

Susan M no longer needs to plan her wardrobe weeks in advance. She now limits her scheduling to a mere three days, the first three days of the week, and she does her planning for those days over the weekend. This leaves Thursday and Friday free of any compulsive activity. Over Christmas, she plans to visit her mother in Omaha. By then, she hopes she will not have to plan her wardrobe ahead at all.

Today is the sixteenth day of October.

David hopes she will make it.

Alex J has fallen in love with the Puerto Rican girl he followed home from the subway again last Tuesday night. He has actually made contact with her. He has approached her on the street, and introduced himself, and told her he found her quite extraordinarily beautiful.

And despite the wife and three children he adores, he has asked if she would like to go to a movie with him one night. Tonight is that night.

As Alex describes her, his face is rapturous.

Moreover, he feels quite proud of himself, having approached this gorgeous "Latina," as she prefers calling herself, in a neighborhood where everyone looked like a dope dealer who would slit his throat for a nickel, and there he was talking to one of their *women* for Christ's sake, "Don't you think that took balls?" he asks David.

David remains noncommittal.

"Well, fuck you," Alex J says. "*I* think it did."

The kids have already watched their Disney fare and are upstairs asleep. The rented movie David and Helen are watching is about a couple going through a very stormy divorce.

"Do you want to watch the rest of this?" she asks.

"Not particularly," he says, and hits the STOP button on the remote control unit. He turns off the television set. The room is suddenly very still.

"Do you believe people really fall in love that way?" Helen asks.

"What way?"

"The way the man and woman in the movie do?"

"I suppose."

"I mean, meeting *cute* that way. In a rainstorm. Sharing an umbrella."

"Well, I guess it doesn't matter how people meet," he says. "*You* were sitting on a park bench when I met you."

320

"Yes," she says thoughtfully. "But in movies, they're always *strangers*, did you notice? Why don't people who *know* each other ever fall in love?"

"Well, they do, I guess."

"In movies, I mean."

"In movies, too."

"No, in movies it's always strangers."

"Well, I guess strangers are more interesting."

"I think two people who know each other could be interesting, too. Finding out more about each other, you know? Learning things they didn't know about each other."

"Well, nobody says movies have to be true to life."

"Only *life* has to be true to life," she says.

He turns to look at her.

She takes a deep breath.

"David," she says, "I'm in love with Harry Daitch."

He keeps looking at her.

"And he's in love with me," she says.

"I see."

"Yes."

"When . . . ah . . . did all this happen?" he hears himself saying.

This is a movie, he thinks.

"Well . . ." she says. "I guess you know that Harry and Danielle were having trouble for a long time . . . well, you've seen him at parties with his hands all over women . . ."

I haven't seen him with his hands all over *you*, David thinks, but that's yet another movie.

". . . which, of course, was a clear signal that he wasn't

too terribly happy with her, otherwise he wouldn't have been fooling around, would he?"

"I really couldn't say."

"Well, men don't fool around with other women unless they're unhappy at home. That's a basic fact of marriage, David."

"Is it?"

"Yes. I'm sure you know that, a psychiatrist. In any event, we got to talking one night on the deck of his house, and I began to realize . . . I'd always considered him nothing but a womanizer, you see . . ."

Gee, I wonder why, David thinks.

". . . but that night . . . this was in July sometime, there was a full moon, I remember. You were in the city, David, this was during the week sometime. Anyway, I discovered that night that Harry was truly a very sad person with depth and sensitivity . . . he writes poetry, you know . . ."

To you? David wonders.

". . . which is unusual for a lawyer, whom one usually expects to be rather stiff . . ."

Great word, David thinks.

". . . and unyielding, rather than . . . well . . . romantic and adventurous. In any event, one thing led to another . . ."

To make a long story short, David thinks.

". . . and by the time you went into the city for your August seminar, I guess it was, we . . . well . . . we realized we were in love."

"In love, I see."

"Yes."

"So this has been going on since August."

"July, actually."

"Well . . . congratulations."

"David, I want a divorce."

"I see, a divorce," he says.

"So Harry and I can get married and go live in Mexico."

"Mexico."

"Yes."

"I see, Mexico. Land of opportunity."

"He *does*, in fact, own land down there."

"I see."

"Why do you keep saying that? It's *infuriating*."

"Well, I *do* see. You love Harry Daitch and you want a divorce so you can marry him and go live on his land in Mexico. Isn't that it?"

"That's *about* it, yes."

"Well, that's about *all* of it, wouldn't you say?"

"Not quite."

"What's the rest of it?"

"I'm pregnant."

"Pregnant, I see. Then I suppose you'll want the divorce in a hurry, so you can rush down there and give birth to a Mexican citizen."

"I *would* like the child to be born in my new marriage, yes. Not necessarily in Mexico."

"Fine, I'll call Peter . . ."

"I've already called him."

"You called our *attorney* before you . . . ?"

"We spoke only in general terms."

"But about divorce, right?"

"Yes. I told him a friend of mine was thinking about divorce."

"Must have fooled him completely."

"I wasn't trying to fool him."

"Just called to ask how this friend of yours should proceed, right?"

"Yes."

"Who?"

"What?"

"Which friend did you say wanted a divorce?"

"Well . . . Danielle, actually. She will, after all, be need—"

"Danielle, perfect. I'd like a drink. Would you care for a drink?"

"No, I don't think so."

"I think I'd like one."

He goes to the bar, pours himself a very hefty vodka over ice, and then stands at the window, looking out at Manhattan, looking out at the heavy snow falling outside, covering everything with white, blanketing the rooftops and the streets and the world and the universe with pristine white. When he hears her coming into the room behind him, he asks, without turning to look at her, "What about the children?"

"What about them?"

"They stay with me, you realize."

"Don't be ridiculous."

"You plan to take *my* daughters to Mexico?" he says, turning to face her, his hand tight around the glass in his hand. "To live with Harry Daitch?"

"Of course I do."

"Over my dead body," he says.

"Well, we'll talk about it when you're . . ."

"We just did. And you heard what I said."

"David . . ."

"You *heard* what I fucking well said!"

"Goodnight, I'm going to sleep."

"Go to hell, for all I care."

Helen stares at him silently for just a moment. Then she merely sighs, and nods, and leaves the room.

He stands looking out at the falling snow. He drains his glass, carries it to the sink, rinses it, puts it on the drainboard. Down the hall, he can hear Helen thundering around the bedroom, preparing for bed. Take *his* kids to Mexico? Over his, fucking, dead, body!

He remembers that the tape is still in the video player.

He snaps on the television set, picks up the remote control unit, hits the PLAY button and then the RW button and sits down to watch as the tape rewinds. As it flickers in reverse, as the actors walk backward out of a room, or move out of each other's arms instead of into them, David keeps watching the flickering images on the screen. The main titles appear, running backward to the very beginning of the film. The movie is almost ready to start all over again. He hits the EJECT button. The tape slides out of the video player with an audible click. He snaps off the set, carries the tape back to where its protective plastic case is sitting on the coffee table.

He stands looking at the blank screen.

He stands looking at it for a long while, as if trying to remember what the movie was all about.

Well, no matter, he thinks.

He finds a blanket and a pillow in the hall closet, stretches out on the couch, and tries to make himself comfortable. At last, he closes his eyes and drifts off to sleep.

He dreams that they are taking a long walk up the beach. He and Helen are holding hands. The girls are running up the beach ahead of them, circling back occasionally to hug them both around the legs, skipping off again, skirting like sandpipers the waves that gently rush the shore.

"Forever, right?" Annie says, turning to look back at him.

"Forever," he says.

Annie leaps over someone's abandoned sand castle, lands flat-footed and crouched on the other side of it.

"Boop!" she says.

And he awakens with a start.